With best
wish
for

Christopher
Crocker
Feb. '07

CAPPADOCIAN MOON
and other stories

Christopher
Arthur

Published by

MELROSE BOOKS

An Imprint of Melrose Press Limited
St Thomas Place, Ely
Cambridgeshire
CB7 4GG, UK
www.melrosebooks.com

FIRST EDITION

Copyright © Christopher Arthur 2007

The Author asserts his moral right to
be identified as the author of this work

Cover designed by Catherine McIntyre

ISBN10   1 906050 02 3
ISBN13   978 1 906050 02 3

All rights reserved. No part of this publication may be reproduced,
stored in a retrieval system, or transmitted, in any form or by any means
electronic, mechanical , photocopying, recording or otherwise,
without the prior permission of the publishers.

This book is sold subject to the condition that it shall not,
by way of trade or otherwise, be lent, re-sold, hired out or
otherwise circulated without the publisher's prior consent
in any form of binding or cover other than that in which
it is published and without a similar condition including this
condition being imposed on the subsequent purchaser.

Printed and bound in Great Britain by:
CPI Bath, Lower Bristol Road,
Bath, BA2 3BL, UK

CONTENTS

1 Cappadocian Moon 3

2 The Cartoon 16

3 Jessica's Gap Year 33

4 Ambrose Prior 45

5 The Postlethwaite Lecture 73

6 The Stain - a Sequel 81

7 A Confession.. 100

8 Part of a Quota 113

9 The Bedroom Window 124

10 Ice-Cold 129

11 The Symposium 150

12 The Menin Gate 167

13 Mr Smedley 174

14 The Fall of the Roman Empire 191

ACKNOWLEDGEMENTS.

I would like to say a warm thank you to Nilda Ginn for casting a critical and constructive eye over each story as it was written and to Mervyn Burleigh for his good advice and for help in establishing the locations of three of the tales.

1   Cappadocian Moon

"It's exactly the same as it was twenty-five years ago," said Simon, who was talking about the moon.

"What else would you have expected it to be?" retorted Wendy.

"You know what I mean: the same big moon hanging up there and flooding those queer old rocks with its light, just the way it has done for what? Hundreds of thousands of years? I don't know. A Cappadocian moon."

Wendy went through the motion of pondering the phrase. "A Cappadocian moon? The title for a book perhaps, but does it really mean anything?"

"Of course it means something," rejoined her husband. "Probably a combination of things; the way it seems to be suspended up there for a start, like a Chinese lantern … the rocks … and the balmy night air … You must admit that taken together they add up to a magical effect, and like nowhere else that I can think of. So, a Cappadocian moon."

"Twenty-five years ago and just married," mused Wendy. "It did look different then."

"But not the moon," insisted Simon. "And the rocks look the same. I know Goreme's grown up a lot since we first came – the tourism and so on – but how do I put it? The genius loci, that hasn't changed."

"And that's why we're here now, back where we began. Because of the genius loci," said his wife.

"Back where we began," answered Simon. "In a full circle. Like that Cappadocian moon."

"Careful," warned Wendy. "Don't stretch it too far. It's already beginning to sound a bit tired."

"What's that supposed to mean?"

"I mean your Cappadocian moon. Once is just about all right. After that it starts to grate."

"I was rather pleased with it." Simon frowned and sipped his wine.

"I know you were."

For a moment they said nothing.

"Anyway," resumed Wendy, trying to make up for her rebuff and to rise to an occasion that meant more to her husband than it did to her, "It looks very pretty, quite marvellous in fact."

A soft breeze had just sprung up, which gave her a pretext for a contented sigh.

Back to where we began. Coming full circle. Poor bloody Simon. That was him all over. It was wretched that they should be going through it at all. For Wendy had already made up her mind. This was where the charade that their lives had become had to end. Once the holiday was over she would quietly go her own way. It was so like Simon to conjure this thing up, as if starting again after a quarter of a century could possibly cancel out all those lost opportunities and everything would work out wonderfully well the second time round – in later middle age. Poor deluded Simon. It was hardly any wonder that he'd never got a chair and that his academic career, once so promising, had run into the sand so that he seemed to be only going through the motions of it until his retirement. And the one thing they couldn't repair was the lack of children. No fresh covenant under a Cappadocian moon was going to do that. Dear romantic Simon; such an optimist despite everything. Wendy knew that she would have to let him down very gently.

Her husband recharged their glasses. "Or would you like something stronger?" he asked. "This wine's got rather warm."

"It'll do," said Wendy as she raised her glass to touch his. "To better times?" she suggested.

"Better times," he repeated.

No, Wendy reflected, let Simon have his fling. I won't spoil it for him now – or try not to, at least. I'll cut the painter when we're back home again. For the time being I'll try to look as if I'm enjoying myself, and anyway, despite his piffle about Cappadocian moons, it's a stunning place, so let's just give in to it. Live for the moment and succumb to its magic …"

This time they were staying in a large tourist hotel and sitting by its swimming pool. Previously, they had stayed in one of the small pensions, half-carved out of the prevailing volcanic tufa and faced with blocks of the same material. But the view was the same – of fantastically shaped rocks, some with chambers hollowed out of them and windows and doorways cut into their sides, standing like the ranks of a silent army or, as Wendy expressed it, like erect penises, especially the ones with capstones perched on their tips. Because of the crisis in Iraq, fewer tourists were coming to Turkey this year and the hotel was half-empty, –which suited Simon. Apart from an elderly Turkish gentleman who was drinking raki and eating a cheese salad by himself in a little summerhouse not far from the pool, no one else was about.

"What about tomorrow?" Simon asked his wife. "Have you any ideas?"

"Not especially. As long as it's nothing too hectic."

"It would be difficult to be too hectic in this place," said Simon. "How about a walk in the Red Valley? And before that we can climb the citadel for the view. And, if you felt like it, we could even have a poke round some of the carpet dealers."

"I'm not sure what I'd do with any more rugs or kilims," replied Wendy.

"It's only a suggestion," said Simon, "but let's kick off with the citadel, shall we?"

"As you wish." Wendy nodded and tried to look pleased at the prospect, though it was a matter of indifference to her.

They forced the conversation along, Simon trying to inject a sense of renewal into the occasion while Wendy pretended, for his sake, that she was sharing it. And then he started to talk for the nth time about the book he was going to write. Wendy had the forbearance not to remind him that he had being talking about the book he was going to write since before they were married and still nothing had come of it. Not that it had stood still. On the contrary, the project had grown more ambitious with the passing years. Outlines had been drawn up and topics listed, mostly in his head, but occasionally committed to paper, which gradually expanded into a scheme for a survey of the entire prehistory of Anatolia from the Palaeolithic period up to the beginning of the Iron Age. But it remained just that, a skeleton of increasing complexity but with no flesh on it. Thus Simon, who found he had to run to keep up with the ever-quickening pace of research, had a plausible excuse for never getting started.

As he dilated on his theme, Wendy thought how endearingly old-fashioned it sounded. No one wrote books like that any more. It was like one of those nineteenth century general histories, an account of an entire epoch that, weighed down by its enormous ballast of footnotes, ran to ten volumes or more.

He seemed to have the structure of it worked out in great detail inside his head: the amount of space to be allotted to the first waves of hunter/gatherers; the early Neolithic farmers and the spread of agriculture; then the Bronze Age and the dawn of literacy– his own specialty: the Hittites had been the great fascination of his youth – and, finally, the first use of iron in the area. In his time, he had kept up a steady flow of papers in several leading archaeological journals, but with the passing years it had fallen away to a trickle before drying up completely. Now, these papers were virtually archaeological specimens themselves, the equivalents, in their way, of the cuneiform tablets of the Bronze Age.

But to be fair to Simon, he had never succumbed to bitterness as his work had been eclipsed by later researchers in the field. No, he decided, he was not a monograph man, but one who preferred to work on a large canvas with a broad brush. He would write the great definitive work about the prehistory of Anatolia, one, moreover, that had literary merit. It would rise above the customary dryness of the professional archaeological publication. For Simon believed that his was a larger spirit than that of the general run of archaeologists.

So now, under the Cappadocian moon, the floodgates were opened yet again, but it was an indulgence tinged with an increasing sense of melancholy because it was clear by now that nothing was ever likely to come of his beautifully conceived plan. But it was an eloquent performance all the same, and of the countless occasions that Wendy had been subjected to it, she could not recall a better one. Thanks to the intoxicating effect of the moonlight, no doubt.

"You know something, Simon," she said when he had fallen silent at last, "you have a marvellous book there. Not quite the one you think you have, but I mean telling the story of the book you intended to write but never did. A book about a book that should have been written but never was. Don't get me wrong. I'm being perfectly serious. Addressed to the right kind of reader it could be fascinating, something philosophical or metaphysical perhaps? You could even call it "Cappadocian Moon" if you liked. It's quite a catchy title."

He gave her a puzzled frown, not sure whether to take her seriously or not. Then he ordered a fresh bottle of wine, recharged their glasses and gazed across at the moonlit rocks. Neither of them spoke. In the meantime, the Turkish gentleman in the summerhouse emerged – a dapper figure in high-waisted fawn slacks and a crisp white shirt, swinging a string of worry beads behind him as he went. He seemed the kind of man who was perfectly at ease with his own company and Wendy found herself trying to invent a biography for him as he ambled past them into the hotel.

"Time to eat," she said, breaking the silence at last.

"Yes, I suppose it is." Simon sounded as if he had been startled out of his sleep. "We might come out again afterwards for a nightcap."

They went into the big dining room in the basement of the hotel, which served a buffet supper.

"Perhaps we should have gone out for something a bit more adventurous," said Simon. "A karishik izgara and a muhallebi would have been nicer."

Wendy shrugged her shoulders in a manner that her husband took for indifference.

"Aren't you glad we came?" he said reproachfully.

"Of course I am, darling. You're absolutely right about Cappadocia. It has a magic all of its own." She tried rather too hard to inject some enthusiasm into her voice. "And you mustn't misunderstand me about the book. It was meant to be a positive suggestion."

"Are you sure you wouldn't like to buy a rug?" said Simon, choosing not to discuss her positive suggestion any further for the time being. "We could look for something old and a bit faded – the kind of thing you like."

"We can think about it, certainly," replied Wendy. "There must be something hiding among all that tourist tat. My God, how the place has mushroomed since we first came here. It's scary."

"I wouldn't say that. In a funny way it suits it," said Simon. "Turkey is a land of small traders. It always has been. The essence of it hasn't changed, even though travelling here is less of an adventure than it once was."

They finished with fruit and a cup of coffee before ordering drinks to be brought out to them by the pool.

The Moon was sinking by now and the light on the rocks was more muted, but they still seemed charged with ancient mystery. There was a loudspeaker system that piped music to the guests sitting outside. It might have been annoying but now it was playing a selection of Aegean guitar melodies, which matched their separate moods and removed the need for conversation.

When it got quite dark under a starlit sky, they went to bed. They had twin beds – a renewal of sexual passion was not part of Simon's agenda, to Wendy's relief – and, for a while, they lay chatting before turning out the light.

"I suggest that tomorrow we have a leisurely breakfast then wander in the direction of the citadel and look at some carpets on the way," concluded Simon. "Then, after lunch, if you feel up to it, we can walk along the Red Valley."

"Sounds all right to me," murmured Wendy, giving a yawn and snuggling down under the sheet. "Night-night."

Simon switched off the light and was asleep almost immediately and started to snore. Wendy, whose little pretence of wanting to go to sleep herself was the means of achieving this, cautiously switched on her own reading light after a few minutes and took up her book. Simon turned over, away from the light, but did not wake up. That was something Wendy could say in his favour; when he slept he tended to drop off like a child, which gave her a chance to do some serious reading. It was a thing she anticipated with relish once their ways had parted: evenings of uninterrupted reading for hours at a stretch.

In the morning, Simon was up first and into the bathroom. Wendy, meanwhile, lay in bed listening to his shower running. Simon, although he was in his late fifties, always whistled while he showered, which somehow made him sound like a younger man. His wife was bemused by his apparently persistent good humour.

In the dining room, they settled with their coffee and rolls at a table next to the solitary Turkish gentleman who had been drinking raki in the summerhouse by the pool.

"Good morning," Simon said to him in Turkish.

"Good morning," he replied in English. "Have a nice day." Without making any attempt to take the exchange further, he got up, bowed his head slightly and left the room.

"I wish he hadn't felt the need to add that ghastly Americanism," said Simon. "But do you know something? I feel like a proper Turkish coffee. Perhaps while we're bargaining for a rug we'll be offered one. A rug is definitely called for."

Simon, who was anything but businesslike, nevertheless fancied himself as a dab hand in the

bazaar. So, after depositing their room key, they strolled down towards the centre of town. Simon started to whistle.

"You sound very chirpy this morning," remarked his wife.

"It's that sort of a day. A beautiful morning and good to be here again. The view from the citadel will be tremendous."

The tourist shops were open for business in spite of the relative lack of customers. They displayed everything from little carvings of the rock formations – rather like clustered phalluses – to copper and brass trinkets, onyx vases, kilims, carpets, cushion covers and garish narghile pipes. In true Turkish fashion, dotted among them were numerous small shops offering quite different things: kebabs, guided tours and confectionary, as well as more mundane things like household hardware.

"You see?" Simon pointed out. "It's still utterly Turkish. Tourism has merely added another layer to it, that's all." It was a perfectly valid point to make – especially by an archaeologist who thought in terms of stratigraphy.

They walked to the end of the road, negotiating a passage round the goods that were piled on the narrow pavement, and then turned in the direction of the citadel. Simon took Wendy's hand.

"Keep your eyes peeled for any nice rugs. But you know the score. Try not to show too much interest," he told her.

Despite the hollowness of the enterprise, Wendy found herself being caught up in it and scanning critically the rugs and kilims that were hanging outside the shops.

"Good vegetable dyes," she observed. "That's what we've got to go for." Wendy liked the bold Cappadocian patterns, especially when the colours had faded down a bit.

Meanwhile, the citadel came into view. It was a natural object – a volcanic plug – but much modified by human hands. Openings had been cut into its sides bringing to light a network of passages and chambers within. One face was entirely smooth and vertical giving it the appearance of a cheese from which a large piece had been sliced. Houses, carved from the soft tufa and dressed with blocks of the same, clung to its lower flanks, the narrow streets winding up to the base of the ancient plug.

There were small pensions with flat roofs where the guests could sit in the evening and, no doubt, enjoy the splendour of the Cappadocian moon, and still more shops which, the further up you went, became more exclusive to the requirements of tourists.

It was a warm day in early summer with just enough clouds to cast dappling shadows and, still holding hands – which Wendy was beginning to find irksome – they walked swiftly up the narrow street where it joined the square in front of the citadel.

"Stop," said Wendy, withdrawing her hand from Simon's. A display of rugs draped across the front of a shop had caught her eye. From the shade within, a pair of eyes watched her, but their owner did not move.

"What do you think?" she said. "I rather like those colours."

"Don't make it too obvious," whispered her husband.

"Shut up, Simon. I wasn't born yesterday."

There was one rug in particular with rather unusual colours. Instead of hot reds and rich blues and the brighter shades of yellow, Wendy was attracted by its relative dullness – the sombre purple, the coffee brown, the muddy green and inky blue of the central panels and their surrounding bands. The pattern was a bold Cappadocian one but was held in check by its muted tones. Exactly the kind of thing she liked.

Simon watched her dubiously as she eyed it. "Easy does it now," he advised.

The owner of the shop emerged from the shade – a short, plump man with a neatly trimmed, grizzled moustache. He dipped his head slightly and smiled at Wendy but said nothing.

"Hm," she said with a frown, trying her best to look thoughtful.

Raising his eyebrows gently, but without saying a word, the man unhitched the rug and spread it in the doorway of his shop.

"Please," he said in English.

Two chairs quickly appeared. A boy standing in the shadows followed them and stood waiting for orders.

"Would you like tea or a Turkish coffee?" the man asked, again in English.

Wendy glanced at Simon who was eying the rug with a frown on his face. She sat down on one of the chairs.

"Coffee, please," said Simon in Turkish, sitting down on the other chair. "And medium sweet," he added, also in Turkish.

"Ah, I see you speak Turkish," said the man, again in English, which he followed with, "welcome," in his own language.

The boy was dispatched to the nearest coffee house and soon arrived back bearing two small cups on a circular tray.

Simon was determined to take charge of the bargaining on behalf of his wife, though the outcome was never really in doubt. They went through the ritual of examining the other rugs that the dealer brought out and laid before them, pretending to consider them with equal care. But Wendy, as she turned over the edges of the ones they had already looked at to make a running comparison, always seemed to dwell on the one that had first caught her eye for a fraction longer than the others. This did not go unnoticed by the vendor who, of course, could read all the signs of an impulse purchase – though he behaved very correctly by going through the business of letting Simon believe that he was driving a hard bargain but getting the price to where he wanted it in the end, which was between the two opening positions but significantly nearer to his own than to Simon's.

Anyway, it was concluded amicably and Simon, who had got his coffee, felt pleased with his effort. The boy immediately fetched a piece of brown paper and string and the dealer rolled up the rug tightly, making a neat bundle complete with a handle improvised out of the string. Simon settled with his credit card and arranged to collect the parcel when they came down from the citadel.

"Are you happy?" he asked Wendy as they set off across the square.

She smiled and nodded, at the same time feeling guilty about it, as if she had just practised a deception on her husband.

Inside the citadel, the chambers hollowed out of its rock were crammed with merchandise – racks of guidebooks in various languages, including Russian, postcards and the usual range of souvenirs. Not a single piece of space was wasted. If it could be filled it was, in a kind of commercial horror vacui.

"So very Turkish," announced Simon. "It might be the bazaar. Nothing really changes here."

They threaded their way up the sloping passage and steps that led to the summit of the citadel. It was packed with visitors, most of them Turkish.

"That's one thing that has changed," pointed out Simon. "The number of Turkish people coming to these places now. Before, it was almost entirely foreigners."

"Because they've got more money and can afford to do it," Wendy said.

They emerged into the daylight on a small platform where Simon took her hand again. "Must you?" she said, a trifle testily, and pulled it away.

"Just as you like." Simon sounded a little put out.

"Don't take it to heart," she said. "We can do the romantic bit when we're on the top admiring the view." She touched his cheek lightly with her forefinger.

They climbed the steep iron steps that led to the top and onto a narrow viewing platform. A couple of shallow graves of the Byzantine period had been scooped out of the rock, beyond which was a natural shelf and, on the other side of that, a drop that fell sheer for about sixty feet.

"How very Turkish," Wendy pointed out, "not to bother about a rail. Really, they're much better out of the European Union with all its ridiculous health and safety regulations."

"And I hope for their sake that they always will be," added Simon, "if only they'd realise it."

Wendy peered over the precipice. "All the same, be careful," she said.

Simon replied by taking her hand.

In the morning sunshine with its scarcely moving banks of cloud, the view was tremendous.

"My God," said Simon in an awed whisper. "I'd forgotten just how good it was."

Wendy issued one of her practised sighs of contentment that stood in for words.

Among and beyond the flat-roofed houses, the ranks of strangely worn rocks lay before them, rank after rank, blurring into the dry hills behind. Their colours stood out clearly with all their fine gradations – dusty pinks and ochres and cream with darker tones here and there between them. The houses, built out of the same soft tufa and indeed cut right into it, seemed like termite mounds, an equally natural part of the landscape.

"Never have the works of Nature and Man been in closer harmony than they are here," declared Simon portentously as he gripped Wendy's hand. He stepped over the shallow scoop of a Byzantine grave and stood on the low shelf at the platform's edge. "Do you see the Red Valley?" He pointed to a strip of darker rocks that crossed the middle of the view.

"Be careful," said Wendy, tugging at her hand, which remained firmly in his grasp.

A breeze, which stirred the clouds before them, started to blow in their direction. Simon threw back his head and drew a deep breath as if drinking it in. "Champagne," he declaimed to the world at large. "Pure champagne." He tightened his grip on his wife's hand and emitted a low trumpeting noise, presumably to express his pleasure.

"Do be careful, Simon," Wendy warned him again. At the same time she drew back from the edge, hoping to take him with her.

"Champagne," Simon announced once more in the same exalted tone.

"So you keep saying. But what exactly do you mean? Why champagne, for God's sake? It's only fizzy white wine. It's getting as bad as your Cappadocian moon. Simon … what the hell are you doing?"

He was rocking backwards and forwards on the edge of the drop with his eyes closed and uttering rapturous little grunts. Wendy gave a sharp tug at her captive hand as he swayed forwards, but he held it in a tight grip and she felt herself being dragged remorselessly after him. Then she felt a firm grasp on her left hand and she was being pulled in the opposite direction. Suddenly, she broke free from her husband.

Simon, his eyes still shut but without Wendy to anchor him, staggered forwards, tottered for a second on the brink and plunged head first onto the rocks below.

Wendy stared down the way he had fallen. She could see him lying face down and quite still. "Simon!" she screamed. "Simon! Oh my God ... what got into you?"

"Come on," a voice said gently in her ear. She had sunk to her knees and she felt herself being raised by a firm hand. Unresisting, she was led to the steps at the back of the viewing platform.

"Simon," whispered Wendy. "Simon ... oh my God."

She glanced up to see her companion for the first time and recognised the Turkish gentleman from the hotel who had been drinking raki in the little summerhouse by the pool.

"There was nothing you could have done to save him," he said in an accent that sounded more English than Turkish.

"Was it an accident or did he do it on purpose?" she asked wildly. "Did I make him do it? Was it what I said ... about the Cappadocian moon ... or champagne just being fizzy white wine? Was that the last straw ...? Did that make him do it? Oh my God, what a bloody awful mess!"

"Come," said the man. "You must try to be brave."

He started to lead her down the steps, pushing against the tide of people flowing in the opposite direction.

"Poor bloody Simon," said Wendy.

"He was enjoying himself – or at least he appeared to be," replied the man.

"Or pretending to. I never could tell with him. I suppose he must be dead, mustn't he?"

"We have to go to him. You must be brave."

By now, they had reached the square outside the citadel. A large bus was dropping a party of tourists. The Turkish gentleman steered Wendy through the throng and, as they passed the shop where she and Simon had bought the rug, the owner ran out bearing a neatly bound parcel.

"Madame," he said, offering it to Wendy.

"Thank you," she answered in Turkish as she took the parcel from him. "Oh thank you so much."

A siren could be heard shrieking from somewhere behind the citadel.

"God, what a ghastly fuss," said Wendy weakly as her companion guided her towards the sound.

2 The Cartoon

It was a scene worthy of Dostoyevski when Gregory Grayling was sick over the table at his grandfather's eighty-fifth birthday party. The greyish-pink sludge, laced with lumps of half-digested lunch, swamped the cake and washed onto the laps of the guests sitting opposite. The stink was frightful. Everyone, apart from Grandpa, jumped to their feet, while Mrs Grayling seized the tiller. Grandpa, in the meantime, remained sitting with a faint smile flickering about his lips, apparently impervious to the effluent and its stench. Some of the sick had landed in his napkin, which he carefully folded and laid on his plate.

"This is the stuff of nightmares," barked Mrs Grayling. "I think we should all move into the next room."

Grandpa was helped to his feet while the guests quietly evacuated the dining room, leaving Gregory slumped at the table with vomit still dribbling down his chin as he gazed with glassy eyes at the devastation he had just wrought.

"Shouldn't we do something about him?" Sarah whispered to her twin sister Georgina. "We can't just leave him here, can we?"

"Can't we just? I see no reason why not. Greg's his own worst enemy – useless bugger," retorted her sister.

"But all the same …"

"I thought Grandpa took it bloody well, didn't you?"

"Bloody well, and it's certainly given everyone buckets to talk about. "Buckets" is the word for it too. It amazes me how much one stomach can hold. I'm sure Grandpa's never had a birthday party quite like this one before. But all the same, we can't leave Greg. He might choke."

"It would serve the little sod right if he did," rejoined the hardhearted twin. But, nevertheless, she took the point. Something had to be done about their younger brother.

"Oh my God," he groaned, as he lifted a hand to his face and smeared it still further with vomit. "Oh bugger all that."

"You've no right to swear," Georgina admonished him. "We're the ones who ought to be swearing. You've fucked up Grandpa's birthday well and truly, haven't you? I'll be surprised if he leaves you anything at all in his will after this."

"Come on, Greg," said his more sympathetic sister. "We'd better clean you up and put you to bed."

"It's more than you deserve. Apart from wrecking the party, some poor sod's got to clean up after you," Georgina complained. "And I know who that is. Mummy certainly won't. You should be made to do the sodding job yourself."

Together they got Gregory to his feet and helped him to the door.

Meanwhile, Mrs Grayling was holding the fort in the drawing room. She was doing what she normally did in a family crisis of this nature – of which she had seen a good number – appearing not to be the least bit fazed by it and talking furiously so that no one else was allowed to get a word in. Above all, she wanted no expressions of sympathy. Once her father had been settled in a chair by the fire, she dilated on her theme of nightmares.

"The stuff of nightmares," she concluded, but then added as an afterthought "His father was just as bad. A tribe of drunkards, the Graylings. You said as much yourself, didn't you, Daddy?"

"You can't say I didn't warn you, Hermione," replied Grandpa. He spoke softly, without a trace of rancour in his voice.

"Anyway, it's made your birthday something of an occasion, hasn't it?" resumed his daughter. "Even if you didn't get to cut the cake."

She turned to her guests. Most of them were family who knew enough about the habits of her late husband Arnold and her son Gregory not to be unduly scandalised by what they had just witnessed, which made it easier for her to ride out the occasion.

"I don't know which is worse when someone's sick – the sight of it or the smell," she declared, as if the topic was worth airing.

"Oh the smell without a shadow of doubt," said her cousin Patricia. "It always makes me want to be sick too."

"Don't you start, for Heaven's sake," groaned her husband Tom.

"I think clearing up's the worst bit," put in Susan, Patricia's sister.

"If only people were like dogs. Then they might lick it up themselves and save other people the bother," opined Tom.

"Talking of which, do you need a hand clearing it up, Hermione?" asked Patricia.

"Not at all," retorted Mrs Grayling. "What are the girls for?"

"Lucky old you, having daughters who are so obliging," mused Susan. "I suppose Gregory's all right?"

"That's his business," said Mrs Grayling, who found Susan disagreeably contentious at times. "No doubt they'll clear him up as well, so put it out of your mind. I'm sorry your cake was spoiled, Daddy."

"Stuff the cake," the old man replied. "What I'd really like is a gin and tonic."

"A bloody good idea," announced Mrs Grayling. "G and Ts all round."

Tom poured the drinks while Patricia distributed them. Then, when they were all clutching a glass, Mrs Grayling raised hers.

"Happy birthday, Daddy," she boomed.

"Happy birthday," chorused everybody else.

Grandpa adjusted his bow tie – which he liked to fasten with a loose, raffish knot – and, clearing his throat, raised his glass in reply. "To absent friends," he said, "above all, to that young scamp Gregory who made it such a special occasion just now."

There were awkward glances all round and a muffled, "To Gregory."

"What about his sisters?" muttered Susan. "Aren't they absent too?"

"I must say that boy has got panache," went on Grandpa. "He chose his ground well and timed it to perfection. I would never have had the balls to do a thing like that at my grandfather's birthday party, though a few of us were a bit the worse for wear at his funeral."

"Well, I'm glad someone enjoyed it at least," said his daughter.

"It saved me having to eat birthday cake, for which I'm deeply in the boy's debt. Do any of you keep pigs?" he asked the company in general.

"I do," ventured Susan's husband Harry, a modest, sandy-haired man who said very little.

"Take it home to them – with my compliments," declared Grandpa. "The contents of the boy's stomach will make a splendid garnish for the icing sugar, marzipan and fruit cake."

Harry looked somewhat baffled by this generous offer until Mrs Grayling came to his rescue.

"I'll get one of the girls to put it in a doggy bag for you," she said. "Or should it be called a piggy bag in the circumstances?"

"Those wretched girls," muttered Susan.

"Well then," declared Grandpa, "that's settled. Now, if you'll excuse me, I'm off to see that young scamp and congratulate him on making it such a lively occasion."

He gulped down the remains of his gin and tonic and, climbing stiffly to his feet, shuffled to the door.

"I'm not sure that he's in a fit state to be seen by anyone just at the moment, Daddy," Mrs Grayling called after him. "You'd better ask the girls."

"Those wretched girls," repeated Susan in a louder voice this time.

"Wretched girls?" challenged Mrs Grayling. "They don't mind a bit. They're as happy as sand boys mucking out the stables, so what's a bit of sick?"

Meanwhile, Sir Barnaby Gillard climbed the big curving staircase to the landing. It was a slow process, but he insisted on doing it by himself and angrily dismissed any talk of installing a chairlift. Moreover, he had insisted on remaining in the Georgian pile that he now shared with his daughter Hermione, the widow of Arnold Grayling, and her grown-up children, the twins Sarah and Georgina and their brother Gregory. The girls were in their late twenties and unmarried, while Gregory was three years younger. His sisters lived at home, but Gregory spent most of his time in London with occasional retreats into the country, usually for financial reasons.

Sir Barnaby found Hermione immensely irritating with her bossy manner – much too like her own mother and not a bit like the Gillards – and wasn't over-fond of her daughters either. They swore like stable lads, a trait he found distasteful in women and one which again reminded him of his late wife, Ursula.

But the arrangement suited him in other respects. He could have gone to share the Grayling house with them instead, which was charming in its way – Jacobean, timbered and built in Cotswold stone – but it would have meant being parted from most of his beloved pictures – the great joy of his life – and putting himself under much closer tutelage.

His own house – built by a nabob ancestor of the East India Company who had laid the foundations of the Gillard fortune, was large, far too large really to rattle around in all by himself, but possible to keep if his widowed daughter and her children shared it with him. Ideally, he would have liked to have had a son to pass it on to, but nature had not been kind to him in that respect. The Graylings were tiresome, but the place was big enough to accommodate them all without too much treading on each other's toes. Sir Barnaby had what amounted to his own apartment on the first floor while the rest of them lived above and below him.

Hermione ruled the ground floor and, taking after her mother, managed the day-to-day running of things, which suited Sir Barnaby even if it meant putting up with irksome family rituals like today's birthday party from time to time – though on this particular occasion, it had turned out to be an unexpected treat.

The stables, which had fallen into disuse with Ursula "s death and Hermione's departure to live under the Grayling roof, were revived and absorbed most of his granddaughters" attention, while Hermione, being practical and hardheaded, soon made the house a venue for local gymkhanas and other more profitable rural events.

None of which interested Sir Barnaby in the slightest – or young Gregory either, for that matter. Gregory had aspirations of an altogether different kind – if "aspirations" was a word that could be used in his case. Assuming that the term "Bohemian" could still be applied on the threshold of the twenty-first century, he might almost have passed for one. In his middle twenties, he had yet to show any creative talent of his own, but, like his grandfather, he had a genuine if flighty feeling for art, which he felt obliged to match with a louche lifestyle. But also, alas, like his own father he had a weakness for strong substances and was all too apt to create minor scandals, of which his recent performance at his grandfather's birthday table was a fair specimen. These, the brusque, horsey Grayling womenfolk took in their stride.

His mother, despite her talk about "the stuff of nightmares" – a typically hackneyed and overworked expression of hers – considered herself and her own to be a cut above the middle-class and what she conceived to be its vulgar hang-ups, and was inclined to rub other people's noses in her own family's messes to make the point. Indeed, she had a formidable reputation for housetraining puppies, while clearing up after Gregory was considered to be a chore on a par with mucking out the stables and a jolly good opportunity for showing the steadiness of the Grayling womenfolk in a crisis.

But Sir Barnaby had his pictures and cabinets of drawings, which gave him infinitely more pleasure than the incompatible brood he shared his house with. The pictures filled the walls of his rooms and he tried to arrange them as a Renaissance prince might have done. For instance, in his bedroom was a reclining Venus, a succulent nude, which, if not by Titian himself, was certainly from his studio. In the room he called his studiolo – it wasn't strictly the real thing since it admitted daylight from a single window – there were several small devotional pictures of the Italian Quatracento, one of which, St Antony in his cave, had been attributed by several experts – all friends of Sir Barnaby – to the great Venetian master Giovanni Bellini.

The sitting room's walls were crammed from dado to ceiling in the manner of an early Royal Academy exhibition, as painted by Zoffani, with works from the seventeenth to the nineteenth centuries, including one by the man himself – a group portrait of East India Company nabobs watching a cockfight in the company of some Indian princes, among whom was Sir Bamaby's own ancestor, Hector Gillard.

The fine walnut cabinet of drawings and etchings, which included a couple of Rembrandts, a Dürer and an early print by Mantegna, stood in the room next to his bathroom, which he styled his dressing room.

Apart from Mrs James who "did" for him, he was seldom visited by anyone – the exception being young Gregory. And if Sir Barnaby could be said to have hopes pinned on any of them at all, it was on young Gregory.

He could hear a bath running on the floor above his own and the sound of his granddaughters" voices. A few pathetic groans indicated the presence of Gregory, who had apparently acquiesced to his sisters stripping him of his clothes and putting him in the bath after giving him their cold shower treatment.

"May I come in?" Sir Barnaby stuck his head round the bathroom door.

"Gregory wants to tell you how sorry he is for buggering up your party," said Sarah.

"Tell Grandpa you're sorry," ordered Georgina.

"You've nothing to apologise for at all, young Gregory," said Sir Barnaby. "It was a bloody bore until you provided a bit of spice. And some spice too, I might add."

"Which we will have to clean up as soon as we've put His Majesty to bed," pointed out Georgina. Like her sister, she found her grandfather's indulgence of her hopeless brother exasperating.

"When you've slept it off and smell of roses once more, I'd like to show you something, young Gregory," said Sir Bamaby to the miscreant "I think you'll find it interesting."

"Thanks, Grandpa. I'm sorry for throwing up over your birthday cake. It was nothing personal, but I think you understand that."

"On the contrary, it was the best thing you could have done to it. The perfect present. I believe your Uncle Harry – you know the one I mean, the dreary fellow with nothing to say for himself – is going to give it to his pigs. In the morning then? Ten o" clock, if that's not too early for you?"

"Thanks, Grandpa. I'll be there."

Georgina pulled out the bath plug with a violent tug, which tore it from its fixture. "Shit. Now look at what you've gone and made me do," she snarled.

Wrapped in a towel, Gregory slunk off to his bedroom along the landing. The bed was unmade and the clues to his condition lay scattered about it: a couple of empty vodka bottles and one that had contained absinthe.

He always brought absinthe back from Prague after one of his binges there. It was his professed interest in late nineteenth century Symbolism that had opened the door to the delights of the turquoise nectar. For Gregory had pretensions of being an art historian. A higher degree to compensate for his weakish second from Edinburgh University was contemplated, while in the meantime, he was learning the trade of a picture dealer with one of the smarter West End salerooms. Not that there was as much room for effete young men in these places as there might once have been, and Gregory, with his louche lifestyle and rather limited concentration span, was hardly equipped for the cut and thrust of an energetic art market. But he had been to a leading public school, spoke well and would wear a good silk tie when he needed to, and faded jeans and an open-necked shirt whenever the occasion called for it.

Behind him, of course, was his grandfather, Sir Barnaby Gillard Bt, and what his name and money stood for in the auction rooms of the West End. Gregory looked and sounded right, though his knowledge was patchy, but the name of Sir Barnaby still had considerable clout on the boards of directors – especially that of Winthrop and Swan where he had once sat.

So, at the beginning of the twenty-first century, Gregory Grayling was being carried along by a combination of charm – he chatted people up rather well at private viewings – a modicum of interest in fine art and a good deal of old-fashioned family patronage.

The only problem was that he was the son of his father – a Grayling with a weakness for intoxicants. This his Gillard grandfather had taken on board and, deep down, he had no very high hopes for young Gregory. He knew enough about the fine art world to realise that his grandson did not really match up, but was simply the best of a bad bunch because he was the only one who showed a glimmer of interest in the things that he loved himself. For this reason, he was prepared to fan the fitful flame.

That by pushing young Gregory he might arouse the jealousy of the other Graylings did not matter a fig to Sir Barnaby. Indeed, he rather hoped it would, and he took a quiet satisfaction in the scandals that his drinking sometimes created, though he wished that they shocked the boy's mother and sisters a bit more than they did. Their stubborn refusal to be fazed irked him.

Of course, he would have preferred it if Gregory could have applied himself and built up a reputation for scholarship, but, failing that, he felt that he could keep his interest alive at any rate, and use him as a stick to beat the rest of the family with. And if he had to drink, at least it was a traditional aesthetes" beverage like absinthe. If he carried on the way he was doing now it would kill the boy before long, but he was almost certain to be dead himself before that time came. And nothing mattered after that.

Gregory slept in a fitful sort of way and managed to drag himself out of bed shortly after nine o" clock the following morning.

He hadn't shaved for three days but, knowing Sir Barnaby's views on stubbly chins, he felt obliged to do so now. His grandfather was the one person who had that kind of effect on him, and he even put on a clean shirt for the occasion. With a floppy tie, baggy grey flannels and a well-worn jacket patched at the elbows with leather, he decided that he had hit the right artistic note for the old man who detested what he termed "hippies" and the whole sixties thing.

Having given himself a generous squirt from the cologne bottle, he settled down to read an old copy of *Country Life* until it was time to go down to his grandfather. At five past ten, he went down. It was an unwritten rule of Sir Barnaby's that he didn't like people to be too punctual, but he didn't like being kept waiting for too long either. Gregory, when he was sober, had the acumen to get that sort of thing right.

As he approached his grandfather's door, Mrs James came out with a breakfast tray. "He's waiting for you," she said, "in the dressing room."

Gregory went through and found the old man in a silk dressing gown and pyjamas, sitting by an occasional table on which a pot of fresh coffee, cups, milk and sugar were awaiting the arrival of his guest. The old man glanced at his watch.

"Timed to perfection, young Gregory," he declared. "Like your remarkable performance at the birthday tea yesterday."

"I'm sorry about that, Grandpa."

"For Heaven's sake, why? Because those two stable wenches told you that you should be?" retorted the old man. "Cherish the memory, dear boy. If you don't, I certainly shall." He chuckled lightly. "Now, pour me a cup of coffee, but preferably not all over the table this time. There's a time and a place for everything."

Gregory poured the coffee and handed his grandfather a cup.

They talked in a desultory way about Winthrop and Swan at first, then a little bit about Gregory's proposed thesis which had progressed no further since they had last discussed it. Sir Barnaby, having shown the right amount of interest in what passed for his grandson's academic aspirations, turned the conversation to Prague. He was very fond of Prague, a city that he had first visited shortly after the Second World War and again just ten years ago. But neither of them had anything much to add to what they had already said about it, so the old man got down to what he really wanted to talk about.

Sir Barnaby liked to be mysterious and to spring a surprise, which usually followed a lengthy preamble.

"There's something I want to show you, young Gregory. But finish your coffee first."

Gregory swallowed the remains of his coffee. "I'm ready when you are, Grandpa."

Sir Barnaby rose stiffly to his feet and lead the way into his studiolo. Behind the writing desk was a cupboard, recessed into the panelling. He went over to it and, giving his grandson a conspiratorial wink, opened it and stuck his head inside. Sounds of rummaging and displacement could be heard before Sir Barnaby backed out with a large portfolio wrapped in a piece of hessian.

"We'll take it to the sitting room," he said.

In the sitting room, he laid the portfolio on a table and started to untie the strings that bound the hessian. Gregory offered to help, but the old man waved him aside. He opened the portfolio and began to sift through various frayed and badly discoloured pieces of paper, separated from each other by sheets of tissue. Carefully, he lifted them out and spread them across the floor.

"Watch where you put your feet," he commanded his grandson.

The papers had markings on them in the form of figures, but were so discoloured that Gregory could not fathom what his grandfather was on about. Sir Barnaby looked at him closely for a second. "Well?"

"Well what, Grandpa?"

"What do you make of them?"

"It's hard to say at a glance," hedged the young man. "I'll have to examine them more closely." He did not enjoy tests of this kind.

His grandfather knelt down painfully and Gregory felt obliged to join him. Together, they scrutinised one of the pieces of paper. Gregory even picked it up to examine it more closely. It was old paper, all right – even he could tell that – dry and very brittle. He gave the old man a puzzled frown.

Sir Barnaby looked at him hard for a second without speaking, hoping, perhaps, that the penny might drop and the young man would come up with an answer, but Gregory said nothing.

"Raphael," said Sir Barnaby.

"Raphael, Grandpa?"

"Yes, Raphael. I'd hoped that you might have spotted it for yourself." There was a touch of reproach in the old man's voice.

Gregory looked hard at the ancient scrap of paper with what he hoped passed for a thoughtful frown. He could make out figures on it, which were vaguely familiar.

"Wait a minute," he cried. "The whatsit?"

"What's the whatsit?"

"The School of Athens."

"At last. For a moment you alarmed me, young Gregory. I very nearly despaired."

"Are you playing one of you little games with me, Grandpa?"

The old man laughed, almost with relief. "Now would I do a thing like that?"

"Of course you would."

Gregory looked at some of the other scraps. He could make out more of the figures. "Is … is this?"

"Pythagoras."

"Yes, of course. This is all stuff actually by Raphael?"

"Probably with the help of his assistants, but in essence his own."

"Bugger me," said the young man. "How long have you been sitting on it, Grandpa? And how did you get hold of it?" He looked at the sheets dubiously. "And, forgive me for saying it, but it looks a bit of a mess."

"Your education is clearly very incomplete, young Gregory," sighed his grandfather. "What did they teach you in that Art History degree of yours? In my day, they didn't give degrees in the subject, so if you were any good you bloody well found out for yourself."

Gregory did not like that last observation, but held his tongue.

"The Papal apartments," explained Sir Barnaby. "Pope Julius II. At the same time as Michelangelo was painting the ceiling of the Sistine Chapel."

"Wait a moment. Raphael was painting the ... the ... Stanza ...Stanza ... della ... della ..."

"Della Segnatura. We've got there at last. That and other chambers."

"And that's where The School of Athens is," said Gregory. "Of course I know all about that."

"All about it? But you do alarm me, young Gregory. Your memory isn't quite what it should be for a man of your age."

"It's all coming back to me now ..."

"It should never have left you in the first place."

"A series of frescoes in the Pope's library, each one with a theme appropriate to the shelves over which it was situated."

Sir Barnaby clapped his hands. "Go on."

"The School of Athens filled the space above the Philosophy section."

Sir Barnaby gave a deep sigh, this time of contentment. "I feel rejuvenated," he said. And now, what can you tell me about the art of fresco painting?"

There was a pause.

"Anything at all?" A disappointed look crept into the old man's eye.

"Sure, Grandpa, I can tell you something, but I know you can tell me a hell of a lot more. The Quatracento is very much your thing. And, anyway, I like listening to you."

"Brown-nosed little sod."

Gregory was startled by the sudden descent into contemporary scatological idiom on the part of his 85-year-old grandparent. But the old man had been flattered nevertheless.

"Well," he said, " for a start do you know how the paint was applied?"

"Yes. A tempora paint was applied to wet plaster, so that when it dried the colour was fixed. A little touching up might be added afterwards on the dry surface. This was known as a "secco'.'"

"This is almost too good to be true," said the old man.

"And," went on his grandson, "because of the speed with which the plaster dried, the paint could only be applied in small sections at a time."

"Which meant?"

"Which meant?" Gregory looked nonplussed.

"Go back to the beginning of the process."

Gregory's face brightened. "Ah. The Cartoon."

Sir Barnaby clapped his hands and pulled himself up painfully into a chair.

"The painter would do a series of studies that he worked into a complete picture, which he scaled up," explained Gregory.

"How did he scale it up?"

"By squaring," said Gregory. "That way he got a drawing which was the right size for the area he wanted to paint."

"And then?"

"He had to transfer the drawing to the wall or ceiling."

"How did he do that?"

Gregory frowned.

"Wet or dry?"

"Wet or dry?"

"Did he transfer the drawing onto a wet or a dry plaster surface?"

"A wet one, of course."

"Of course. But how?"

"By "spolvero'."

"Your knowledge of Italian astounds me. By "spolvero', which means?"

"A series of holes were pricked into the outline of the drawing and charcoal was pounced through them onto the plaster."

"I like "pounced'. But if the painter wanted to be quick he could sometimes press his outline into the surface of the plaster by running a stylus along the lines of the cartoon. But it wasn't quite as straightforward as that."

Gregory frowned.

"Remember the wet plaster – which dried quickly." The old man leaned forward and picked up one of the fragments of old paper from the floor. He handed it to Gregory. "What did he do with his cartoon?" As he spoke he ran a finger along the broken edge of a second fragment.

Gregory frowned.

"Of course. He couldn't use a large piece of paper if he was working on a small patch of wet plaster. So he cut his cartoon up – into separate pieces."

"Look at it closely. What else can you see apart from the outline of a figure?"

"I think I can make out the holes for the charcoal," said Gregory, "and squares. They're still quite distinct."

"There we have it then. This is the very cartoon that Raphael used to transfer his original drawing onto the wall of the Pope's library." Sir Barnaby leaned forward and gave his grandson a chaste kiss on his forehead.

Meanwhile Gregory picked up a few of the scraps of paper and eyed them rather dubiously.

"You see, we already have a cartoon by Raphael for The School of Athens," went on Sir Barnaby. "But there is one thing wrong with it that for a time puzzled the scholars."

Gregory looked at him blankly and said nothing.

" A perfect cartoon, but without one thing. There were no squares."

"No squares?"

"None. So what do we conclude?"

"That it was never intended for use on the wall?"

"Correct. It was itself a marketable work of art by the hand of the Master, no less. Like those drawings by Rembrandt that I have in my cabinet."

"So what you've got here is the actual working cartoon?"

"Indeed. The one that was used on the wall of the Pope's library. That's why it's in pieces and looks such a mess."

"This is fantastic, Grandpa. Does anyone know you've got it?"

"You do now – and the man who sold it to me, if he's still alive. It was shortly after the end of the war and among a lot of material that – how do I put it – walked during the German occupation of Italy. I was part of a commission for the restitution of looted works of art." The old man chuckled. "And, as no one else seemed to interested in this particular instance, I thought I might do a little looting on the side myself. I paid something for it, of course. Call it a notional sum."

Gregory gaped at his grandfather. "I would never have believed it of you, Grandpa."

"Does it shock you?"

Gregory thought for a second. "No, Grandpa, I don't think it does. Should it?"

"The man who sold it to me hadn't the faintest idea what it was. And anyway, there were so many more obvious masterpieces lying around at the time that no one noticed. Raphael was very much my subject, so I had a pretty shrewd idea what I was looking at as soon as I opened the portfolio."

"And you never told anyone?"

"You understand the purpose of a studiolo? The place where a lover of beautiful and fascinating things could enjoy his treasures in solitude and reveal to his fellow connoisseurs only the things he wanted to reveal. You're the first, young Gregory, to be so honoured in this particular case. It could be your very own little scoop when I'm gone."

"I'm sure you're going to be with us for a long time yet, Grandpa."

"Bollocks. Now off you go and don't breathe a word of any of this to the rest of them – especially those stable wenches."

"Mum's the word, Grandpa."

"And certainly don't tell your mother. This will be yours one day, so now you can help me pick it up off the floor before you go."

Gregory picked up the fragments, examining each one carefully as he placed them on the table.

"Thank you, Grandpa. This is a moment I shan't forget."

"Don't sound so bloody mawkish. Just piss off."

"Thank you, Grandpa," said Gregory again.

Sir Barnaby waved a dismissive hand.

On the following morning, his grandson looked in to say goodbye before going back to London and no mention was made of the cartoon. But it was the last time he ever saw his grandfather alive.,

Sir Barnaby died very cleanly in his sleep as the first daffodils bloomed, just over a month later. Mrs James went in with his breakfast and, instead of being up and in his dressing-gown, he was still in bed – stone dead with his mouth wide open.

The funeral and subsequent entertainment passed off without incident – Mrs Grayling drew the line at her son upsetting that particular occasion. Gregory stayed on for a few days to hear the will read out by the family solicitor, Mr Findlater.

The big surprise was what Sir Barnaby did with his art collection. Sarah and Georgina were fully expecting him to leave it to their useless brother, the so-called artistic one. But no. Nor did he bequeath it along with the rest of his possessions, which he left for his kin to fight over among themselves. Instead, he gave the entire collection to a well-known national institution, not even stipulating that it should bear his own name. Only one item, the portfolio of the Raphael cartoon fragments, did he leave to young Gregory, without stating their actual identity in the will. That was something for his grandson to publish and reveal to the world.

But Gregory was not pleased and felt cheated by his grandfather. He had hoped to become the owner of his entire collection, thus giving lustre to his image as a gentleman/connoisseur without having to lift a finger to do much about it. Now he would have to sit down and write a fucking thesis to establish himself well and truly in the fine arts world.

When the day for the division of the spoils arrived, the portfolio was placed on a table with a lot of lesser items. His relatives were naturally intrigued to see what was in it for the old man to single it out specially for his grandson.

They were predictably sniffy and both of the sisters gloated over the fact that nothing else was coming his way – Georgina especially. Rather than listen to them, Gregory took the portfolio from the table and slipped upstairs. First, he went to his own room where he collected a bottle of absinthe and a tumbler, then he went down to his grandfather's apartment, which, without its owner and stripped of its treasures, had all the chill of a tomb. In the sitting room, he placed the bottle and the glass on the floor beside a remaining chaise longue and, opening the portfolio, he spread the discoloured fragments of the cartoon about him where he could contemplate them as he stretched himself on the couch. There was an unwritten rule in Gregory's life that if something could be done lying down it was better to do it that way.

Having filled his glass, he sipped the absinthe and looked at the scraps of paper on the floor beside him. They might just as well have been decorator's rubbish, left behind after the room had been papered. And strictly speaking, that's all they were – except that the decorator in this case happened to be Raphael. But did that really make any difference? Indeed, should it make a difference? It was an unusually profound thought for the likes of young Gregory.

"Bugger Grandpa," he muttered as he took a large pull at the glass, which made him wince. "Why did he have to give everything else away and leave me with just this?"

He recharged the tumbler with turquoise nectar and what followed can be swiftly told. Soon, Gregory was hopelessly drunk and, as was commonly the case with him, massively sick, so much so that it was a miracle that he hadn't choked by the time Sarah discovered him. But he still breathed and his sisters did him the usual honours, while the gory business of clearing up the battlefield was left, on this occasion, to Mrs James.

"What shall I do with all these bits of paper?" she enquired of Mrs Grayling, as she eyed with distaste the fragments of cartoon that showed through the surface of the lake of vomit.

"Throw the bloody things out," Mrs Grayling commanded her. "And for God's sake open the windows and get rid of the appalling stink."

3   Jessica's Gap Year

Coming home after her gap year was always going to feel strange to Jessica. She had never been away from home for so long before and it seemed as if her existence had been split between two quite separate worlds: the world of Ukraine and all that had happened during the ten months she had just spent there, and the one she had grown up in. Somehow, the two did not meet. They might have existed in parallel universes. But nothing had prepared her for what she found when she got home and, full as she was of everything that had recently happened to her – especially Sasha – it left her feeling utterly dazed.

She had caught the train from London at the last minute and, as no one at home had answered her call to tell them when it would get into York, she had taken a taxi from the station.

It felt odd coming home to a strange house because her parents had moved during the time she had been in Ukraine. They had discussed the possibility before she had left so it was no surprise to her, but naturally she was concerned that none of her things had gone astray in the process.

It turned out to be a substantial thirties suburban house overlooking Clifton Green and within comfortable walking distance of the centre of town. Jessica liked York, a town she had visited on a number of occasions.

The door was locked so she rang the bell. "I hope they're in," she thought, "But I shan't tell them about Sasha straight away."

Someone approached the door and Jessica could hear the Yale lock being lifted. It was a stranger, a woman with thick, wavy, grey-blonde hair and rather heavy make-up.

"I'm sorry, I must have come to the wrong house," Jessica faltered. She picked up her holdall and stepped back from the porch. But the number on the jamb was the correct one.

"This is Water End?" Jessica asked with a frown.

"Of course it is, Jess," replied the woman in a husky voice. "And welcome to your new home." She laughed awkwardly.

"You know who I am? Are Professor or Mrs Stallard at home? They do live here now, don't they?"

The woman laughed again, making an oddly deep-throated sound.

"They moved while I've been abroad, so this is my first time here," explained Jessica.

"Welcome home, Jess."

Jessica stared hard at the strange woman who looked back at her a shade nervously. "My God, it's Dad, isn't it?"

"Not any more, Jess."

Jessica shook her head in disbelief. "What's been going on? Have you gone utterly mad?"

"No, Jess. Just woken up."

There was a pause while neither of them spoke.

"Sorry if it's a shock to you, Jess, but the truth had to come out one day. And we thought this was the best time for it – when you'd left school and were about to start university." The voice was unmistakably her father's and, in a creepy kind of way, the wig suited him.

Jessica sank onto the step. "Oh my God," she said in a weak voice. "And what about Mum? What does she make of it?"

"You could say that I'm Mum now," said her father, "but you don't have to call me that if it'll be difficult for you."

"And I suppose Mum's Dad."

He/she did not answer, but the silence was enough to confirm her suspicion.

"What's got into the pair of you?" said Jessica in a tiny voice. "You've gone quite mad."

"We'll talk it through, Jess, and then perhaps you'll understand." The woman who used to be her father picked up her holdall. "I know it's hard to come to terms with straight away, but before we were living a lie. Really we were, Jess. We kept it up until we felt you were old enough to understand and then my retirement provided the break."

"So I suppose having me was a kind of a lie too, was it? It has to be, doesn't it? I mean if you were both the wrong sex at the time, or perhaps I should call it 'gender'?"

"Come on, Jess, you know things can't be as simple as that."

"And what are you doing with yourself now that you've become Mum?" rejoined the girl.

"I'm still working on my book and writing the odd review. They keep me busy. None of that's changed."

"And what about Mum? Or should I call her Dad?"

"Not if you don't want to, Jess. Just take it in stages. But she – he's – fine. You see, Jess, we're free at last. We've started to live a real life. No more play-acting. You have to try and see it that way.

"So it would appear. And other people? Do they see it that way?"

"That's for them to work out for themselves," replied her parent. "But, as I've told you, we were living a lie before."

"And Uncle Bill and Aunt Susan? What do they make of it?"

She – or he – shrugged his or her shoulders. "What would you expect them to make of it? You know what they're like. And anyway, it hardly matters what they think."

"Hardly matters?" Jessica shook her head and buried her face in her hands.

"Don't just sit there," pleaded her parent, trying to ease the rucksack off her back. "Welcome to your new home."

She did not speak.

"Won't you come in and see Mum? He won't mind you calling him that until you've got used to things. And tell us all your news. We're dying to hear."

"Just leave me alone for a minute. I've got to think this thing out. Surely you can see that." Her parent took the luggage inside the house and hovered in the hall.

"Come on inside, Jess."

"Just leave me for a minute. God, I don't even know what I'm meant to call you. I'll come."

Her thoughts flew back to the past months of her life in Poltava and how straightforward it had been compared with what she had just come home to.

Jessica had got good A level grades in Russian and French and was intending to read Modern Languages at Durham University in the coming academic year. For her gap year, she had been attached to School Number Three in Poltava in central Ukraine. This had been arranged for her by her Russian teacher who had met and befriended the deputy director of the Poltava school, Ludmilla Mikhailovna, at a conference.

So Jessica had lived with a family and taught a thing that was loosely described as "British Culture'. It had been a challenge because she had none of the things that she would have taken for granted at home, no visual aids or access to a photocopier even. And virtually no books – just a few tattered leftovers from the Soviet era. Chalk even had to be foraged and wasn't in the form of a stick, but was a nugget that you grasped in the palm of your hand and was often too greasy to make a proper mark on the board.

The school had run on a curiously ad hoc basis, probably because of the dead hand of bureaucracy that hung over it – a power that issued binding decrees, which generally went unheeded.

Though casual about their attendance, her pupils were bright and willing enough when they were there. Interestingly, School Number Three was an elite kind of establishment that tended to collect the offspring of journalists, university and institute teachers, lawyers, engineers and officers of the security police – members of the privileged professions, in other words. So, apart from the sudden unnerving demands of the authorities for completed registers and the like, there was little stress as long as Jessica could find enough things to fill her lessons with.

And then there was the English Club, which met in the Poltava Musical Institute a couple of evenings a week. Though there were several members of the United States Peace Corps in Poltava, Jessica was the only English person, which made her something of an event, and her standard received or classical English – as her friends preferred to call it – was in great demand.

The English Club meetings were arranged by Eleni Nikolaevna, the Institute's deputy director. They were popular and attracted a wide variety of people of different ages and occupations, ranging from the misanthropic Boris Babko, a former state interpreter whose grandmother, a hanging judge under Stalin, had been murdered by Ukrainian nationalists, to Sergei, a mathematician who had worked in western Europe, to Viktor, a tenor teaching in the Institute itself, and finally to Sasha and Anya, the youngest members of the group who had just left school.

Sasha used to collect the money for Eleni Nikolaevna at the end of each session and then made a point of walking with Jessica up Oktobskaya Street to her lodgings in a small apartment block not far from the central circus. In this way, he could continue practising his English. Sometimes Anya would come with them as well, but though they were old school chums, she and Sasha did not appear to be particularly close.

Jessica, who was the same age, fell in with them straight away. Of the two, Anya was the more fluent, though Sasha was more voluble and bubbled with humour. He had a flattish, Slavic nose, a round, almost baby like face and large playful eyes, which reflected his nature. All of which Jessica found very appealing.

And he was brimming with irreverent humour, which Anya thought he was inclined to push a little too far. Having grown up under communism, he had an ample store of the kind of cynical jokes that sustained the more thoughtful people during that time. This was something new to Jessica – an eighteen year old who spoke in the tones of one who had seen it all and did not expect a very great deal from life, whatever system he lived under.

But, at the same time, Sasha expressed himself with such panache and charm that she swiftly fell under his spell. And their surroundings helped in a way too. Despite its post-Soviet shabbiness, Poltava had claims to elegance with its neo-classical central circus – Kruhla Ploscha – and the Column of Glory, raised to commemorate Peter the Great's victory over Charles XII of Sweden in 1709. The circus and the buildings in the streets radiating from it were dressed in white stucco, reminding Jessica of some of the swankier streets in London. Indeed, a Governor Kuragin in the early nineteenth century had set out deliberately to emulate St Petersburg and the centre of Poltava, with its spacious tree-lined streets, retained much of the refinement he had aspired to. A great deal of the city, of course, was like any other in the former Soviet Union – high-rise kruschevkas with Stygian stairwells, dreary emporia with half-empty shelves and mangy, neglected spaces between its buildings.

But it was easy enough to walk out of the town, past old-fashioned isbas and the brash edifices of Ukraine's new rich, to relatively open countryside with its untidy clusters of wooden dachas and rubbish tips. Scruffy in a characteristically Slav kind of way, it was innocent of environmental considerations.

And it wasn't long before Sasha and Jessica were walking through these fields together on Sundays in the early autumn sun. Of course, Sasha was learning English by leaps and bounds while Jessica's Russian – never mind her Ukrainian – was hardly advancing at all, but she saw into all sorts of nooks and crannies on the outskirts of the town that she would not have discovered otherwise because her companion, who was an imaginative guide with an eye for the eccentric, saw it as his side of the bargain in return for the free English lessons she was giving him.

They visited the Khrestovozd Monastery – which had started to function again not long before – and wandered in the fields and woods beyond, past ugly iron garages and the sprawl of dachas to the rather neglected botanical gardens – a place they would make a regular haunt. They visited the battlefield of Poltava where a Russian army decisively defeated a European one for the first time. Sasha explained the action in detail, showing Jessica where the redoubts had been, but without a hint of triumphalism. He was a Russian who refused to speak a word of Ukrainian, yet he took no aggressive pride in his own country's military achievements.

They wandered through the streets of the town too, where Sasha helped Jessica with her shopping and explained the buildings to her and even introduced her to his old history teacher, Ivan Ivanovich who, as a teenager, had seen Von Paulus" doomed Sixth Army pass through Poltava on the way to its nemesis at Stalingrad and had actually set eyes on Hitler on one of his fleeting visits to the Eastern Front.

One day when Jessica met Sasha at their usual rendezvous at the foot of the Column of Glory in Kruhla Ploscha, she found him wearing a pair of dark glasses. But instead of coming forward to meet her as he usually did, he seemed oblivious of her presence. She walked right up to him.

"Sasha, have you gone blind or something?" she said.

"Is it you, Jessica?"

"Yes, it's me. Why are you wearing those glasses all of a sudden?"

With a flourish, Sasha whipped them from his face and slipped them on Jessica's.

"I can't see a thing!"

"Does that surprise you? They're Soviet sunglasses."

Jessica removed them and held them to the light. "They're completely black," she said. "Are they made for blind people?"

Sasha laughed and a wicked glint came into his eye. "In a way – for people who were meant to be blind – how do you say it?"

"Kept in the dark?" Jessica frowned.

"Kept in the dark. They belonged to my mother," Sasha explained. "My father bought them for her back in the days of Comrade Brezhnev."

"But they're useless!"

"Of course they are. And when my mother took them back to the store to change them, she found that every other pair she tried was just the same. They could only be worn by someone who was blind. So she couldn't change them and they didn't give her the money back either. Two months later they were still being offered for sale. I keep them and will give them to one of my children – when that time comes."

It was the middle of autumn and there was a fresh breeze. It had rained steadily all night but now the day was fine with a few clouds scudding across the sky.

"I have something else to show you," Sasha announced. "More of our old Soviet Union. Are you interested?"

"Of course I am," said Jessica.

"Pashlee. Let's go then."

"Where are we going?"

"That's my surprise."

They walked to a place on the edge of the town that they had not visited together before. The lanes were muddy after the recent rainfall. Sasha took Jessica to the end of a little street of isbas, which looked the same as others they had visited. There had once been an attempt to metal the road, but now it was a mass of potholes filled with water. The houses with their overgrown and cluttered yards had a dejected air.

Sasha stopped and looked at Jessica, his large eyes twinkling with mischief at the thought of what he had in store for her.

"Can you read the name of the street?" he asked her.

Jessica read the faded Cyrillic sign. "Communism Street," she said.

Sasha nodded and led the way up the road, picking a path around the puddles.

"Where are you taking me?" Jessica demanded to know.

"Wait and see."

The muddy street did not change but, if anything, seemed to be getting narrower. Finally they stopped when their way was barred. In front of them was an enormous puddle, almost a lake, with odd bits of household junk sticking above its scummy surface.

"There," said Sasha triumphantly. "That's where Communism Street ends."

A dirty puddle. Seventy years of history in a nutshell. The most turbulent, idealistically driven and misguided event of modern times.

"Is there any way round it?" asked Jessica, for the stagnant pool appeared to lap the very fronts of the houses.

"That's a good question," replied Sasha. "We might be able to find a way, but it will be difficult and take time." He started to lead the way cautiously along the foot of a fence.

Winter followed autumn and brought snow with it, which sometimes lay thickly over everything and sometimes melted into slush only to freeze once more. It curtailed the walks but Sasha and Jessica continued to meet and he to regale her with stories of the Soviet times. For instance, he told her about the wall that had been covered with old party slogans, which were deemed to be redundant in the days of Perestroika. He and several of his classmates had been given the task of covering them with a coat of paint. But no matter how many coats they put on the wall, the slogans still showed through.

At last the snow gave way to a soggy aftermath and the dregs of winter sprouted with new life. Sasha and Jessica were drawn into the open countryside once more. The botanical gardens bloomed and people could be seen returning from them with armfuls of lilac that grew in abundance there.

Sasha's fund of anecdotes at the expense of the Soviet Union tailed off for the time being, as something more primal took their place. They were young and falling in love while, at the same time, the lilac that grew on the banks that bounded the botanical gardens was out in all its glory.

Other people had the same idea, but Sasha managed to find a place deep inside the bushes that was safe from prying eyes.

"You've done this before," Jessica said to him as he led her by the hand into what seemed like the heart of the lilac grove.

"But never like this," he told her as he pressed his lips to hers.

It was the first time he had done it. Sasha had always seemed oddly old-fashioned in the way he approached Jessica. He loved to amuse her and to show her little gallantries and, in a way, those were the things she cherished most about him because, in truth, Jessica was an old-fashioned girl. "I'm not a sixties kind of person at all," she had once complained to her parents, and her betrayal of their own youth and all it had seemed to stand for was a shock to them.

"Oh dear," her mother had said. "Did we fight that war for nothing, then?"

The metaphor of war coming from her peace-campaigning mother, of all people, had struck Jessica as odd at the time.

But if Sasha was innocent of the finer points of lovemaking, his instinct was true. He broke off the lilac blooms and made a bed with them and then, withdrawing discreetly into the bushes, he took his clothes off while Jessica did the same in the nest that he had prepared.

And when he returned, with hardly a word passing between them, the two virgins made love on the lilac bed. Their subsequent lovemaking, technically more accomplished though it became, never quite achieved the sheer rapture of that first essay on the lilac bed.

That is where it began and it flowered long after the lilac had faded. Jessica had met Sasha's mother – who was divorced from his father – of course, and they became good friends. In common with many Russian and Ukrainian families, Sasha was the only child and his mother doted on him, as the numerous photographs of the different stages of his childhood in their flat testified. How deep her son's relationship with Jessica went, she probably did not fully grasp, but she expressed her gratitude for what she was doing for him, meaning his progress with English – an impression that Sasha did everything to foster by his readiness to demonstrate his skill as an interpreter. Tatyana Andreyevna watched his performance with a mother's pride and only chided him gently that he left her to do all the work at the dacha while he spent his weekends with Jessica. But it was a very mild rebuke because she was very fond of the girl. Jessica wished that her own mother was more like Tatyana Andreyevna.

But the summer drew on and Sasha was due to visit his father who lived in St Petersburg, and Jessica's time was running out. Her communication with her own family had been sporadic – they hardly seemed to miss each other – but she had been told about the move north to York and they had said something about "starting a new life" without giving her any more details. She knew that she would have to return in good time before her university term began.

So, after the last bell and the ending of the school year, the day came when she would have to make her break with Sasha. Of course, it was only to a temporary one – both parties insisted on that – and a visit by Sasha to England was discussed as a possibility, so there was no feeling of finality. Indeed, Jessica felt quite the opposite, that something much larger was stirring. Perhaps this was only normal in a nineteen year old girl, but she had good grounds for thinking so, which she was keeping to herself – for the time being, at least.

Almost as a commemorative gesture, they made love on the eve of her departure in the lilac grove on the edge of the botanical gardens, though, of course, the bushes were no longer in flower. And then they took a stroll down Communism Street, which they had not visited since Sasha had first shown it to her. The lake had shrunk considerably and now the passage around its margin was much easier to negotiate, though even more household detritus had been exposed in the process.

"Better, but still a long way to go," Sasha observed, eying the scruffy spectacle critically. "The smaller it gets, the more rubbish you can see."

They parted at the entrance to Jessica's apartment. The Director of School Number Three was to take her to Kiev at one o'clock in the morning. So it was a lingering kiss and only a brief word spoken. Jessica promised to return and Sasha who, for all his cynicism, had the Slavic propensity for large promises that were seldom kept, believed her. He was only nineteen and in love.

And what made it so perfect for Jessica was that it was a journey out of innocence that they had made together. The inexpert fumbling followed by the ecstatic climax was a mutual discovery, one that upheld the purity of their relationship – a pair of wholesome young creatures doing exactly what nature expected of them.

So, with a reluctant heart, Jessica flew home and, after a day spent in London, took the train to York and the curious state of affairs that awaited her in her new home. Quite unexpected but not altogether surprising, she decided, after she had time to reflect on it.

When the person who was formerly her mother came out to coax her into the house, the sight shocked her less than the encounter with her erstwhile father in drag. Her mother had always preferred to wear trousers and had kept her hair neatly cropped in boyish fashion, so the transformation was not so blatant. Now she was wearing men's chinos and a sporty checked shirt, while her hair had been swept forward to rise in a trendy tuft over her brow.

"Shouldn't you grow a beard as well to complete the effect, Mum?" suggested the girl unkindly. "You'd really make your point if you did."

The onetime Mrs Stallard took her taunt with good grace. "If only I could tell you how much more like my true self I feel now, Jess, you'd understand why we've done it."

"What am I supposed to call you? I can hardly call you Mum anymore, can I? And Dad sticks in the throat, somehow,"

"Why not call me Fran?"

"Short for Frances, you mean?"

"Or Frank if you'd prefer. It's a plain, honest-sounding name."

"And shall I tell you my news … Frank … since we're being so honest and open with each other?"

"Oh yes, dear, of course you must, we're longing to hear, aren't we, Bobby?" Her partner had been "Bob" before and "Bobby" would just about do for a woman.

"We're all ears," said Bobby.

Jessica followed Frank into the kitchen while the professor followed with her luggage. The girl looked at her parents with a triumphant gleam in her eye. "I'm going to have a baby."

"Oh my God, you're not, are you?" said her onetime mother, sinking onto a chair. "I suppose you'll get rid of it."

Jessica looked hard at both of her parents who exchanged anxious glances with each other.

"You will, won't you Jess?" her former father said at length. "I mean it would be the most sensible thing to do now that you're just starting university, wouldn't it?"

"You take my breath away," replied the girl. "I'll do no such thing. I'm surprised that you of all people should say a thing like that. But no, on second thoughts, I'm not a bit surprised. Just sad, that's all."

It was not difficult to arrange a fresh invitation to Ukraine where Jessica had her baby, a little boy that they called Anton who naturally had his father's full name, Alexander, as his patronymic. She married Sasha, of course, despite both of them being so young and, with the support of the child's grandmother, was even able to carry on with her studies. Meanwhile, Jessica's own parents continued to live their more truthful lives, untroubled by a critical daughter who might disrupt the newfound harmony of their relationship.

4 Ambrose Prior

It was a warm day of mixed cloud and sunshine in late June. Ambrose Prior was leaning against the railing of the Spa Bridge and looking across the bay towards Scarborough Castle on the hill above the town. He felt as content as he ever did these days. For one thing, it was summer and he could sleep out. And a spot of rain didn't matter much because he slept in the loggia on Plantation Hill, a short walk from where he was standing now – just as long as there wasn't a gale blowing to drive the rainwater into his shelter.

Naturally, he preferred to have the place to himself. Despite having come in contact with all sorts and conditions of people in the course of his life, he found the alcoholic maunderings of his fellow vagrants tedious. And, unless an interesting conversation was available to him, he preferred to be left alone with his own thoughts.

It had not been a bad day – in the morning there had been that pair of nice-looking boys in the Olympia Amusement Arcade on the front. He'd hovered in the doorway and admired their postures as they operated the machines. But that was as far as such matters went these days since the balloon had burst. Not that it had ever amounted to much more than that anyway. It was the pictures that he had downloaded and filed with his own pithy captions and comments that had been his undoing. He had built a whole shelf full of dossiers but had never laid hands on a single boy in the whole time he was doing it. But, as a barrister, he had realised that when he was eventually tracked down he hadn't got a leg to stand on. He could only go down with the ship, salvaging as much dignity as he could and then vanish from view.

So he still treated himself to the sight of a good-looking boy in the arcade. He wasn't hurting anyone by admiring them, but then he had told himself the same thing before his arrest. They all said that. He'd enjoyed his work as a criminal barrister and had only just taken silk when the calamity struck. Yet, in a perverse way, he had embraced his martyrdom. But martyrdom to what exactly? Even his own fertile imagination couldn't come up with a good answer to that.

On the face of it, his case was cut and dried and he could see that justice of a kind was being done. He had offered no defence and had bowed his head with due humility when the judge, in his sentencing, drew attention to the special shame of one in his position – a distinguished and rising member of the Bar, blah …blah …blah. And yet… and yet a part of him had felt outside it all – the public humiliation, the scandal in the tabloid papers – a mere onlooker, just as he did now that he was leading a vagrant's life.

And it all might have been a good deal worse. Six years before, Cassandra had divorced him, decamping with their two teenage children who, if anything, were relieved by the collapse of their parents" marriage after the domestic gloom that had led up to it. Cassandra had married again and left his life completely before the balloon had burst, so it was less messy than it might have been.

He had shaved in a public convenience early in the morning – something he liked to do at least three times a week if possible. His money was lasting out – he still had access to considerable funds, but chose to live on what he described to himself as "a tramp's wage" – and he could afford to feed himself on sandwiches till the end of the week in four days" time. The weather was kind and he had a warm sleeping bag and a book to read – a secondhand copy of Evelyn Waugh's *A Handful of Dust*. So, taking it all together, he felt reasonably at peace with the world. When it eventually grew dark, he would settle down in the loggia and think of those lads he had admired in the arcade.

As long as he could be sure of being left alone. That was one reason for choosing to live the way he did – that and to avoid causing embarrassment to the people he knew. Of course, he was not the real thing, but a vagrant with a still valid credit card and the means of retreating to a more comfortable existence if he chose. Still, for the moment at least, he was wedded to the idea of the nomad's life. After two years he had grown quite used to it, though when age started to take its toll and his tracks had been sufficiently obscured he felt he might return to something like the existence he had previously known, living abroad perhaps. No, he knew perfectly well that he was not the real thing. But, come to think of it, had he ever been that? From his childhood onwards he had been living a lie of one kind or another.

He ambled towards the Spa and, finding a bench with a pleasant view across the bay, lit a cigarette he had cadged earlier in the day from a holidaymaker on the front. He cadged his cigarettes because he knew that it was the kind of thing tramps were meant to do, though begging still didn't come naturally to him.

There was a distant murmur of voices from the front and the sound of the occasional motor vehicle, blurred by the distance. On the sands immediately below him children were still playing before the tide came in. Would their mothers be letting them do that if they knew the kind of man who was watching them? He smiled at the thought, knowing that they were in no danger from this particular paedophile at least.

It was growing dark when he decided to have a drink. He had enough for half a pint of beer. Gone were the days of champagne and fine wines. But, on his strict budget, he allowed himself enough for a daily half pint of beer and admired his own self-discipline. At the same time, while his clothes were shabby and worn and had been slept in, they were not yet in a condition to draw unwelcome attention to him in a crowded bar.

In the pubs of his choice he had even made one or two acquaintances, but he was careful to keep them at a safe distance and not talk too much about himself.

Being a warm evening, the pub had spilled out into the space behind where there were tables and benches. There was a holiday mood, which he did not particularly feel like joining in with, so he took his glass to the edge of the car park and settled down on a low brick wall from where he could watch the other drinkers. It was a solitary pleasure that he had always enjoyed – giving them imaginary names and writing their biographies in his head. Indeed, with his background in law, he was able to come up with some colourful fancies, often out of pretty unpromising material. That was one of the things that had never failed to fascinate

Ambrose – how commonplace even the most vicious criminals looked in real life. But now a particular face caught his attention.

It wasn't an exceptional face – a middle-aged, fattish one with close-cropped, steely-grey hair. He envied people with a good crop of hair. His own wispy, sandy kind had started to thin at an early age and, though it had looked not undistinguished in its way and was no doubt easier to manage under a barrister's wig than a full head would have been, he nevertheless regretted the loss of youthfulness that it implied.

But he knew the face. It was one he had come across in the course of his work – not that it made it easy to place because he had seen a good many faces during his time at the Bar. It was not someone he had defended – he felt fairly sure of that – but it was probably a face from the dock.

Someone he had prosecuted, then? The fellow lookedplump and well-heeled – much more so than he did himself – so whatever he had been up for at the time it didn't appear to have done him much harm in the long run.

The man glanced his way but, as soon as their eyes met, each averted them again. Ambrose tried to study another face, but his gaze kept coming back to the first one. And, again, they caught each other's eye. This could be embarrassing, Ambrose thought, so, swallowing the remainder of his drink, he got up to go.

Emerging from the pub, Ambrose turned towards Plantation Hill, while someone came out after him and set off in the same direction.

Ambrose didn't look back and walked briskly on – he had yet to acquire a tramp's shuffle. On his back he carried a small rucksack with a change of underpants and a shirt, his washing tackle and his sleeping bag. When he got to Plantation Hill, he could see a huddled form in the loggia. From it came the sound of heavy snoring.

"Bugger," Ambrose muttered to himself as he settled at the far end of the loggia, as far as possible from the sleeper.

Taking off his coat, he folded it into a pillow and brushed the space he had selected clean before unrolling his sleeping bag and laying it out.

For a while, he lay on top of it without getting in. Apart from its other occupants, he had grown quite fond of his loggia, which, being acquainted with the classical orders, he had noted was in the Tuscan style. Although he was in his mid forties, he had got used to sleeping on the hard ground surprisingly quickly, but it was still pleasant to lie on top of the soft quilt before getting into it.

The snoring persisted and he thought of crossing to the sleeper and waking him with a plea to desist, but the man was clearly drugged or drunk and he felt it would be a wasted effort. So he lay on his back with hands behind his head on his makeshift pillow and thought about the lads in the Olympia Arcade. He would go back in the morning after he had been to the library to read the papers.

The ragged snoring continued and, as he didn't feel particularly sleepy, Ambrose lit a cigarette while his thoughts turned to his father who had fallen face-first into a bowl of game soup in his club, dead of a massive heart attack when Ambrose was still a schoolboy. He had followed him to the Bar, though he had specialised in criminal work rather than libel, which had been his father's speciality. Nathan Prior had become something of a celebrity in his own right as a result of the high profile cases he took on. While Ambrose, for his part, was fastidious about such noisy acclaim and had preferred the relative twilight of criminal practice. He thought about it – how his father had hoped that he would follow in his footsteps. But now what would he have made of his son? He had never liked his father very much – not least because he was inclined to treat the members of his family as if they were in the witness box to be bullied. No doubt he would have been appalled by his son's disgrace, but that thought did not trouble Ambrose in the least. In fact, he rather enjoyed it.

As he pulled at his cigarette and thought of his parent, he saw a man standing at the far end of the loggia, contemplating the sleeper and nudging him with his toe. Then he wandered over to where Ambrose lay in the shadows, drawn, no doubt, by the lighted cigarette. When he lent over him, Ambrose recognised the man he had observed in the pub.

"Mr Prior?" the man said.

"Yes?" Ambrose replied nervously. "How do you know my name? What do you want?"

"I thought it was you, Mr Prior. But don't look so frightened. I don't bear grudges. I'm not that sort of man. Quite the opposite, in fact."

"Well, that's a relief," said Ambrose, trying to sound as relaxed as possible.

"I must say this has come as a bit of a surprise, Mr Prior," the other went on.

"Yes, I expect it has."

"Quite a turnaround as a matter of fact." The man spoke with a strong Teesside accent and his tone was not unsympathetic.

"It is, isn't it. Mr …?"

"Tapner."

"Tapner," repeated Ambrose, searching his memory.

"You probably won't remember me. You must have seen so many sent down."

"I suppose I have." Ambrose sat up and tried to get to his feet.

"No, no, Mr Prior. Stay where you are." Tapner squatted on his hams beside him.

"You must be wondering what I'm doing here. The great prosecuting barrister reduced to sleeping in the street," said Ambrose.

"One of the things I learned in the slammer, Mr Prior, was not to ask too many personal questions. I did read something in *The Sun* at the time, but let's just say you've hit a sticky patch."

"You're a gentleman for putting it in those terms, Mr Tapner."

"Coming from a proper gent like yourself, Mr Prior, that really means something to me." Oddly enough, he sounded as if he meant it too. His voice stirred Ambrose's memory.

"Armed robbery, wasn't it? And ten years?"

"Got it in one, Mr Prior. Good old-fashioned armed robbery. A clean sort of crime. Nothing to spoil the rest of my life."

Ambrose did not reply to this.

"I did five years. The best thing that ever happened to me. I have you to thank for that, Mr Prior – and the judge, too. I mustn't forget him."

"Well, that's good to hear. Not many of them say that, I'll bet. And I've met a few."

"I'm sure you have, Mr Prior. And as you're down on your luck, I owe you a favour."

Ambrose looked at him as closely as the light permitted. "You're not taking the micky out of me by any chance, are you?"

"Of course not, Mr Prior. I never was a good liar, as no doubt you realised."

The case had come back to Ambrose now and he could hardly believe that the man did not harbour a grudge against him. He could, of course, be taking a subtle form of revenge by patronising him now that the tables were turned, but Tapner's tone suggested that he meant what he said.

"And how does a gentleman like yourself enjoy sleeping rough? I did plenty of that in the army, but I never really took to it. I certainly couldn't do it now," the man went on.

"Like most things you have to do, you get used to it if you have to," said Ambrose. "You probably don't need me to tell you that. Anyway, it's a lot better than sharing a cell with a man who farts all night."

"Have you done that too, Mr Prior?"

"I think we might draw a veil over that one," said Ambrose.

"Quite right. I respect your feelings, Mr Prior. But you don't need to, you know."

"Need to what?"

"Sleep like this."

"I really don't mind – not in the warm weather, at least," insisted Ambrose.

"Why not sleep at my place? I've got a spare bed." It sounded perfectly reasonable.

"I couldn't possibly do that!" exclaimed Ambrose.

"You're not a snob are you, Mr Prior?"

"God, I hope not," returned Ambrose, knowing perfectly well that he was. "But in view of the circumstances, I mean. After all, I was responsible for putting you away, wasn't I?"

"The judge did that," said the other firmly. "You were only doing your job. And anyway, haven't I just told you it was the best thing that ever happened to me?"

Ambrose pondered the offer. This is a very odd turn up for the books, he told himself. The sheer absurdity of it tickled his fancy. "All right," he said at length. "If it's not too much trouble to you. One night in a proper bed would be rather nice."

"It's no trouble at all," replied Tapner. "You can stay longer than that if you want to."

"I'm sure one night will set me up," said Ambrose. "It's really very kind of you, Mr Tapner. Where do you live?"

"A short walk from here," Tapner told him. "Up on the Esplanade."

"Wow!" exclaimed Ambrose. "The Esplanade. You certainly haven't let the grass grow under your feet since you came out, have you?"

"As I keep telling you, Mr Prior, it was the best thing that ever happened to me. I've never looked back since."

Ambrose climbed to his feet and Tapner started to roll up his sleeping bag for him. "In here?" he said, indicating the rucksack. With Tapner carrying his belongings, Ambrose followed him down the path that led to the Spa Bridge and then up the other side to the Esplanade, Scarborough's swankiest street.

This is ridiculous, Ambrose told himself as he walked behind Tapner. What if he changes his tune once I'm inside the house? But something told him that the man wasn't likely to do that. He recalled the case now. Tapner had robbed a building society with a sawn-off shotgun. It wasn't his first offence and the police had run him in pretty quickly. The case had been concluded in a day, though the prisoner had gone through the motions of pleading not guilty. There had been something transparent, almost guileless, about him. A decent sort of cove – and, of course, he had never discharged his weapon. Not a man to bear grudges either, it seemed, despite his tendency towards extreme behaviour. But was he the sort who detested gays? He didn't seem to be.

Well, time will tell, Ambrose told himself. Meanwhile, the novelty of his situation appealed to him, as did the prospect of a comfortable bed for the night.

It was a handsome neo-classical terrace house, not unlike the one in which Ambrose had lived in his piping days, and he was curious to see what Tapner had made of it. It was difficult to imagine a man of his kind possessing the aesthetic refinement to do justice to it, and Ambrose, who prided himself on his own excellent taste, was ready to wince – unless, of course, he had made the matter over entirely to a professional designer, which would also be a giveaway.

So before they had even arrived at the first floor landing where Tapner lived, Ambrose's curiosity was thoroughly whetted.

The flat was neither of the things he had imagined. There was little to suggest the flashy taste of the barrow boy and certainly nothing of the designer magazine interior where a newspaper or a plate of sandwiches carelessly set aside could ruin the effect. It was quite nondescript, a blank canvas waiting to be addressed by an artist. Tapner watched Ambrose as he cast his eye round the sitting room.

"Perhaps you could advise me, Mr Prior," he said. "You see, there's no Mrs Tapner and I'm not very good at these things."

Ambrose did not speak.

"I need someone to advise me about putting this place right," Tapner explained. "An educated sort of person who understands these things. Someone like you, Mr Prior, who knows how things ought to look."

Ambrose hedged. "I'm not sure that I'm quite the man you want, Mr Tapner. You can afford professional advice, surely."

"I'd rather this was kept between you and me," the other replied.

Ambrose looked at him sharply, to be met with an ingenuous smile and a shrug.

"You must be tired, Mr Prior. Would you like to go to bed?"

"Thanks. If you don't think me rude, I think I would."

"Of course I don't think you rude, Mr Prior."

"The name's Ambrose, by the way. You don't have to call me Mr Prior."

"That's nice of you, Mr Prior," replied the other. "I'm Steve."

They shook hands.

"I'll show you the bathroom," said Tapner.

It was splendidly old-fashioned, white-tiled and panelled in a dark wood. The bath had not been boxed in and the lavatory, with its ample mahogany seat and lid, stood throne-like on its own plinth.

"Whatever else you do, you mustn't touch this," said Ambrose.

"Do you think so, Mr Prior?" Tapner sounded doubtful.

"Ambrose."

"Ambrose then, but it doesn't come naturally, Mr Prior. Though you can still call me Steve," Tapner added hastily.

The spare bedroom was a surprise. A small room at the back of the flat, its walls were covered with a boy's bedroom paper – all aeroplanes and helicopters.

"This is rather jolly," said Ambrose.

"I thought you might like it, Mr Prior. I do."

The two men exchanged a glance, which, in Tapner's case, almost amounted to a wink.

"Time for some shut-eye," said Tapner. "I'll fetch you some pyjamas."

They were on the large side, but silk, which brought back agreeable associations to his guest.

"Night-night, Mr Prior," said Tapner. "Sleep as long as you like. There's no hurry in the morning. The bathroom's all yours."

Ambrose took off his things and slipped into the pyjamas. He sighed with pleasure at the feel of silk against his body once more.

Despite the disconcerting turn in his fortunes, he slept well – the comfort of the bed saw to that – and he drifted off, thinking pleasant thoughts about the boys he had watched in the amusement arcade.

It was late when he woke and as soon as he was fully conscious he sat up, alarmed as he recalled last night's strange business. What the hell had he let himself in for? Accepting favours from a convicted criminal – indeed, one he had once helped to put away for armed robbery.

He could hear slippered feet softly padding up the short passage past his door and he lay down again but kept his eyes open. Meanwhile, he examined the boys" wallpaper and pondered Tapner's comment about their both liking it. Was that mere naivety on the man's part? There was a cautious knock at the door.

"Are you awake yet, Mr Prior?"

"Come right in," replied Ambrose. "I've had my best sleep in ages."

"I'm glad to hear it, Mr Prior," said Tapner, entering the room with a tray. "I don't know what you like for breakfast. I forgot to ask. I like the full works myself – black pudding, the lot – but I've done you some toast. I drink coffee, but if you'd rather have tea I can give you that instead."

"No, no. Coffee'll do nicely. This is really most kind of you."

"No trouble at all, Mr Prior." He retreated to the door. "As I said last night, there's no hurry. Take as long as you like. The bathroom's yours and help yourself to the lounge."

"Gosh, I don't know how to thank you ... Steve," gushed Ambrose.

"I'm going out. I've a few things to see to. Can I get you a paper?"

"That would be very decent of you. Can you get me a *Telegraph* or a *Times*? There's money in my pocket." Ambrose started to climb out of bed to reach his trousers on a chair by the wall.

"Stay where you are, Mr Prior. We can settle that later," said Tapner, backing out of the room and shutting the door after him.

Ambrose munched his toast and inwardly commended his host for his brand of coffee. It was interesting how quickly some of these criminal types got the hang of things. He was warming to Tapner, though he knew he had to be careful.

"But then," he reflected. "I can hardly sink much lower than I have done already, can I?"

He lay in bed for another half an hour, contemplating the wallpaper. The room was sparsely furnished but looked clean. Did Tapner do his own housework or did he have someone to do it for him? Then, rather regretfully, he heaved himself out of bed and went into the bathroom where he ran a bath and enthroned himself on the lavatory. He had forgotten just how nice it felt to do one's business on a wooden seat. A fresh towel had been provided for him and he noticed that his host had set out his own toothbrush and shaving things, which he must have removed from his rucksack.

He was still luxuriating in the bath when Tapner returned.

"I've got you a *Times* and a *Telegraph*, Mr Prior, but don't worry, just take your time," he called through the door.

Ambrose felt that it would be impolite to linger too long, so he got out of the bath and appeared in the kitchen where his host was drinking a mug of coffee and reading *The Sun*.

"Coffee?"

"Thanks."

Tapner pushed a plate of biscuits across the table to him and indicated the two newspapers he had bought him.

"They're a bit heavy for me," he explained, "but I'm sure you'll enjoy them, Mr Prior."

Ambrose fished in his pocket for the money to pay for them but the other stopped him.

"No, no, Mr Prior. You're my guest."

"Well, if you insist."

"Of course I insist."

It started to feel awkward, especially when Tapner began to read aloud from the sports page about the sacking of a football manager and make the kind of comments that required answers from his guest, which Ambrose, who wasn't remotely interested in football, was ill equipped to provide.

"Who do you support, Mr Prior?" asked the man after listening to Ambrose's limp reply.

"I used to support Middlesbrough," said Ambrose, "but I don't really follow it much these days."

"Oh, you should, Mr Prior. Everyone should follow football."

"Don't Scarborough have a team?" offered Ambrose.

"They're nothing. Just bugger all, a load of shite," said the other scornfully.

"Cricket was more my game," said Ambrose.

"Cricket?" queried the other in a tone of mild disbelief.

"Yes. Cricket. A bit of a Yorkshire fan."

Ambrose felt that it was time to take his leave, so, folding the newspapers, he got to his feet.

"Well, I must be on my way," he said.

"Where are you going, Mr Prior?" Tapner sounded put out by the suggestion.

"You've been wonderfully kind," said Ambrose. "That's been the best night I've had since I don't know when. And a first class breakfast too. I must congratulate you on your coffee."

"Mr Prior," replied the other, "I thought you were going to help me."

Ambrose looked puzzled.

"You haven't forgotten already, have you?" Tapner's voice was reproachful. "I mean with the house. I'm not educated the same as you, Mr Prior. I don't have taste. You've got taste. I need you," the man pleaded. "And besides …"

"Besides what?" said Ambrose, eying him closely.

"You might be able to advise me on other matters, too."

"Such as?"

"Things to do with the law. That kind of thing." Tapner looked at him bashfully.

"No can do," Ambrose told him firmly. "But I daresay I could help with the house. Mind you, it won't come cheap. I have expensive tastes."

"That's my problem. Then you'll stay?"

There was a pause. It was a situation fraught with danger. But, Ambrose told himself, I think I might be able to handle this man. I could make this place into what I want it to be. It depends on the kind of company he keeps, of course.

Tapner was watching him hungrily.

"I'll take a walk and think about it," said Ambrose.

"Remember, you could make this place really nice, Mr Prior."

Ambrose glanced out of the window. It was starting to rain and a cold easterly wind was driving in from the North Sea.

"Don't stay out too long, Mr Prior. You'll get wet."

"I won't," answered Ambrose. "I just want a bit of fresh air."

Tapner was reassured by the fact that he removed only his light waterproof from his rucksack, leaving his other things behind.

It was early afternoon when Ambrose returned and found Tapner watching a quiz show on television. It was a massive state-of-the-art set which seemed to fill an entire wall.

That'll have to go for a start, Ambrose told himself. "May I?" he said, sitting down beside Tapner.

"Of course, Mr Prior. Have you made your mind up?"

"Yes," Ambrose replied. "I've decided to take you up."

"That's very good to hear, Mr Prior. Exactly what I hoped you would say."

"However ..."

Tapner frowned. "Go on."

"I can't possibly live off you. You may have found me sleeping rough, but I have got some money. And I want to do the right thing."

"As far as I'm concerned you'll be doing the right thing if you make this place nice for me. And I bow to your judgment in everything, Mr Prior, except I insist on one thing."

"Oh? And what would that be?"

"The spare bedroom," replied the other. "We wouldn't want to change that paper, would we? A real lad's room, that."

There was a pause.

"It's just a little fancy of mine," said Tapner at length.

"There is one other matter," said Ambrose. "I don't quite know how to put this. You seem to be doing very well for yourself and money seems to be no object. How's it done?"

"You lawyers," replied Tapner. "Always asking nosy questions."

"But I need to know. You see I don't want to land myself in the shit for a second time. I've had enough of it already."

"You won't do that, Mr Prior, I promise you. But I think my money's my business, don't you? I will tell you this, if it'll put your mind at rest. Whatever I get up to, no one who's innocent ever gets hurt."

"Well, I suppose that's something."

Ambrose could make a few shrewd guesses at how Tapner earned his living, and his concept of innocence might be food for discussion. But then he didn't really need to know – indeed, it was much better if he didn't. And anyway, he did not intend to stay for very long – a week or two at the most.

"All right," he said. "But you won't let me down, will you?"

"And don't you let me down either, Mr Prior." Tapner offered his hand and the two men shook on it.

"Now, if you don't mind, I'll lie down for a while," said Ambrose.

He took the papers and went to his room where, propping himself on the pillows and stretched luxuriously on the bed, he started to read. After that he fished in his pocket for a biro and tackled the *Telegraph* crossword. He completed it in fifteen minutes flat.

It was five o'clock when Tapner knocked on the door. "Are you awake yet, Mr Prior?"

"Come in, come right in."

Tapner put his head into the room, but did not follow it. "Tea, Mr Prior?"

"Thanks."

"Milk and sugar?"

"A dash of milk and no sugar." Ambrose swung his feet off the bed.

"Stay put, please, Mr Prior," the other insisted. "I'll bring it to you."

Ambrose lay down again and Tapner shut the door after himself. It was then that Ambrose thought he heard whispered voices, but could not make out what they were saying, though he distinctly heard his host's voice saying "sssh". Then he heard a door open and close softly. Tapner said nothing about his visitor when he returned bearing the tea and a biscuit on a tray with a doily.

"Mr Prior," he said, "I'm going out for an hour or two, so help yourself from the fridge and make yourself at home. The lounge and telly are all yours. Use the CD played too if you want. "And," he added, "it might be a good time to look the place over and get a few ideas."

Ambrose waited until he had gone before he sallied forth. Having the place to himself was pleasant and he hoped that his host would be in no hurry to return.

The CD player stood on a low table next to the black leather sofa, which faced the state-of-the-art television. Tapner's musical taste seemed to be surprisingly good, though hardly well informed. Apart from a stack of pop CDs, his collection consisted largely of selections from the better-known classic operatic arias, violin concertos and pieces like Handel's *Fireworks Music*. Clearly, the man had aspirations and Ambrose began to see a vocation for himself as his cultural mentor.

"This man is worth it," he told himself.

His inspection of the rooms did not take him long, for there was not very much to see. The furnishings were sparse and there was nothing to hurt the eye so much that it cried out for instant replacement. The television would have to go, of course, and the black leather sofa and the two armchairs, but the walls were bare of pictures. The rooms were spacious with high ceilings and handsome moulded cornices, which would need to be painted or papered. As for what went on them, he had carte blanche.

"This requires a trip to Harrogate," Ambrose decided – an agreeable prospect if he had a generous supply of someone else's money to spend. "And, before that, a visit to a decent tailor to replenish my wardrobe."

Ambrose spent a pleasant afternoon shopping for clothes. There were several good men's outfitters in the town and he came home with a tweed jacket, two pairs of trousers, several shirts – pure cotton, he wasn't an artificial fibre man – a new pair of shoes – handcrafted by a well known shoemaker in Richmond – fresh underpants, socks, two pairs of pyjamas and half a dozen silk bow ties.

But it was nearly midnight before Tapner returned, in no fit state to discuss improvements to his flat, so Ambrose decided to postpone it till the morning and ordered him to bed. He preferred not to think about the kind of company he might have been keeping and what else he had got up to. The truth was that if he was to have a free hand with the flat it wouldn't do to enquire too closely into Tapner's extra-mural activities, though he could try to do something about his domestic ones.

In the morning, Ambrose was up early, before his host, who was suitably subdued when he woke with a thick head.

"I am sorry, Mr Prior," he mumbled.

"Stay put," ordered his guest. "I'll bring you some black coffee."

Ambrose returned with the coffee.

"It's really very kind of you, Mr Prior, doing all this for me," said Tapner, struggling up into a sitting position.

"Not at all. You've been good to me, so it's the least I can do. I've looked over the house, by the way, and got a few ideas."

"Ooh, have you Mr Prior? You don't waste much time, do you?"

"When you're up and dressed I'll explain. Not until," said Ambrose firmly.

"Right you are, Skipper."

Ambrose went into the kitchen, made himself a piece of toast and poured a cup of coffee. He liked the 'skipper' bit, which seemed to put the relationship on the right footing. "This is damned good coffee," he told himself. "The man certainly knows where to find his substances."

When Tapner had finally risen and showered, his guest ordered him into the living room.

"This could be a fine drawing room, but of course it isn't. At the moment it's nothing. Absolutely nothing at all. In fact, it's worse than nothing," he added, warming to his theme. "It's utterly without character, downright insipid."

"If you say so, Skip," replied the other, startled by his show of feeling – something new to Tapner who had never known anyone get so worked up about the look of a room before.

"But I think I can make something of it," Ambrose went on. "You'll have to shell out. And I doubt you'll get away with less than fifteen grand."

Tapner blinked. "If you say so, Boss."

"Leave it to me, then. You'll need to drive me over to Harrogate. I know a dealer in Montpelier Parade where we can make a start. And afterwards you can buy me a cream tea at Betty's."

"If you say so, Boss," repeated Tapner.

"Tomorrow then. It's a Thursday so it should be fairly quiet."

At ten o" clock the following morning they left Scarborough in Tapner's Jag. Ambrose was wearing his new clothes with his bow tie set at a suitably raffish angle.

"Please drive carefully," he admonished Tapner. "You don't have to impress me with a macho performance at the wheel, you know."

Tapner said nothing, just bit his lip and slowed down.

"That's better," said Ambrose. "It would be a pity to be killed at this stage in the proceedings."

The journey continued with little said between them, which suited Ambrose who did not rate Tapner's conversational skills very highly.

In Harrogate, they left the car in a multi-story car park and walked briskly to Montpelier Parade.

"Leave me to do the talking," ordered Ambrose. "You don't even have to be around – in fact, it would be much better if you weren't – but I'll have to have your card when the time comes to pay and you'll need to be there to sign."

"Oh, I've got the cash," Tapner informed him airily. "You said fifteen grand would cover it, didn't you, Mr Prior?" He took a wad of notes out of his pocket and riffled it through his fingers like a pack of cards.

Ambrose was impressed. "We won't need all of that straight away, and for God's sake don't let anyone see you've got it."

"Mum's the word," replied Tapner with a wink.

Ambrose was starting to find his clichés tiresome but, in a way, they added to his own sense of power over the man.

The shop was Allison's – an antique dealer from whom Ambrose had bought in the past – and it was reassuring to find them still in business, though he did not recognise the rosy-cheeked young man in the thornproof tweed suit who hovered discreetly while his customer cast an eye over the goods. It was one of those softly lit, uncluttered establishments whose muted tones suggested good quality, the kind of place where Ambrose felt at home. A high-backed settle in a relatively restrained rococo style caught his eye first of all. Its damask upholstery was pleasantly faded, but he wondered how it would stand the test of Tapner's bulk. It didn't look particularly comfortable either.

Why not combine it with something modern? Ambrose told himself. That's the trick – never be a slave to a particular style; stick your neck out; be bold and eclectic.

By the time he was examining a couple of early eighteenth century walnut occasional tables, the young man in the thornproof tweed suit had presented himself. He had the high colouring of a country man, which matched his plummy voice and his brogues.

Ambrose closed on the tables, prevaricated about the settle and drew a Georgian sideboard into the debate. He talked about it in a knowledgeable way, examining closely the patination and the condition of the handles, but all the time keeping an eye on Tapner outside the shop. He had loitered on the pavement for a minute or two, clearly at a loss about where to put himself, before drifting onto the green across the road and sitting on a bench.

Ambrose talked easily and well and soon put together a package, which the young man had to ring through to his superior to confirm.

"You're not in this line of business yourself, by any chance, are you?" he enquired of Ambrose, impressed by his knowledge and bargaining skill.

"Not yet," Ambrose replied. "At the moment it's just a hobby. But it might take off any day."

The upshot was that after thirty minutes he had spent eleven thousand pounds of Tapner's fifteen, but arranged a healthy discount in the process by offering cash.

"I'll be straight back," he told the man. "Give me ten minutes." He crossed the road to Tapner who, by now, was pacing about on the green looking bored.

"Done," announced Ambrose. "I've got you a Georgian settle, a pair of occasional tables and a walnut sideboard with superb patination for the dining room as well, all for eleven grand. By offering cash I managed to get a thumping good discount – so that was good thinking on your part." He thought it expedient to give the man some credit.

It was on the tip of Tapner's tongue to say that it was a fuck of a lot of money to spend on a few sticks of furniture, but he restrained himself and counted out the money instead.

"I expect you know what you're doing, Mr Prior," was all he said.

"We can fill in the gaps with modern stuff," explained Ambrose. "If you get it right, the effect can be quite striking."

"If you say so, Mr Prior."

"In the meantime, we've still got a little to play with so, after I've settled with Allison's, we might look at some carpets in the shop further down," went on Ambrose. "And then you can stand me tea at Betty's; it's just at the top here – we passed it."

He gave the young man the cash, took his receipt and arranged for the carriage of the goods to Scarborough.

The same procedure was followed in the carpet dealer's. Ambrose managed to bring the man down to £3,500 from five for a handsome Bokhara rug, suitably worn and faded, which would set off the furniture admirably. At the same time, he reflected that something would have to be done about the fitted carpet already in place in Tapner's flat.

"Well, that's a start at least," he told him as they set off back to Scarborough after their cream tea. "And you've even got some change out of your fifteen grand."

"Five hundred bloody quid," observed the other ruefully. "There's just one thing I'd like to ask you, Mr Prior. Why do things have to look old? I mean that carpet. Why couldn't we have got a nice new one with bright colours? It would have been cheaper too."

"Don't you want to live like a gentleman?" retorted Ambrose.

"I'm not a real one like you, Mr Prior, am I? But if you think I should try, I'm game," replied Tapner.

"We might buy some pictures next, don't you think? Fancy a trip up to London?"

"Sure, I'll go to London with you," said Tapner. "I know some places you might like."

The two men glanced at each other but said nothing.

As on the journey out, conversation was fitful, while Tapner drove with an almost servile deference towards his passenger – so much so that Ambrose felt that he ought have been sitting in the back seat.

There was something canine about Tapner, he reflected, and, inevitably, he found himself wondering how such a meek giant had managed to make quite such an enormous pile in his chosen field – whatever that was, which wasn't hard to guess.

When they reached the landing outside the flat they could hear loud pop music coming from inside.

"Hullo, hullo, hullo, we've got visitors," said Tapner.

For the first time since he had moved in, Ambrose felt nervous. He had hoped his host would keep his chums – who were likely to be a pretty unsavoury lot – at arm's length.

"You let somebody have the key?" he asked him.

"Only Terry," replied the other airily. "You'll like Terry, Mr Prior."

"Are you quite sure about that?" Ambrose gave him what he hoped was a meaningful frown.

"Terry's a chum. You'll get on fine. Not jealous by any chance, are you, Mr Prior?" The man immediately corrected himself. "Sorry, Boss, I shouldn't have said that. Spoke out of turn. You know I didn't mean anything by it."

"When we've set the place up, you'll have to be careful who you give a key to," warned Ambrose. "Otherwise the place'll be stripped in no time".

"Terry's my chum," insisted the other.

Tapner opened the door and a blast of sound from the sitting room hit them like a hot gust. Ambrose winced. Tapner went ahead into the room and the volume of the music immediately dropped.

"You can come in now, Mr Prior," he called.

As he crossed to the sitting room, Ambrose could hear urgent whispering going on.

When he went in, he saw Tapner standing over a young man with dark, spiked hair and an earring lying spread-eagled across the sofa.

"Meet Terry," said Tapner awkwardly. "Terry, this is Mr Prior. I told you about him."

"Pleased to meet you," Terry replied in a tone that was intended to show that he wasn't particularly. He made no effort to move.

For once, Ambrose was at a loss for words. The young man was very attractive in a sulky, proletarian sort of way. Rough trade, Ambrose reflected. And not bad either.

"Steve called you Mr Prior," the boy said, pronouncing the name in an affected upper-class voice. "What's your proper name?"

"What do you mean my "proper name'?" Ambrose eyed the cheeky boy sternly but appreciatively. He looked hardly a day older than sixteen.

"I'm Terry. So who are you?"

"My name's Ambrose."

"Ambrose? Fucking hell, is it really?"

"He's Mr Prior to you, if you don't mind," cut in Tapner. "He's a gentleman who's helping me to put this place straight."

"Fucking hell. Tell me another one, Steve," exclaimed Terry. Or should it be Mr Tapner now?" Again, the toff's voice.

"I'm not having you being rude to any friend of mine. And mind your fucking language," responded Tapner, "or I'll …"

"You'll do what?" Terry sat up and put his feet on the floor.

"You know what I mean. Now bugger off and get us an Indian. You'd like an Indian, wouldn't you, Mr Prior?"

"Christ, the things I do for you," complained the young man, getting to his feet. "Do you really want an Indian, Ambrose? What about a Chinese?"

"Anything suits me," replied Ambrose with a shrug.

"Mr Prior to you, you cheeky cunt," Tapner called after Terry as he left the room.

"Sorry about the bad language, Mr Prior, but you mustn't mind Terry," he explained as soon as the front door was shut. "He's a good lad really."

"I met quite a few like him during my leave of absence from the Bar and, indeed, before that in the course of my work," said Ambrose. "We usually rubbed along quite well in the end."

"I'm quite sure you did, Mr Prior. It's rather your way, isn't it? I mean rubbing along with people."

Ambrose looked back at him, surprised by the bluntness of the innuendo, but said nothing.

"Sorry, I didn't mean anything by that, of course."

"No, I'm sure you didn't, so no offence taken. Well, if you don't mind I'll go and lie down for a few minutes. All that bargaining has taken it out of me." Ambrose forced a little chuckle.

He lay on the bed, smoking a cigarette and reading the copy of *The Times* he had brought back from Harrogate, but he was thinking about Terry. When he heard him return, he was half-minded to get up and speak to him. But softly, softly, he told himself. The lad did not look a day over sixteen, despite his spiked hair and earring. A right little oik; but, of course, that was a large part of his charm. No doubt he pushed drugs for Tapner, the loveable scamp, and was bloody good at it too. But he was still a child and Ambrose warmed to him. No, he'd not rush things because he felt that he'd be seeing quite a lot of Terry in the coming weeks.

And so it went from there. Quite rapidly, Terry got used to Ambrose's presence in the flat and was fascinated by his transformations. And, for his part, Ambrose came to the conclusion that the lad was not quite such an oik after all. He genuinely appreciated what he was attempting to do and even ventured his own suggestions, which showed some flair – untutored and naive, perhaps – and that he had an eye for such things.

Tapner, meanwhile, seemed happy that his young protégé got on with his guest, until one day Ambrose suggested that Terry should come with them on another trip to Harrogate and even accompany them to London on the projected picture hunt.

"Are you sure that would be wise, Mr Prior?" said Tapner dubiously.

"Why on earth shouldn't it be? I think that lad's got a bit of an eye."

"An eye?" echoed the other. "But are you sure it won't go to his head?"

"Isn't that where eyes are supposed to be?" said Ambrose.

"Joking apart, Mr Prior, are you not spoiling the lad a bit?"

"Spoiling him?"

"I mean it might be kind of corrupting him."

"Why should it be corrupting him?" responded Ambrose tartly. "I thought you'd done that already."

"Terry assists me with my work," replied Tapner stiffly, "and you don't have to be very clever to guess how, do you – especially a brief like yourself, Mr Prior – it's bread and butter, and that's all there is to it. He's an innocent kid and must stay that way – at least as long as I've got anything to do with it. After all, the lad isn't even eighteen."

Ambrose laughed. "OK, if you're worried about his morals, we'll forget about London for the time being and try him out in Harrogate. He might have some good ideas about wallpapers."

Tapner still looked dubious. "All right, Mr Prior, if you insist. I don't suppose looking at wallpapers will do him much harm."

And so it was arranged. Terry joined them on the next run to Harrogate and looked at wallpapers with Ambrose, where his contributions added an agreeable freshness to the business. Tapner hung about in the background, saying nothing.

He's a bright enough lad, thought Ambrose for the umpteenth time. It's such a pity he has to waste himself pushing coke for the likes of Tapner in a seaside town. And it was while listening to the lad's naive but enthusiastic comments about the wallpapers that Ambrose decided to rescue Terry.

But he knew next to nothing about him – his family, his home, even where he was living right now, nothing at all. That Tapner kept him seemed pretty obvious. But the lad was sharp and articulate in an uneducated way – and was quite a beauty with his sullen, dark features. Ambrose would have liked the chance to have a real heart to heart with him and, above all, to make sure that even if he traded in the things, he didn't touch the drugs himself.

On the latter point he felt curiously confident, for he sensed in Tapner a perverse regard for the lad's moral welfare. Despite being a criminal, the boy appeared to be in safe hands. It wouldn't do if he were to end up a rent boy, of course. Ambrose felt strongly about that. And he felt pretty sure that Tapner did as well.

Yet Tapner was the obstacle. If Ambrose was to help the lad to make something of his life, he needed to be separated from his present protector. So, after the customary tea in Betty's, he brooded on the problem on the drive home to Scarborough.

It was a delicate matter and he knew it would take time. Meanwhile, he must humour Tapner and really deliver the goods where his flat was concerned. So the round of art and antique dealers continued. Together, they scoured the North and West Ridings of Yorkshire. Tapner seemed resigned to Terry accompanying them on many of these jaunts, but still drew the line at London. About that he was adamant. The boy had to be kept away from the stews of the capital at all costs. Meanwhile, Ambrose managed to acquire some fine eighteenth century landscapes in the Dutch manner through a branch of one of the leading London salerooms a few doors down from Allison's on Montpellier Parade. It made a good start to the picture collection he was planning and, moreover, Terry liked them – which mattered much more than anything Tapner might think.

Terry was growing rather cocky, earning the occasional glare from his protector, but Ambrose laughed along with the lad, which annoyed

Tapner even more. He was a quick learner and Ambrose wondered what had gone so wrong with his young life that he had ended up in the hands of a drug dealer.

"You know something, Terry?" he said one day when Tapner was out of earshot in an antiques emporium where they were examining a Bristol Blue glass decanter together, "you should learn this trade. It's much better than what you're doing now."

"Steve's doing all right, isn't he? He couldn't afford all this stuff if he wasn't."

"True. But how long for, Terry? The bubble's going to burst one of these days. Either he'll be snuffed out or he'll have to spend the rest of his life behind bars. Sooner or later, one way or the other, it's going to happen."

"He's been a real dad to me, Steve has. I never knew the other one."

"I can see all that, Terry. But think about it. You've got a very good eye and you'll train. You might have to posh up your accent a bit and wear the right kind of clothes, but you can take that in your stride, I'm perfectly sure. I've seen a lot more of the world than you have and, believe me, I know."

"It's nice of you to say so, Mr Prior. Or can I call you Ambrose since a certain person isn't listening?"

"Of course you can. I'd be only too delighted. But just be careful when he's around, that's all. He's a bit stuck in his ways." It gave Ambrose a thrill just saying that.

And now the flat was looking really magnificent.

"You'll have to have a house-warming party," Ambrose suggested to Tapner, but immediately regretted saying it.

"No danger of that, Mr Prior," Tapner said. "Apart from young Terry here, I keep business and home separate."

"Quite right too," replied Ambrose and meant it.

Terry took to the splendid new surroundings like a duck to water and started to spend as much time in them as possible, which didn't altogether please Tapner.

"You've got work to do, young man, so bugger off out and get stuck in," he would order him.

Tapner's manner towards Ambrose began to change and, as the makeover drew to its conclusion, he started to drop heavy hints that the time might be approaching for him to move on.

"I love having you here, Mr Prior, make no mistake, and in certain legal matters I would like your advice from time to time, but ..."

"Just tell me when you feel it's time for me to go," Ambrose told him. "I won't stay a day longer than you want me to. But I think we need some watercolours for the passage first, don't you? And I've been having second thoughts about that boys" bedroom wallpaper. We talked about it once, if you remember. Terry doesn't like it."

"What does he know about it?" growled Tapner.

"He's still a boy himself and I thought he might have a view on the matter," said Ambrose warily.

"He doesn't have to see it, does he?" retorted the other, turning on his heel.

"No, I don't suppose he does."

"So don't bring him into it. He's got enough to do without worrying his head about fucking wallpaper."

Ambrose couldn't help noticing that there were a good deal fewer "Mr Priors" now and more four- letter words creeping into Tapner's conversation.

"I must get that lad out of here before he's arrested," he told himself. "But I still know next to nothing about him, who his own people are and so on. And if I try to take him under my wing with my record ..."

It was a growing conundrum. He tried to talk to Terry about his family but gleaned little. Both his father and mother had decamped, the father leaving first. Terry thought that he had come originally from Glasgow but his mother was local. There were no brothers or sisters – or at least none that he had heard of. Of course, he had skived off school and had started pushing coke for Tapner at the same time, working the school gates. Strictly speaking, he should have been attending school until the end of the summer, but no one had followed him up, tacitly accepting the fact that he was a tearaway and turning a blind eye. His disappearance from local society would not be missed. Needless to say, he could hardly read or write and Ambrose saw a mountain to be climbed ahead of him. But it was one he desperately wanted to climb – and not for any carnal satisfaction either. Despite his appreciation of the boy's beauty – and he really was beautiful – the old dirty little bursts of lust did not seem to bother him in this case.

No, he would have to get the lad away from Tapner and, at the same time, put his own affairs on a footing whereby he could maintain him properly. It would mean abandoning the vagrant life – which had been an interesting interlude and of a piece with his days in prison. A small place in the south of England or perhaps Burgundy would do. He had always fancied a pied-à-terre in or near Dijon. That would be preferable; a discreet establishment in Burgundy; something he felt he could afford with his funds, which had been gathering interest during his time in gaol and on the road. My God, France was just the place to turn Terry into a civilised human being. For the first time in his life Ambrose felt that he had a real calling.

He must put it to Terry and urge complete discretion. Not that he felt no sympathy for Tapner because, in his way, he loved the lad as well. It was difficult to say in what way exactly; there appeared to be no girl friend in Tapner's life and he never discussed women, but like his lack of hard feelings towards Ambrose for helping to put him away, the man had a sense of fair play and doing what was right. In very different circumstances he might have been a good scout master. It was just difficult to square with flogging coke at school gates, that was all. Should he explain to Tapner that he would take the boy away from him for his own good? He dismissed the idea at once. There was no other way – he had to hurt the man who had taken him in off the streets.

But first, Terry. And when Ambrose whispered his plan to him in a picture gallery in York, his eyes lit up at the prospect, but then his thoughts turned to Tapner.

"Christ, Ambrose, there's nothing I'd like better. There'd be no stopping me then. Christ, France, but …" He hesitated.

"But what?"

"There's Steve. He's been a real dad to me."

"Steve'll be fine, and in any case, there's no reason why he shouldn't stay with us in France – when he needs a break."

It took time – the opportunities to work on him were not plentiful with a watchful Tapner around, especially as the makeover of his flat was drawing to a close and his treatment of Ambrose was growing less deferential by the day. It took time, but the boy was dazzled by the prospect of the new existence opening up before him.

The final plans were hatched in the flat on the Esplanade one afternoon when Tapner had gone out and Terry had slipped in. They sat side by side on Ambrose's bed, surrounded by the childish wallpaper.

"Christ, this paper," exclaimed Terry. "Great, isn't it?"

They spoke in low voices and kept an ear open in case Tapner should suddenly return.

"There's only one thing I need to know, Ambrose," said the boy.

"Yes?"

"It's about you."

Ambrose felt the room go chilly. "Go on," he said.

"It's something Steve once said. Are you gay? He said you fancy boys."

"Good God," laughed Ambrose. "I'm quite harmless. It's the sort of thing people usually say about you when you've come unstuck, but there's nothing like that about me."

"How did you come unstuck, Ambrose? Steve says you were a very good lawyer. A Q ..."

"A QC – Queen's Counsel. Oh yes, a rising star, but ... how do I put it? When you get mixed up with the likes of Steve – and in my line it happens all the time – you can land yourself in the shit, to coin a phrase."

"And that's what happened to you?"

"That's what happened to me."

But, for the moment at least, the boy was too captivated at the prospect that Ambrose dangled before him to want to entertain any serious doubts about him. It was settled, provided steps were taken to assuage Tapner's wounded feelings.

A letter was written and left on the kitchen table, promising to be in touch with Tapner soon and, of course, to let him know where they would eventually be living. Nothing was said about France. They both thanked him for all he had done for them. Terry then opened a drawer in the kitchen and put his hand into the back. He drew out a wad of twenty-pound notes.

"Christ, Terry, you can't do that," exclaimed Ambrose.

"Why can't I? He owes it to me."

"Then at least leave him a note saying what you've done."

"You do it, Ambrose."

"All right then, but I don't like it. I've got enough money to see us through. We don't need it."

"It's my money," said the boy firmly.

Ambrose counted it out – all of five hundred pounds – wrote an IOU and made Terry sign it

"Now, if you don't mind, I've got to see my nan," said the boy.

"Your nan? You never told me about her," said Ambrose

"Didn't I? Everybody's got a nan. I've got to say good-bye to her, haven't I?"

Ambrose looked at him dubiously.

"I suppose so, if you must, Terry. But be quick about it for God's sake. Don't be late. The bus station in one hour. I'll be in the cafeteria. Got it?" Ambrose ordered him.

"Got it. See you there. In the caff."

"God bless you, Terry," said Ambrose, squeezing his hand.

Terry let himself out and Ambrose went back to his bedroom to put together his things in his old knapsack. While he was doing it he heard the door open. Oh my God, he thought. Couldn't he have stayed away for just another ten minutes?

He heard Tapner go into the kitchen and, shortly after, a howl of anguish followed by a torrent of expletives.

Nothing else for it, he told himself as he tiptoed out of the room and started across the hall towards the door.

"You bastard – still here are you? What have you done to my Terry?"

Tapner rushed from the kitchen and grabbed the collar of Ambrose's coat.

"Think you can sneak away like that, do you? Fucking smart-arse of a brief. You sent me down once and now you want to ruin my Terry. Well, I'm not going to let you, Mr Smart-arse fucking Prior QC, lord chief fucking paedophile …"

He hurled Ambrose across the hall and sent him sprawling on the sitting room floor.

His nose bleeding, Ambrose was aware only of the lozenge in the rug's central panel, its muted tones defiled now by the garishness of his own blood. He did not feel what came next as he slipped into the dark …

5 The Postlethwaite Lecture

Angela Tasker had spent a lovely day in London. It was good to escape there from time to time and lose oneself in the anonymity of the crowd – to know no one and to be known by no one. She had looked at pictures: an exhibition of nineteenth century Russian painters – the Itinerant School – at the National Gallery. She preferred these small-scale exhibitions to blockbuster shows, which, despite the marvellous things in them, left her feeling drained. This had been followed by her customary early evening walk in Chelsea, peering discreetly through lighted windows to inspect the insides of the houses – a furtive pleasure not untinged by envy – and an early supper at a snug, yet inexpensive, Polish restaurant in South Kensington. It had been a satisfying day and now she was on the nine o'clock train back to Durham from King's Cross.

She had booked a seat in the quiet coach to avoid the mobile phones, which bothered her more than tobacco smoke did, and she settled down in good time with a copy of *The Literary Review*, which she had bought at the station bookstall. Meanwhile, as the seats filled up, she eyed the other passengers, hoping that none of them would infringe the rule about mobile phones. It always annoyed Angela how many people disregarded it and she had remonstrated with them on a number of occasions. She hated having rows, but was prepared to do it when others were too spineless to make a fuss.

A loud, rather tanked-up foursome of Geordie salesmen settled at a table on the opposite side of the aisle from her and she looked at them anxiously, praying that they would obey the rule because she didn't want to scrap with people of their kind if she could help it.

The carriage had almost filled up when an elderly man, with an untidy shock of grey hair and a strikingly large nose, rushed along the platform and climbed aboard just as the guard was slamming the doors. Breathlessly, he dumped a holdall bag on Angela's table and started to take off his coat. As he did so, he brushed his bag onto the floor.

"Damn and blast," he exclaimed with surprising heat. "Is this seat taken?" he asked in a strong central European accent as he retrieved the bag and sat down opposite Angela without waiting for her answer. Then he opened the bag and, uttering another expletive, poured a heap of loose colour slides onto the table. With an exasperated sigh, he glared at Angela through his thick glasses.

"They were perfectly arranged," he groaned, "and now I have it all to do again." He rummaged inside the holdall to produce a sponge bag, a couple of paperbacks, pyjamas, a pair of slippers and, finally, several plastic slide racks, all of which he set out on the table before peering into the depths of the bag. "Damn," he exclaimed. "Blast and bugger."

"Is something the matter?" Angela rather pointlessly asked.

"Of course something's the matter, bloody seriously the matter," the man snapped back. "The Postlethwaite Lecture is at four o'clock tomorrow afternoon and now I am completely buggered." He fished in the bottom of the bag, this time producing a pair of socks. "No, it's not there," he declared with a heavy groan.

"Can I help?" offered Angela.

"What possible good could you or anyone else do? It's my viewer, isn't it?" he said. "How do you expect me to arrange my slides again without my viewer? Just answer me that, if you can. Oh my God, I should have put them in a box. Everything is utterly buggered."

"If the lecture's not until the afternoon, you'll have time to find another viewer in the morning, surely," suggested Angela.

The man winced as if she had said something particularly crass. "That's quite out of the question," he declared in a withering tone. "In the morning I have a very important engagement with Professor Clarke. And then in the afternoon I have to deliver the Postlethwaite Lecture. So where do you imagine I can find the time to go shopping for a viewer? Eh?"

"Perhaps Professor Clarke could lend you one," said Angela.

It seemed a perfectly reasonable suggestion to make, but the man raised his eyes as if she had again said something so utterly ridiculous that it was unworthy of an answer.

"Aren't your slides labelled?" asked Angela sharply in response to his rudeness.

"I have only just got back from America," explained her companion, speaking slowly and deliberately as if he was trying to make himself clear to an idiot or a small child, "so there has hardly been any time, has there?"

"If you held them up to the light you might possibly be able to recognise them and I could stack them up for you," spelled out Angela, as if she too was talking to a simpleton.

The man looked appalled. "This is the Postlethwaite Lecture," he exclaimed. "It's very important that none of it should get into the wrong hands."

"Which mine are," retorted Angela. "I was simply trying to be helpful."

He frowned and blinked unhappily, perhaps aware at last of the negative effect his churlishness was having. "It would be quite impossible to tell what the correct order is in this light, so thank you for your offer, but it is out of the question."

Angela did not reply, though the man felt obliged to offer her a fuller explanation.

"I have been very busy in America where I had very important meetings with Dr Paling and Professor Chernovski, and my slides were arranged in racks in readiness for the Postlethwaite Lecture," he explained. Picking up a slide, he held it to the seat light and groaned. "It's quite impossible to see this properly without a viewer," he said. "Oh bugger, bugger, bugger."

Angela picked up another one and held it to the light. She could make out what looked like a red figure Attic vase – the kind of thing she enjoyed looking at in the British Museum.

"This looks interesting," she said.

With a look of horror, the man snatched it from her hand but, at the same time, realised that he had gone too far.

"I'm sorry if I appear rude," he gasped, "but this is the Postlethwaite Lecture."

"As you've never stopped reminding me," returned Angela frostily. "I mustn't be nosey, must I?"

Then she regretted saying it, because the man really did have an exceptionally large nose. Indeed, he looked a positive Cyrano de Bergerac.

"Are you an archaeologist or an art historian?" she ventured after a difficult pause. The man looked at her as though she should hardly have needed to ask.

"I am Professor Edelman," he announced with a show of affected patience, almost as if he expected Angela immediately to say, "Of course you are. Silly me for forgetting."

"I love this kind of thing," she went on. "I spend hours sometimes browsing in the BM. But I really know very little about it. I'm strictly a dilettante, I'm afraid."

This display of humility in the face of his own eminence had a mollifying effect on Professor Edelman and he rewarded Angela with a vinegary smile while, with yet another massive sigh, he started to shovel his slides back into the mouth of the bag.

"And I am Angela Tasker."

"It's a pleasure to meet you," responded the Professor without meaning it, but managing a token display of good manners at least. "The Postlethwaite Lecture is a very important occasion in the academic calendar," he explained, "but my flight from New York was delayed on account of the terrorist threat and I have had no time to prepare it as well as I would like to have done. A very regrettable state of affairs."

"Where does it take place?"

"In Edinburgh, of course. In the University. Where it always has done." A note of his former petulance crept back into his voice because this was surely something she shouldn't have needed to ask.

"I wish I'd studied fine art or archaeology," mused Angela. "I'm afraid I missed the boat on that one."

Professor Edelman managed to look very mildly sympathetic and, for a second, his testy manner seemed in danger of melting into something more benign.

"What about your slides?" asked Angela. "Hadn't we better put them back in their racks, at least? We can wrap them so that they don't fall out again."

The Professor shook his head emphatically. "Thank you. I will attend to them myself later."

With that relatively mild rebuff, Angela took the opportunity to retreat into her copy of *The Literary Review* while Professor Edelman peered out of the darkened window for a minute or two, then shut his eyes, relieved, no doubt, that for the time being he was spared the discomfort of any more tiresome conversation.

Meanwhile, the Geordie party across the aisle was warming up, as Angela feared it might. But so far it had not become intrusive. The four men, who looked to be in their thirties, were keeping themselves well supplied with beer, which they were working their way through – a boisterous group of bonding males, they nevertheless had an amusing run of patter. Angela, who was single and the wrong side of forty but no prude, found herself wanting to laugh – especially when one of them, a big fellow with a shaved head and an ear stud, did a demonstration sales pitch with a Geordie wife, trying to convince her that she really did need to install a set of french windows. The word 'pet' was reiterated throughout the performance and Angela started to smile. Meanwhile, Professor Edelman, with his eyes tightly shut, was pretending not to hear. But he pursed his lips and frowned as the volume increased. Angela caught herself savouring the contrast between the Professor's scarcely contained irritation and the comic performance going on across the aisle.

One of the foursome went for fresh stocks of beer and, as he got up, a plastic cup was spilled on the table to raucous exclamations. And then one of the men noticed Angela laughing. He pointed at the comedian beside him and winked at her.

"What do you think, Pet? Would you buy a set of windows from him? I wouldn't, not if I was you, Pet."

"He's quite funny," Angela said.

"Funny, Pet?" said the man. "You call that funny? He's just bigheaded, him."

Professor Edelman opened his eyes, glanced at Angela, blinked uneasily and assumed the attitude of sleeping once more.

The man who had gone to replenish the beer stocks returned with a dozen fresh cans and several bags of crisps. He lurched unsteadily along the aisle, nearly landing in somebody's lap on the way. When he reached his friends, he dumped his load noisily on the table and started to scrabble about on the floor. Angela hastily retreated into her copy of *The Literary Review* while Professor Edelman screwed up his eyes even more tightly than before, chuntering angrily to himself at the same time.

But the man had not sunk to the floor because he was too drunk to remain on his feet. He quickly stood up again and placed something on the table. It was a handful of Professor Edelman's slides that he had failed to retrieve in his haste to shovel them back into his bag. He winked at his companions who, with sly glances in the Professor's direction, started to examine them by holding them up to the light. Immediately, there was a series of muffled snorts, which Professor Edelman seemed not to hear. Angela glanced up from her magazine and, looking across at the others, exchanged a conspiratorial smile.

The slides were being passed round the little group from one to the next while snorts of ill-contained mirth issued from them. The Professor still had his eyes firmly shut, apparently oblivious of the use to which the precious material of the Postlethwaite Lecture was being put.

"Take a look at this one, Pet," said the comedian with the shaved head and ear stud to Angela as he leaned across to her with a slide.

Casting a glance in the direction of Professor Edelman, Angela held the slide up to the light. She could make out the inside of an Athenian red figure drinking vessel where a bearded man was sucking a youth's penis. She stifled a laugh.

The salesman put a finger to his lips and passed Angela a second slide. This time a gang of satyrs with enormously dilated penises was chasing a pair of nymphs round the circumference of a vase. Two naked boys masturbating one another came next.

Angela's attempt to suppress her mirth provoked the others to fresh splutters, which were fast getting out of control.

"Do you like them, Pet? Pretty, aren't they?" one of the salesmen said to her.

Angela gave him a saucy smile, which was quite unusual for her. Then, apprehensively, she glanced at the Professor, who opened an eye. As soon as he saw his slides in the profane hands of the salesmen, his jaw dropped and his eyes became huge behind his thick glasses. A burst of laughter greeted him from the opposite table, followed by a cheer.

"How dare you?" shrilled Professor Edelman. "What fucking business is it of yours? It's the Postlethwaite Lecture. How dare you?"

"I've never heard it called that before," joked one of the salesmen.

There was general laughter at this sally, which Angela did her best not to join in while the Professor leaned across the aisle and furiously snatched at his slides.

"It's none of your fucking business," he shrieked.

"Allahu Akbaaaarrr!"

The cry sounded from the far end of the coach. "Allahu Akbaaaarr!"

Screams came from the same direction. Angela turned to see a figure with its head wrapped in a red and white chequered cloth rushing down the aisle towards her, lashing out with a machete as it came.

"Allaaaaaahu Akbaaaaaaar!"

All hell had broken loose. Passengers were screaming and trying desperately to duck under the tables as the wild-looking figure approached. One foolhardy individual who tried to restrain the assailant was cut down with a blow across his face while cries of pain and terror were mingled together. There was a mad stampede towards the door at Angela's end of the coach. She and Professor Edelman were blocked into their seats, so she tried to duck under the table as best she could. Then the man was upon them, slashing at the passengers ahead of him as they attempted to escape into the next coach. A man fell to the floor beside where Angela was crouching, a gash across the back of his head from which the blood poured onto the floor in a torrent and over Angela herself. From the place where Professor Edelman was cowering came a terrible shriek.

Then, into the mayhem, came the sound of brakes squealing and the train began to grind to a halt. It stopped and everything suddenly seemed oddly still. Groans, sobbing and expletives could be heard the length of the coach while, from the one beyond, the drawn-out call of "Allaaahu Akbaar!" rang out one last time before ceasing once and for all.

The passengers who had escaped injury picked themselves up and set about comforting the less fortunate ones, lifting them onto the seats and attempting to staunch the bleeding with their handkerchiefs and paper napkins. A ticket inspector and a guard appeared, calling for calm and assuring them that help was on the way.

Angela pulled herself stiffly from the floor back onto her seat. The comedian on the opposite side was groaning, his head lying on the table and bleeding profusely. One of his chums was pressing a blood-soaked handkerchief to his face. Angela noticed a part of his ear, cut clean off and lying on the table beside him. The stud in its lobe sparkled in the light from above the seat.

But opposite her, Professor Edelman, who had not moved quickly enough, sat rocking and moaning horribly, his hands pressed over his nose.

"Let me have a look, Professor," said Angela gently. She came round and lifted his hands from his face. It was a gruesome sight, though hardly fatal. The bridge of his enormous nose had been sliced clean away, leaving a bloody hollow just below the line of his eyebrows. Then a clever thought suddenly came into Angela's mind.

"Do you know who you remind me of, Professor?" she blurted out, as she applied her scarf to the gaping wound. "The Duke of Urbino in Piero della Francesca's profile portrait of him – you surely must know the one I mean – the one that shows him without the top of his nose. You're in very good company."

"Bugger the Duke of Urbino," groaned Professor Edelman. A series of loud jangling noises came from down the coach.

"Switch those bloody mobiles off," blazed Angela. "You know perfectly well you're not supposed to use them in here."

6 The Stain - a sequel

Mr Salmon had arranged the taxi that picked Cyril up at the prison gate and went with him to the station. He had provided him with his own telephone number, at the same time urging him to only use it in extremity. He also told him to contact his own parish priest – he had provided him with a covering letter – and offer to help him in the ways that had made him so useful in the prison chapel. He was ready to speak to the vicar on his behalf if he needed convincing but, beyond that, Cyril was to try to make a go of things himself. And, with that, he had put a miserable Cyril Crackenthorpe, who was fighting back his tears, on his homebound train.

Cyril felt like a lost dog. The home in Highgate, which he had left just four months earlier when he was sent down for stalking Virginia Howell of New Millennium Kitchens, no longer felt like one. He pined for his snug little cell – the cell he had kept so shipshape that it had impressed the governor and helped earn him the full remission on his sentence, which he would much rather have done without. Indeed, to Cyril, the remission was the real sentence – the pain of having to live once more in the outside world.

The house had not been touched since he had left it so abruptly and it smelled stale. There was a heap of mail lying on the doormat, which he shifted listlessly with his foot, not even having the heart to pick it up and arrange it neatly. And dust. Dust was everywhere. The sheets on his bed were exactly as he left them four months earlier. They felt damp and gave off a sour smell, but he felt no inclination to change them, let alone Hoover them as he had been in the habit of doing before he went to prison.

He had been sent down in the summer and now, four months later, it was a dank, grey day in December and he felt cold, so he did, at least, turn the storage heaters on before slumping into his familiar armchair in the drawing room where he sat bleakly contemplating the dust on the tables and shelves and comparing the cheerless scene about him with the spick and span little box that had so recently been his home.

Eventually, in the late afternoon, he stirred. He needed something to eat. But going out into the street was an ordeal that he was reluctant to face. Would he be recognised and pointed out as a convicted felon, a jailbird? Inside the prison, nothing like that mattered: no one pointed him out as something unnatural or stared at him with contempt. Here it was different. He had memories of the 'rough boys' of his own childhood, who used to jeer at him for being posh and chuck stones at him. Ever since then, he had dreaded being picked on by their kind.

With a cap pulled down over his face, he managed to supply himself with some tins of baked beans and sliced peaches from his local supermarket. Those, along with a packet of tea and some milk and sugar, would keep him going for a day or so until he could start to pick up the threads of his old life again. All the time he was in the supermarket he was terrified that he might be recognised and publicly shamed. So he was careful to join a queue at the checkout where there was a girl that he had not seen before, though with his cap pulled so far down over his face he attracted more suspicious looks than he would otherwise have done.

But once the ordeal was over, he locked himself in the house and was opening a tin of baked beans when the telephone rang. At first he felt too frightened to answer it, but it persisted, so in the end he did.

It was Mr Salmon, making sure that he had got home safely and urging him to get in touch with his own vicar as soon as possible. Cyril, who had not been a churchgoer before his imprisonment, said he would try, but already the more urgent need of keeping the world at bay was reasserting itself. Though his days under lock and key had already become a source of nostalgia, he was ashamed to reveal to anyone – no matter how sympathetic they pretended to be – the thing that had taken him to prison in the first place. So he agreed to everything that Mr Salmon told him while he knew that he was very unlikely to do anything about it.

Besides, he realised that he was going to be a busy man – tackling all that dust, for a start, not to mention polishing the silver and brass after four months of neglect. And then, in his absence, objects had got seriously out of line: pictures hung crooked on the walls, rugs lay at funny angles and were crinkled in an irritating way, and even pieces of furniture had wandered mysteriously from their true alignments with each other. He would have to go to work with a tape measure to restore them all to their proper relationships.

And there was that pile of mail still sitting on the doormat. That would have to be sifted, filed away and answered where necessary. But the latter was a task he could look forward to because at least it gave him the opportunity to put his calligraphy to good use – that laborious, Gothicised script that Mr Elcox had taught him all those years ago in the handwriting class at his prep school. He sighed every time he thought of Mr Elcox. The headmaster had been a terror with his gym shoe, but Mr Elcox had been different – rather, it had been a meeting of minds – and, as well as teaching him to write beautifully, he had helped him lay out his stamp collection. His schooldays and the past months safe in his prison cell had been the best of times.

But after a couple of days of such reveries, Cyril started to draw his life together again. Mercifully, the telephone did not ring and he was left alone to concentrate on the important tasks around him.

Dusting was his first priority, and then cleaning the windows on the inside – the outside didn't matter. Cyril was not bothered by the outside of the house, anyway – he had abandoned the garden to nature long ago – but indoors it was a different story, where there could be no backsliding.

And once he had got to the stage of checking the alignments of every visible object in the house in its relationship with its neighbours, he rose to the challenge. He had kept notes of where everything should be, but now he even risked a few minor alterations. It was fascinating work, which, while he was at it, took his mind off the menace lurking in the streets outside.

But there came a time, about ten days after his release, when his creative energy started to flag and it was then that he noticed the state of the walls. The first intimation of this had come to him when he was straightening and cleaning the pictures and he discovered the dust marks behind them, but he had put it to the back of his mind while he was busy with his tape measure. Now it had to be faced. The walls needed to be painted.

It was a tricky situation because it would mean disarranging things while the work was being done, but at least he had noted carefully where everything was meant to be so the job of restoration would not be too difficult. And anyway, Cyril felt that without such obstacles to be overcome his life was meaningless.

The application of a damp sponge revealed to him just how dirty the walls were, so he steeled himself for what had to be done: The hall, stairwell and landing all had to be painted. Once he had identified the problem there was no way that he could back away from it. But it was going to involve bringing in an outsider because he did not have the ladders or the other equipment that was necessary to reach the ceilings and especially the stairwell – always a challenge to a decorator. He contemplated using a roller on the end of a long pole – but what if he had an accident with the paint? How was he going to repair the damage then? No, it would have to be done professionally, albeit to his own exacting standards.

His pension had been accumulating in the bank while he had been away, so he was in funds and it was money that simply had to be spent. But what if the decorator found out who he was – the man who had been sent to prison for stalking Virginia Howell?

He looked in the yellow pages at the list of decorators and settled on a Mr Higgs who appeared to live a safe distance away. Hopefully, he did not use the same shops or have friends in the neighbourhood. There was also something reassuringly English about the name Higgs.

Mrs Higgs answered the phone – a homely voice without a hint of suspicion in it when he gave his name and address. Yes, her husband could probably be round tomorrow evening to see what needed to be done and to give him a rough estimate. About six o'clock? He'd get back to him if it wasn't possible. It was a homely voice that seemed to match the name, and Cyril felt relieved. So far so good.

Mr Higgs arrived in his overalls from another job. He was a short, sandy-haired man with a shiny forehead. Cyril did not ask him to remove his shoes as he usually did with visitors, but to wipe his feet instead as the floor had 'just been done', which the man obligingly did. Then he showed him the offending walls while Mr Higgs wrote the information down in a notebook – which, in Cyril's eyes, was a mark in his favour.

"We'll start with the hall, stairwell and landing," explained Cyril, "but I'm sure the rest will have to be done before long, as well."

"And what about the colour?" Mr Higgs asked. "The same again?"

"Of course," answered Cyril, shocked at any suggestion that it might be different. "I would never dream of having anything else. It was the colour my mother chose and she would be most upset to know that I'd altered it."

Mr Higgs looked at him a little oddly and then at the walls. "Hmm," he said with a frown and sucking his pen. "Cream. I'm pretty sure we can match that, though it might be called something different. It wouldn't be a bad idea to look at a colour chart and make quite sure. I'll drop one in tomorrow."

"When can you start?" asked Cyril.

Mr Higgs burnished his forehead. "It would have to be after the New Year. We'll soon be into the Christmas holiday."

"Oh dear, as late as that?" complained Cyril. "I had hoped that you'd be able to start straight away. All sorts of things could go wrong between now and then."

"Don't worry, sir, I'm sure the house won't fall down in the next few weeks. It looks as if it's stood for a good bit of time already."

"It's a fine house," declared Cyril. "It belonged to my father and mother before me, so of course I'm very proud of it."

"It's nice to find someone still living in the house he grew up in," said Mr Higgs. "There can't be many people like that these days."

"I love it dearly," said Cyril. "It has wonderful associations for me."

"I'm sure it does," replied Mr Higgs with the faintest trace of a smile. "Anyway, I'll drop the colour chart off tomorrow and try and fit you in as soon as possible after the New Year. Will that do?"

"I suppose it'll have to," admitted Cyril reluctantly.

And, with that, Mr Higgs was gone. But what he had said stuck with Cyril for another reason quite apart from decorating the walls. He had reminded him that Christmas was upon him and he had done nothing about his Christmas cards.

In fact, he had a further reminder the next morning with the arrival of his sister Georgina's annual letter from New Zealand. It was the usual insipid affair – saying nothing of any interest –but mercifully showed no sign that she had heard of his disgrace. Normally, he wrote to her in good time before Christmas, so he knew he must do it soon or else she might smell a rat. Not that Georgina had much of a nose for rats, but then you never knew. It meant buying a couple of boxes of Christmas cards. One card would have to be despatched to New Zealand, and he thought perhaps it would be a nice gesture to send one to Mr Salmon as well. He even toyed with the idea of sending one to Mr Higgs and his wife. She had such a homely voice and was probably a Christmassy sort of person, but then he remembered the trouble he had got into with Virginia and did not want to have any more dangerous entanglements with outsiders. No, his relationship with Mr and Mrs Higgs must remain a strictly professional one.

The rest of the cards, of course, he would address to himself, the way he always did. It was nice getting the cards that you liked instead of having to put up with someone else's poor taste. And then it was fun sticking on stamps – placing them so that they were an equal distance from the top and the side of the envelope was a challenging business – and it was exciting to use both first and second class stamps and to see which cards got back the quickest. It was surprising how often the second class ones arrived before the first. He liked to stagger them, too, so that something arrived each day right up to the final post on Christmas Eve. So, all in all, Christmas was a time for fun.

In his letter to Georgina he outlined his plans for the house, assuring her of his trust in Mr Higgs and what a nice person his wife had sounded on the telephone. He dilated on the problem of keeping silver clean and of rugs that crept, but was careful to avoid giving the impression that he needed to restore the house after being absent from it for a long time. Not that he told her a lie – Cyril would never have done that – he simply omitted any unpleasantness that might have upset the tenor of their relationship.

And then there was the fun of inscribing the cards. It was an excellent opportunity to practise his handwriting and for a trip down Memory Lane. Cards were received from Mummy and Daddy and Granny Crackenthorpe and Auntie Ada and Uncle Roger. But Granny Nicholson didn't send him one because she had died before Cyril was born. Mr Elcox, his old schoolmaster who had taught him handwriting, sent one too, of course. And then there were the jokey ones from people like the Prime Minister. An especially handsome one was bought separately and came from the Queen herself, whose signature he worked very hard on. So, one way and another, it provided Cyril with plenty of Christmas cheer.

But he had to be careful not to get carried away. There were still sterner duties to perform – the house could not be neglected – dust still had to be attacked, furniture and silverware polished – for on Christmas morning the house had to sparkle like a new pin.

A card arrived from Mr Salmon, which Cyril compared unfavourably with the one he had sent him. It was funny how remote that cosy little cell was starting to become.

Christmas passed without a single interruption, which was exactly the way Cyril liked it. The night before, he spent touching up the rooms so that they sparkled, and then he hung the decorations of his childhood on a plastic tree – Cyril was not going to have a real one shedding its needles in the house. There were fairy lights, too, from the same era. All had been lovingly wrapped in the very same tissue paper that his mother had used and placed in the very same black cardboard box in the very same cupboard on the attic landing.

And over the holiday, Cyril made plans. The way lay open for some exciting developments in the days ahead. For one thing, he thought of reviving his lodge. It had fallen into abeyance during the unfortunate affair with Virginia, but now he put his mind to work, devising some new ritual. Not that he would make any radical changes – that was not Cyril's way – but he would build on what he had already achieved. So a large part of Christmas and Boxing Day was devoted to inventing new steps and signs and jotting down on a piece of paper some additional passwords. For instance, Cyril decided that before entering a room at each stage of the ritual, a password as well as a manual sign was necessary. He thought back to his prep school scripture classes and then went to the old family Bible to check out suitable names.

And then he had a daring idea. Why not mount a display of some of the old family possessions that remained tucked away in the roof space and in various cupboards? The idea of laying out and labelling an exhibition really took a hold of him. The only drawback was the loft – it might release an awful lot of dust into the house when it was opened. But then that was part of the challenge. "Nothing ventured, nothing gained," Cyril stoutly told himself.

It was heady stuff and he had to force himself to think in practical terms. It was so long since he had last looked in the roof space that he could not even remember where the ladder was. Certainly it was nowhere in the house, he was quite sure about that. So the only place it could be was in the jungle outside, a place he never ventured into. No doubt it was half-buried and rotting in the rank grass, which would mean buying another ladder and carrying it home, a daunting prospect. Then he thought of Mr Higgs. Surely he would lend him a ladder to climb into the loft? He might even help him get things down, but he didn't want to count on it.

Cyril had no real idea what the loft contained. He had a vague memory of dust sheets covering things – what they were he did not know – but he thought there might be a dessert service that had belonged to Granny Nicholson before being passed down to his mother. That would be an interesting thing to display – especially if he could locate the cutlery to go with it.

And weren't there some old pictures in gilt frames? The prospect of their frames excited Cyril much more than the pictures themselves did.

Yes, he reflected, there was plenty to be going on with. He would definitely consult Mr Higgs about the ladder. He was sure he would oblige because he had that kind of feeling about Mr Higgs – he was an obliging sort of man, one whom he could trust. And that was so important – being able to trust people. Such people were, alas, few and far between – the ones you could genuinely trust. He recalled Virginia and immediately put the unpleasant thought out of his mind.

So Cyril planned and waited eagerly to hear from Mr Higgs who he felt sure would not let him down. Anyway, he had his colour chart and he was hardly likely to forget a thing like that. Then he thought he might ring him. Perhaps he might speak to that nice wife of his again.

But Mr Higgs rang first and a date was fixed for the third of January. He would arrive at nine o'clock and no, Cyril did not have to worry about protective covers for his carpets and furniture, Mr Higgs would provide them himself, though it would be a good idea to shift any ornaments that might be in the line of fire. Cyril thought about asking him about the ladder there and then, but decided it would be more tactful to mention it later.

The removal and storage of the ornaments took Cyril the best part of an afternoon, largely because he had to find alternative space for them. Should he place them elsewhere where they might be seen, or should he clear some cupboard space for them? And if he did the latter, what about the things that would have to be shifted to make that space available? It proved quite a headache and he finally resolved the problem by packing them in a couple of his parents' old suitcases and storing them under his bed.

January the third arrived and with it Mr Higgs – just seven minutes late. He found Cyril looking fretfully at his watch, but merely raised his eyebrows by way of enquiring if there was anything the matter, while Cyril managed to rein in his impulse to complain. He even failed to remind him about wiping his feet as he entered the house.

Mr Higgs went swiftly to work with his ladders and protective sheets while Cyril looked on anxiously. He was fearful that there might be traces of fresh paint on the covers that would mark his furniture or carpets, but Mr Higgs seemed unconcerned and whistled as he went about his work. That irritated Cyril but he knew he must say nothing, so he shut himself in the kitchen and pretended not to hear. He had enough sense to realise that he would only make matters worse if he watched what the man was doing. He was sufficiently strung up as it was.

Mr Higgs tackled the hall first, painting it cream as Cyril had ordered. For an hour or so, Cyril stuck to his resolution of not interfering with him while he worked, but after that his anxiety got the better of him. And horror of horrors, the paint that the decorator was applying was darker than the colour it was replacing. There was no doubt about it because he could see the line between the two.

"This isn't the same colour," he protested in an anguished voice. "It's too dark."

Mr Higgs stared at him for a second, nonplussed by his obvious distress.

"That's nothing to worry about, Mr Crackenthorpe," he assured him. "Fresh paint is always like that. It'll dry lighter. Look," he said, pointing at the surface he had first applied, "you can see it's already starting to dry down to the right shade."

Cyril examined the place he had indicated and was forced to admit that it was indeed lighter than the area on which Mr Higgs was presently working. "It's almost the same colour, but not quite," he said. "It's still a bit darker."

"That's because it isn't completely dry," the decorator explained patiently. "Just give it a chance, Mr Crackenthorpe, and you'll see that it's all right. I know what I'm talking about."

He resumed his work and began to whistle softly to indicate to Cyril that it was time to leave him alone.

And when he inspected the newly painted wall in the daylight the following morning, Cyril was forced to admit that the decorator had been right.

So, with his peace of mind restored for the time being at least, he decided to raise the delicate matter of borrowing a ladder to reach the loft – all the more reason, he reflected, for not antagonising the man.

But what was the best time to ask him? That was the question that vexed Cyril. Best leave it until he had finished for the day and ask him if he could do it after he had completed the painting, he decided. Because Cyril's brain was teeming with so many ideas, he was desperately eager to see what treasures the loft contained.

The work progressed into the second day while Cyril dreamed of the Aladdin's cave awaiting him. It was funny that he had never thought of it before, but then if Mummy and Daddy had put things away in the loft it must have been for a very good reason, and he was the last person to upset their arrangements. But now he reached the conclusion that they had done it knowing that one day he would do the very thing that he was now contemplating – he would enter the treasure house and follow it up with something to hallow their memory, like mounting an exhibition.

That was the most likely explanation he could think of, because there had always been a good reason for everything they did.

That Granny Nicholson's dessert service was up there he felt fairly confident, but what about the other things? He had no idea. He imagined pictures in big gold frames – the kind of thing that his grandparents might have had – and sets of cutlery, which he hoped wouldn't be too difficult to get clean again, and perhaps there were stuffed birds and animals – he wasn't so happy about those – and books. A game he had liked playing as a child was guessing the number of words on a page in a book, then counting them to see how close he had got. He had been hopeless at first, but it was surprising how good he had become with practice. It might be fun to try that again with any old books that he came across.

But then, while Mr Higgs was into his second afternoon of work, something happened that shattered Cyril's dreams. He was sitting in the kitchen with a plan of the spare bedroom, working out a tentative scheme for displaying Granny Nicholson's dessert service – a somewhat premature undertaking as he was still not certain that it was in the loft at all and, even if it was, how many pieces it contained, but he was burning with impatience and wanted to get ahead of the game – when there was a knock at the door and the decorator put his head round it.

"Mr Crackenthorpe?" Mr Higgs said. "Might I have a word with you?"

"Yes, Mr Higgs. Is it important?" Cyril's voice was a compound of irritation and alarm.

"There's something I think you ought to see."

"Oh dear, there hasn't been an accident, a spill of any kind, has there?"

Alarm was gaining over irritation.

"Nothing like that," the decorator assured him, "but you ought to come and have a look all the same."

In a fever of anxiety, Cyril followed him to the first floor landing.

"Do you see that?" said Mr Higgs, pointing to the wall behind where a chest of drawers normally stood.

On the wall was a stain, an ugly blotch covered in a furry film. He touched it with his finger and showed it to Cyril. His fingertip was covered with a greenish mould.

"Could be dry rot or a leak of some kind. Is this an outside wall? If so, it might be a blocked gutter."

Cyril's horrified gaze passed from the damp patch on the wall to the decorator's finger and back again.

"Oh my God," he moaned. "Oh my God."

"It's not as bad as all that," replied Mr Higgs, who was finding it difficult to repress a smile. "But I think you may need a plumber."

"A plumber?" repeated Cyril, aghast.

"It looks like a plumber's problem, but I daresay I could have a look at your gutters myself."

"But what about the painting?" muttered Cyril. His head was starting to swim.

"That shouldn't be a problem," the other said. "I can do the rest and leave this bit. It won't show if it's behind the chest of drawers. But it's no good trying to paint over it."

"It won't show?" expostulated Cyril. "What do you mean it won't show?"

"No one'll see it," the decorator explained a trifle testily, "because it'll be hidden behind the chest of drawers".

Cyril stared at him in disbelief. "But it will still be there," he protested. "I'll know it's there, even if no one else does. It would be telling a lie, and that's something I'll never sink to."

"As you wish," said Mr Higgs with a shrug. "But it's no good trying to paint over it until we've found out what's causing it and given it time to dry out."

"And when will that be?" cried Cyril.

"It depends on what your plumber finds."

"My God," groaned Cyril. "My God, why this?"

"I'll finish the rest in the meantime," said Mr Higgs, turning away. "But you'll have to make your own mind up about it."

The decorator's patient approach to Cyril was now touched with a note of exasperation that the latter could not help but notice. His mind in turmoil, Cyril groped his way back down the stairs.

"Why this?" he muttered as he went. "Why this?"

He flung himself down at the kitchen table. "Why me?" he complained out loud. "Why does a thing like this have to happen to me?"

Meanwhile, on the landing above, Mr Higgs had resumed his whistling.

Half an hour later, he stuck his head round the kitchen door and asked if he could have a cup of coffee. His mildly truculent manner showed that he assumed it as his right – it was something which Cyril, who was unused to having workmen in the house, had overlooked. Cyril stirred himself and set about making the coffee.

"Would you like a biscuit as well?" he asked.

"Yes, please."

"You'd better have a plate," said Cyril. "It'll make a lot of crumbs."

Mr Higgs set off with his refreshments but stopped at the door and turned back to Cyril.

"Don't take that mark on the wall too much to heart, Mr Crackenthorpe," he said. "It's often the way when you have the place painted, you find all sorts of other things that need doing."

"It's come as a terrible shock," replied Cyril. "It's the last thing I was expecting."

The other chuckled lightly. "What? A little bit of dry rot or a leaky gutter? The way you're talking you'd think the house was about to fall down."

"Please don't say such dreadful things," remonstrated Cyril, putting his hands over his ears.

"I tell you what, Mr Crackenthorpe," said Mr Higgs. "I'm coming back tomorrow to finish off, so it'll be no trouble for me to take a ladder round and look at your gutters myself. How about that then? It ought to set your mind at rest."

"Thank you," mumbled Cyril in a choked voice. "I would be most grateful if you would."

The other plans he had been entertaining for the decorator's ladder had quite escaped his mind by now.

Cyril passed a bad night. He could put his mind to nothing and before he went to bed, and a couple of times after that, he kept returning to examine the offending stain on the landing. He touched it with his finger the way Mr Higgs had done and examined it under his magnifying glass – the very same that he had used as a boy for his stamp collection – but it showed no signs of going away. It was as stark and malignant as it had been when he had first set eyes on it.

And when he did finally drop off to sleep, shortly before six o'clock, it took over completely – getting larger and larger until it covered the entire landing wall and had started to spread down the stairs. Mr Higgs was there, scraping off dollops of the fungus with a kitchen spatula and stuffing them into his mouth. He kept telling Cyril how good it tasted and how he could make a fortune harvesting the stuff.

Cyril woke when he heard an urgent ringing on the doorbell. He sat up and looked at his alarm clock, which he had forgotten to set. It was after nine o'clock.

"My God," he said. "Is that the time?"

The bell went on ringing while he tore downstairs in his dressing gown and slippers.

Mr Higgs was waiting for him on the doorstep. It was odd seeing him there so soon after he had been on the landing, stuffing his face with fungus.

"I was about to go away," he said gruffly.

"I'm terribly sorry," replied Cyril. "I slept in."

"So it appears, Mr Crackenthorpe."

"I was having a dream – not a very nice one, I'm afraid. The stain was spreading over all the walls and you were there, eating the fungus and telling me how good it tasted."

Mr Higgs frowned and said nothing.

"But come on in," said Cyril hastily. "I'm sorry to keep you waiting out here."

He realised it had been a mistake mentioning his dream to the decorator and tried to sound as calm and in control of himself as possible.

"Would you like a cup of coffee?" he asked.

"I'll have one later, if you don't mind," answered Mr Higgs and set off up the stairs.

"I haven't inspected the damage yet. In spite of what I dreamt I hope it hasn't got worse during the night." Cyril tried to make a joke of it, but it didn't sound like one.

"After I've finished I'll have a look at the outside. It's probably your gutters," said Mr Higgs.

Cyril, meanwhile, went to the bathroom and began the complicated ritual of his morning ablutions, followed by vacuuming his sheets to remove the dust mites. That was one of the few things he hadn't liked about prison – he hadn't been allowed to vacuum his sheets.

By the time it was over and he was ready to go downstairs again, Mr Higgs was waiting for him on the landing.

"I'll have that coffee now, if you don't mind, and then I'll look at your gutters," he said.

Mr Higgs swallowed his coffee and went out of the house.

Cyril, meanwhile, decided to sit out the inspection of the gutters in the drawing room, where he tried to ease his agitated mind by playing the counting game with a book from the shelves, but found he couldn't concentrate and lost count before he was halfway down the page.

Twenty minutes later he could hear Mr Higgs coming back into the house and went out into the hall to meet him.

"It's like the Amazon jungle out there," remarked the decorator, "but I managed to fight my way through."

"Well?" asked Cyril.

The decorator burnished his forehead. "I'm afraid your gutters are in a bad way, Mr Crackenthorpe. One piece has come right away from the wall and has been pouring water down the side of the house, and the others are choked with leaves. I expect it was the weight of the leaves that brought the other piece down in the first place."

Cyril stood with his mouth opening and shutting, gobbling like a newly landed fish while the decorator was speaking to him.

"So what are you going to do about it?" he asked at length.

"What am I going to do about it?" retorted the other. "I cleared some of the leaves out, but they're right down inside the pipes. It looks like a builder's job."

"A builder?" Cyril almost shrieked. "But you told me a plumber just now."

"I'm afraid it's gone beyond that. It's got to be a builder. I haven't mentioned the pointing between the bricks. A lot of it's been washed out and some of the bricks are quite loose. It's a builder's job."

Cyril sank onto a chair and buried his face in his hands.

"I'm sorry, Mr Crackenthorpe," went on the other, "but you wanted my opinion and I've given it to you. You'll have to get a builder in to see to the outside of the house and then perhaps I could paint your windows for you because they're in a bad way as well. In fact, some of the sills have rotted right through and need renewing. Anyway, rather than taking my word for it, I suggest you take a look yourself. And before you do anything else you're going to have to cut back the jungle."

Cyril said nothing, but groaned, leaving the decorator feeling sheepish.

"That's the score, Mr Crackenthorpe, I'm afraid. If you like, I could have a word with a builder for you and he could come and look at it." The decorator shuffled his feet and then started up the stairs to collect his things.

"I'll think about it," Cyril muttered at length.

"Well don't think too long, Mr Crackenthorpe, because it's looking pretty sick."

"Sick?" exclaimed Cyril. "What do mean sick? Is it contagious? Will it spread?"

"It needs a builder," explained Mr Higgs patiently. "I'll speak to one if you like."

"You mean a doctor – if it's sick."

"I meant a house doctor – a builder," said Mr Higgs, as if he was speaking to a child. "It was just a way of speaking."

"Well why not say what you mean then?"

"Come along, Mr Crackenthorpe, there's no need to take on like that with me," retorted the decorator.

"I'm sorry," said Cyril. "I didn't mean to be rude, but what you have just said has given me a nasty shock."

"It's hardly the end of the world, is it? The builder will put it right for you."

"The end of the world?" queried Cyril. "My God, I hadn't thought of that. Is it really that bad?"

"I said it's not the end of the world, but you know what I mean. Just in a manner of speaking. If you get the job done in good time you'll have nothing to worry about."

"But you said something about the end of the world just now. What if it spreads?" demanded Cyril.

"The sooner you get it done the better," said Mr Higgs, but as he spoke he realised that this was not the wisest thing he could have said. "Forgive me for saying this to you, Mr Crackenthorpe," he resumed, "but mightn't it a good idea for you to see a doctor – I mean for yourself – because you're taking everything I say in quite the wrong way, you know. He might give you something to settle you down a bit, if you see what I mean."

The decorator sounded apologetic. It was not the kind of thing he was used to saying to his customers.

"Why should I see a doctor?" Cyril flashed back. "You said just now it's the house that's sick. It's the one that needs the doctor, not me. You said that – I know because I heard you and when I asked you if it was contagious, you deliberately avoided giving me a straight answer."

The decorator sighed. "Well, I've told you what I think. I can't do more than that, can I?" He started to shift his things to his van that was parked outside.

Cyril sat gazing at the floor, not saying anything.

"Well, I'm off now, Mr Crackenthorpe. I'll drop the bill in at the end of the week when my wife has had time to make it out. And you've got my telephone number when you've decided what you're going to do about the outside of the house."

With that, he was off, and Cyril did not even manage to say good-bye to him.

He sat for a long time slumped in the hall. What he had heard had left him feeling numb. He had realised that the stain was unhealthy and unwholesome, but that it was contagious hadn't occurred to him until now. And it was spreading through the house, for the moment largely unseen, working its way below the surface of the plaster and insinuating itself into the skirting boards and the very joists that held the floors up, sending its tentacles out everywhere until the whole house was rotten from top to bottom and came crashing down, when it would cross to the neighbouring ones – the wind would see to that if nothing else did – until the entire street was eaten up. And the people too, for it wasn't going to stop at bricks and mortar and timbers – that was only the beginning – but living things were grist for its mill as well – living things like himself. But what had caused it? It could only have started when he was away, so it had had four months to take hold. Was it terrorists? It was the kind of thing they were doing now. Spreading fatal sicknesses through the population. That explained it. If only he had been here they wouldn't have had a chance. That's what comes of leaving your house standing empty. Dangerous people take advantage of any opening you give them.

For the moment, while this obvious explanation was beavering through Cyril's mind, he didn't hear the bell ring. It was only after it was repeated several times that he finally registered.

"Is that them now?" he wondered. "Come to inspect their handiwork? Right, if that's the case, I'll confront them. I'll take them head on. They won't catch a Crackenthorpe running away."

With that, he flung open the door. "I know what you've been up to while I've been away," he bellowed. "I've rumbled your little game. But it's not going to work because I know what you've been up to. You thought I'd be a pushover, a soft touch, didn't you?"

He stopped to draw breath and the startled middle-aged man in spectacles blinked at him.

"Cyril?" he faltered. "It is Cyril, isn't it?"

"You think you've got a hold on me by knowing my name, do you? Well, sir, it won't wash with me. It won't wash."

"I don't think you quite understand …"

"Oh, I understand right enough. You're not pulling the wool over my eyes."

"No one's pulling the wool over your eyes, Cyril. I'm the vicar of St Barbara's – your parish priest. Dickie, Dickie Doare, that's me," explained the man, putting out his hand.

"Try pulling the other one, Mr Dickie Doare," sneered Cyril. He felt uplifted by his own performance, so much so that he could hardly believe he was doing it.

"I'm not pulling your leg," replied the other quietly. "It was Andy – you know Andy – Andy Salmon – your chum, who asked me to look you up."

Cyril released a loud guffaw of concentrated disbelief – a sound he had never uttered in his life before.

"If it's not a good time, I'll call another day," suggested Dickie.

Cyril discharged another mighty guffaw. "Over my dead body, you will. And if the house comes crashing down it'll take me with it. You can come and inspect your handiwork then, and only then, Mr Terrorist Doare – Mr. Smartypants Doare." He hadn't called anyone 'Smartypants' since he was at his prep school.

Cyril slammed the door and sank onto a chair, astonished by the majesty of his utterance. "Crackenthorpes were always fighters," he told himself. "Over my dead body," he repeated, and went on doing so at least fifty times.

Of course, this time it wasn't prison. He was taken away, yelling defiance at the terrorists who were bent on destroying his house and the rest of the country as well. For several weeks after his admission, he had carried out a detailed inspection of the walls and fittings of his new room to see if the sickness had reached them yet, as he knew that, one day, it inevitably must. But he felt drowsy a lot of the time and slept a great deal, until one morning he woke feeling suddenly refreshed, and when he examined the walls he knew them to be clean.

And then there was nice Miss Belfrage – the junior matron who would read the boys a story before they said their prayers and it was lights out.

And then Mr Elcox came – yes, it really was Mr Elcox, the kindly schoolmaster who had taught him to write with the beautiful hand that had won The Junior Handwriting Prize, the crowning triumph of his schooldays – but, of course, he had never been away at all. So, from then on, Cyril was able to spend his days blissfully covering sheet after sheet of lined paper with the script that was his master's legacy and his own greatest pride and joy.

7   A Confession

The walls of the reception area were beige and on them were hung reproductions of Van Gogh's *Sunflowers* and Monet's *Poppy Field* in pale wooden frames. In her light blue uniform behind the desk sat Pearl, young and blonde and as bright as a button, while a Chopin waltz wafted from a discreetly located speaker system into the air-conditioned space like an audible perfume. When it came to dying, the Hawthorns Hospice for the terminally ill was a pretty good place to do it.

Sitting hunched on a tan leather-covered sofa opposite the reception desk was Father Spottiswoode. Despite the purpose of the place and his advanced years, he was an unlikely figure in such surroundings. He was small and wrinkled like a shelled walnut and not entirely at ease with the soft furnishings. Not that he had come here to die; he was expecting to do that somewhere else, probably in the mission school in Tanzania where he was passing his final years in a kind of semi-retirement. He had spent the best part of a lifetime in Sierra Leone where the conditions had been a great deal harder than in the mission school in its relatively cool uplands. But, all the same, it was a far cry from the Hawthorns with its restful music and pictures and comfy sofas.

Meanwhile, Sandra appeared at the summons of Pearl. She was dark and olive-skinned with carefully penciled eyebrows – a contrast to Pearl's Saxon blondness – and wore a light-blue nurse's uniform. Father Spottiswoode noted the uniform with approval. He liked uniforms on nurses and school children, a point on which he was at one with his African flock. Trained originally in the Classics, he believed that 'a touch of Sparta' and the self-effacement and sense of order that a relatively severe uniform imposed did not go amiss.

"I probably don't have to tell you, Father Spottiswoode, that Dr Hollingside is not going to be with us for very much longer. But he has had his medication and is quite chirpy. Shall I tell him you'd like to see him?" said Sandra.

"Just say it's a friend – an old friend. Don't tell him who I am."

Sandra frowned.

"It's perfectly all right," the priest assured her. "I just want to make it a little surprise – for him to find it out for himself. You see, it's been a very long time."

"As you wish, Father, but I don't have to tell you of all people, I'm sure, not too much excitement and not for too long. He tires very quickly. They all do at this stage."

"Of course. I'd hardly have expected anything else."

"Would you like to come this way?"

Father Spottiswoode got to his feet, exchanged a nod with Pearl and followed Sandra.

"It's so peaceful here," he said. "I rather fancy the idea of passing away to the sound of Chopin."

Sandra smiled. "We only play that in the reception area – more for the visitors really. It's not compulsory listening for our patients."

They went down a corridor, which was carpeted from wall to wall and painted beige like the reception area. Yet more Van Gogh reproductions and a variety of easy-on-the-eye Impressionist paintings hung on the walls, but the sound of Chopin had faded. Dr Hollingside's room was the last one at the end of the passage. Sandra peered through the little window in the door and nodded to Father Spottiswoode.

"You can go in. He's awake," she said. She held the door open for the priest.

"You've got a visitor, Dr Hollingside," she called to the patient and withdrew.

Propped up by a couple of large pillows, Dr Hollingside was reading a paperback with a pair of demilune glasses perched on his beak of a nose. His features were wasted with his fatal illness, though there was a glint of vitality yet, of mischief almost, in his eyes. Glancing over the lenses of his glasses he frowned when he saw the priest's clerical collar.

"Jumping to conclusions, aren't you? I'm not ready for anything of that kind," he declared sharply, "and I shan't be either when the time finally does come. It's hardly a question of meeting my maker, is it? What can a being that has ceased to exist possibly say to one that has never done so in the first place? Or vice-versa? Eh?"

Father Spottiswoode paused on the threshold. He was not taken aback by what he heard. Indeed, he was half expecting something of the kind. He was struck only by the vehemence with which the sentiment was expressed by one on the final leg of his earthly passage.

"Come in anyway," said the patient, managing a skeletal smile. "You won't change anything, mind, but I'm ready for an argument if you're looking for one."

"You mustn't tire yourself," replied Father Spottiswoode.

"A platitude," the patient snorted and, laying aside his book, pointed to a chair by the side of his bed. "You feel obliged to say that kind of thing because I'm a dying man."

The two elderly men looked at each other for a moment without speaking.

"Well?" said Dr Hollingside at length. "Have you come to garner up my soul? To attempt to comfort this bundle of neurological functions with delusions of its survival as a conscious entity in some future state of existence? You'll have your work cut out for you if you try to do that, I can tell you. I may be on the brink of oblivion, but I'm not about to succumb to wishfulness."

The priest smiled with a benevolent tolerance, which struck the sick man as patronising and caused him to turn away.

"Do you recognise me?"

Startled into a response, Dr Hollingside turned on his pillow and stared at the wrinkled features. He frowned. "Am I supposed to? It's a very long time since I've mixed with people like you."

"After all these years it's hardly surprising that you shouldn't. But then the circumstances of our last encounter ..."

The patient stared hard at the features, which the priest lowered for his closer inspection.

"It's so long since I've had any dealings with clergymen of any kind," replied Doctor Hollingside. "Our paths have seldom crossed."

"Not even in intellectual matters?"

"Least of all in those," retorted Dr Hollingside. "As one who has placed his trust in the rational observation of the universe, I have found nothing in the speculations of theologians that was of the slightest value. I'm sorry if that sounds offensive to you, but truth would be my god if I was forced to have one."

"And mine too," replied the priest. He looked intently at the sick man. "But was it always that way?"

"So, the Inquisition has come to press its charges on my deathbed, has it?" observed the sick man crisply. "You've done your homework, haven't you? Yes, I did have what you might call a vocation for the priesthood once upon a time. I would prefer to describe it as a lapse into youthful morbidity. Presumably that's what you're referring to ... that callow flirtation with irrationality?"

The priest nodded. "Yes, though I wouldn't have described it in those terms."

"No, of course you wouldn't. But why me? It was many years ago and you must have seen plenty of other sheep stray from your fold in that time. So why pick on me?"

"You're a distinguished man, Dr Hollingside, a figure of considerable academic prominence."

"And for that reason a good catch, no doubt. Do you attend the deathbeds of many so-called prominent men in the hope of landing a big fish? And who are you anyway? You still haven't told me your name."

"I must apologise," said the priest. "We've been talking all this time and I still haven't told you."

"Apparently I'm supposed to know, but it appears to have slipped from my mind completely," answered the other.

"Spottiswoode. Adrian Spottiswoode."

"Of course it is," said Dr Hollingside. "That rings a very loud bell. If you'd only said so in the first place. The University chaplaincy. We were both much younger men then – in fact, not much between us – and we've changed a very great deal, but it's hardly a name to forget. So why all the beating about the bush? Why not come out with it at once? Direct answers are not part of the Catholic Church's remit, I suppose."

There was a pause in the conversation before the patient resumed.

"No doubt you have come here with the best of intentions, Father Spottiswoode, but you're wasting your time. I don't think you and I have much to say to each other. Yes, the scales fell from my eyes once and for all not long after we last spoke, when I set out on a new path – one that I've never once regretted following, I might add. And now I'm prepared to die with the convictions that have sustained me for the best part of my life. You find them cheerless, even abhorrent, no doubt, but I stand by them with the tranquil mind of an Epicurean."

"Your conscience doesn't trouble you – even now?"

"Trouble me? There are things I regret doing in my life, of course. But what's done cannot be undone. And rather than waste my brief span in fruitless self-reproach, better to make amends by living as usefully as possible – which, on the whole, is what I've tried to do." Dr Hollingside shut his eyes firmly and turned his head away on the pillow. "Now leave me, please. This is turning out to be a rather pointless conversation and I'm beginning to feel tired."

But the priest did not budge. Instead, from the small briefcase he was carrying he removed a sheet of paper.

"Dr Hollingside, would you care to cast your eye over this? It won't take long. Though, if you prefer, I could read it out to you." He looked over his shoulder towards the door. "Quietly, of course."

"I asked you to go, didn't I?" The patient's eyes remained firmly shut.

"I don't want to tire you, but you might find it interesting."

Dr Hollingside did not reply, though he made no attempt to summon the nurse.

Father Spottiswoode sat silently for a moment and then started to read aloud from the paper. He did it softly, in a practiced, mellifluous voice and Dr Hollingside listened to him with his eyes closed.

"Summary of a confession made to myself, Father Adrian Spottiswoode, in the Roman Catholic Chaplaincy of the University of Cambridge in June 1951. 'Father, I have a grievous sin to confess to you. Something worse probably than any you have heard before'."

"Did I say that to you?" said the patient, still with his eyes closed.

"Your own words."

"And you wrote them down? Hardly the ticket, was it?"

"The circumstances were rather unusual."

"The circumstances were rather unusual." A dry chuckle came from the bed. "I suppose they were. Do you want me to tell you the rest?

Actually, I'd rather hear it from you, Father. You've got rather a good deathbed voice. A touch sepulchral without sounding too Gothic."

" 'Worse than you ever will have heard before. Father, I have murdered someone'."

The priest paused and Dr Hollingside chuckled. "That's pretty ripe – not the kind of guff you normally got from an undergraduate, was it?"

"Naturally, I checked you before you said any more, but let's leave those bits out."

"Quite right. Let's not sully the tale." Dr Hollingside folded his hands on his chest, settling himself comfortably as if in the expectation of being pleasantly entertained. "I have murdered somebody," he repeated.

"Murdered somebody ... Then I said ..."

"Murdered somebody. Leave what you said out of it," snapped the patient. "We've just decided that, haven't we?"

" 'In my wildest dreams I would never have thought it possible. It was four years ago when I was doing my National Service in Germany. If it had been in the heat of some battle or other it might have been different, I suppose. As you know, I was a public schoolboy, but I wasn't commissioned and I felt like a fish out of water; an ordinary soldier stuck in the ranks. I loathed every second of it, as a matter of fact, and was counting the days till I was free. I suppose I'm a snob. I confess that, Father ...'."

The priest paused.

"Did I really talk that way?" said Dr Hollingside. "Yes, it was a grim old time – despite having survived a public school up on the Yorkshire moors. But at least I was among my own kind there – under the beady eyes of those Benedictines."

" 'I had been drinking, of course, and I wasn't much good at it, and no good at all at the other thing – you know what I mean, Father. Soldiers always go on about it – that and football. They seem to think of nothing else'."

Father Spottiswoode paused.

"My goodness, how circumspect we once were," chuckled the patient. "I had never fucked a woman and didn't want to say that to you directly – especially since you were a priest – even though I was just about to tell you that I'd murdered one. That's what comes next, isn't it?"

The priest did not speak.

"Well, shall I tell you out of my own mouth now, and we'll see if it corresponds with what you've got on your piece of paper?" He paused and cleared his throat before beginning. "It was Berlin – just after the war – 1948. A group of us young soldiers were drinking and she was a prostitute. And, of course, the topic of my virginity came up – as it always did. They were a merciless bunch who made my life hell because of my posh accent and the other signs of a more polished upbringing than their own. But, in the best Benedictine tradition, I gritted my teeth, determined to see my time through – those bare knees and runs across the moors had taught me staying power of a kind – but we were due home soon, so this time they were going to set me up, put me through the hoop at last. They had even made a collection to pay the woman. I went along with it, of course. I felt I had to. But I was scared stiff – though that's probably the wrong word to use in these particular circumstances. Is that what you've got written down there, Father?"

The patient opened his eyes and the priest nodded. "More or less, but not that last bit."

"Well, to cut a long story short, I went off with her. She wasn't remotely attractive to me – quite the opposite in fact. She looked well past thirty, with muddy blonde hair, in full war paint, of course. But if she'd been a more sympathetic and mothering sort, even, she might have been the right thing for a shy young man who was keen to break his duck. How am I doing, Father?"

"Time has improved your memory. I don't recall the muddy blonde hair."

"We went into a bombed-out building. Berlin was full of places like that then. Anyway, she seemed to know where to go. She stripped off her blouse and undid my flies and started to work on me in a desultory kind of way …"

He fell silent and the priest looked at him anxiously. "Is this making you too tired?" The haggard face grinned at him from the pillow.

"And you know what, Father? I felt nothing – absolutely bugger all. Sorry, that last bit wouldn't have been in a confession. A good trollop would have worked me up somehow, but not this bitch. Oh no. Was it revenge for the war? Had she lost a boyfriend or a relative? I don't know. But you know what she did then?"

The priest nodded. "I think so."

A Confession

"She bit my cock. Sunk her teeth right into it and laughed in my face. Then I saw red – I'd been drinking, after all, and what followed seemed to be over and done with before I understood what I had done. Does that tally?"

"Pretty well."

"I choked her with my bare hands; squeezed her windpipe and the rest wasn't so difficult – even for a callow ex-public schoolboy like me – not in Berlin in those days. I buried her under a pile of rubble near to where we were. They were still dragging bodies out of the ruins three years after the war had ended. And anyway, I was posted home a week later. I told the others I'd broken my duck, of course – it made life a bit easier."

"And the only person you've ever told was me?"

"That's right," Doctor Hollingside said. "And I never did what you told me was the right thing to do either. I never handed myself in."

"Or the other thing, the one I even recommended to you as being the more desirable course," the priest replied in a soft voice, "the thing I have carried round with me ever since."

"Good Heavens, have you really? Did you take it that seriously? After all, it was just after the war and life was still pretty cheap – especially in a place like Berlin."

"That's not what I'm saying to you. It was a terrible crime, not to mention a mortal sin, no matter when or where it took place – we both knew that – but the fact is that you betrayed me."

The patient gave a dry little laugh. "I betrayed you? That's a bit over the top, isn't it? What difference did it make to anything? She was a hard-bitten old whore, after all – not exactly your Mary Magdalene type. She ran the risk – as her tribe always have done – and paid the price. That's all there was to it."

"You renounced your Christian faith within weeks of making that confession – and made no secret of it. Trumpeted it for all the world to hear, as a matter of fact."

The patient raised an eyebrow. "Which was insensitive of me – and not a little ungrateful."

"The fault was possibly mine, in part at least," went on Father Spottiswoode. "You recall, no doubt, that I'd made a kind of bargain or pact with you – or thought I had – something that on the face of it was, canonically speaking, very dubious, but at the time seemed to me to be serving a higher good."

"A higher good? My word, we are moving above the moral snowline now, aren't we?" said the other with a distinct note of sarcasm in his voice.

The priest chose to ignore his tone. "We valued the quality of your mind," he went on placidly. "At that time we felt a particular need for men of your calibre to fight our intellectual war for us."

"That was very flattering of you. It was the early days of the Cold War when Stalin sneered about the lack of divisions at the Pope's disposal, and you were longing for some new Aquinas? A great synthesiser who would carry conviction in those leftwing intellectual circles, which seemed to be carrying all before them, one who would check the tide of dialectical materialism, the Great Satan?" The fire in Dr Hollingside's eye blazed up and, despite his wasted features, it was difficult for a moment to think of him as a dying man.

"And I told you that in return for your commitment to join my order, I would bury the unfortunate incident in Berlin – after a few notional acts of contrition followed by absolution, of course. Hardly very exacting. You would receive absolution and your sin would be subsumed in the devotion of your life to the service of the greater good, so to speak. With your slate wiped clean your intellect would be deployed where it would be of the greatest advantage in the ideological battle of the times. And, what's more, you gave me your word."

"To take the Cross?"

"To take the Cross, if you like to put it that way."

"And I let you down, leaving you lumbered with my guilt, in a manner of speaking?"

For a moment, neither of them said anything.

"This tortured Christian conscience thing seems so utterly remote," said Dr Hollingside, breaking the silence eventually. "To belong to a different age and universe, even. To have absolutely no meaning at all in our modern – or should I call it postmodern – world. I simply can't fathom it. Who do you think cares about a thing like that any more?"

"I do, for one. Which is why I'm here."

"And for that you have come all the way from wherever it is to confront a man on his deathbed?"

"From Africa – Tanzania. I am here on leave – probably for the last time."

"So you decided to kill two birds with one stone when you heard of my condition?"

The other did not speak.

"I still don't understand," went on Dr Hollingside. "What drives someone like you? You are suggesting I deserted to the enemy, leaving you to carry the weight of my sin on your own shoulders? I betrayed your trust when you had bent the rules, so to speak, possibly putting your own soul at risk on my behalf? Do you really believe that? You could have denounced me as a murderer – but the confessional is sacrosanct, so that option didn't exist for you. But you chose not to press the matter with me because you felt you needed me for some larger purpose in your ideological war. I was to be your Werner von Braun – your Nazi rocket scientist."

Father Spottiswoode nodded. "In a nutshell."

"In a nutshell. And I ought to feel tremendously flattered. But you actually believe in that tortured conscience stuff, don't you? It really means something to you, doesn't it? Marxists are every bit as dogmatic. Endless doctrinal hairsplitting and, in their own way, just as wishful. And, at the end of the day, is there a grain of truth in any of it? Talk about the number of angels dancing on the head of a pin. The truth I fear is that we are risen apes whose existence has no more significance than … than …" He searched for a comparison, "than that of one of the dust mites that still infest these sheets despite the best efforts of my nurses."

"And even as a dying man, conscience or remorse mean nothing to you at all? But as an atheist I suppose that makes sense. It's consistent, at least."

"I completely fail to see why you should carry this thing about with you like a millstone around your own neck after all this time," said Dr Hollingside. "Is it some kind of score settling? Or merely a way of setting the record straight? Of squaring the books at the end of the day? I wouldn't suggest anything so mean-spirited as mere vindictiveness, of course. A Christian of your calibre wouldn't sink to that."

"I'm glad you make that concession at least."

A dry chuckle came from the bed.

"So, what am I expected to do about it?" asked the patient at length.

"Just sign this confession and die in peace. I will submit it to the proper authority – which I suppose means the German police – after you are dead."

For such a sick man, Dr Hollingside's snort of derision was extremely powerful. "And what interest could the German police possibly have in the murder of a single prostitute in the ruins of Berlin more than fifty years ago following the most destructive war in human history?"

By way of answering his question, Father Spottiswoode held out the paper and a pen.

The patient took it and signed with a flourish. "There, if that makes you feel better. It's no skin off my nose, or my next of kin's either. The family all flew the nest years ago and if it ever gets back to them they'll probably be rather tickled."

The priest took the paper. "Don't you want to read it?"

"What on earth for? We've been through it, haven't we? And what difference would it make? So what are you planning to do now then? Go back to Africa to die? You could do a lot worse than to do it here, but I expect that would be out of character."

The priest went to the door. Sandra was hovering anxiously outside though she could not hear what had been passing between them.

"Good-bye, Father. I'm sorry to sound so grumpy," said Dr Hollingside. "By the way, there is just one other thing – a point in all this that perhaps you haven't considered."

"Oh?" The priest raised his eyebrows.

"Did it ever cross your mind that the whole thing might have been a lie? A hoax? A rather cruel undergraduate prank played at your expense?"

"Of course it did. But I rejected it. As I do now."

"How can you be so sure? After all, I'd known you for the best part of three years before raising the matter, so why would I leave it so late? If it had been genuine, you would have thought I'd have tried to get it off my chest a bit sooner than I did, wouldn't you?"

Father Spottiswoode fixed an intense gaze on him.

A Confession

"I know because even now – after all this time – I can read you like a book … Geoffrey. You don't mind if I call you Geoffrey, do you? I always used to."

"Wasn't it Geoff? There always was a bit more to it than my powerful intellect, wasn't there?"

"Geoff then," replied the priest. "Call us brothers in the Theban Band, paired by mutual love in a common struggle. No doubt there are more trendy psychological explanations for it in these times of rampant paedophilia. But I prefer the Theban Band. You weren't lying when you confessed to me that time, Geoff, and, what's more, I guessed the real reason why you made such a hash of the business – with the prostitute, I mean."

"And then I betrayed you? My Theban brother?"

The priest did not speak.

"And now we're a couple of sad old men. One actually knocking on Death's door and the other with not much time left before he's doing the same thing. And it all might have been different." Dr Hollingside chuckled. "What a corny old script this is, eh? It stinks."

Father Spottiswoode grinned. "It does rather, doesn't it, Geoff?"

"Then let's wind it up before we start repeating ourselves or, even worse, get tearful," replied Dr Hollingside. He dragged himself painfully into a sitting position against the pillows. "I won't say 'will you hear my confession, Father?' That would be too maudlin for words and highly embarrassing for both of us. The worst possible ending. After all, I embarrassed you that way once before. Just say a blessing for me, Adrian, and go back to your Africans in Tanzania or wherever they are."

Dr Hollingside folded his hands on his chest and, with his eyes closed, inclined his head forward as he used to do at school for the mealtime grace while the priest raised his hand, made the sign of the Cross and pronounced a Latin blessing in a clear voice.

"Amen," said the patient when it was done. "Thank you, Adrian."

Father Spottiswoode leaned over him and kissed his forehead. "Good bye, Geoff – for the time being."

Dr Hollingside winked at him. "Don't you count on it," he said.

He shut his eyes and settled back on the pillow. Sandra was already standing anxiously at the door.

As he left, the priest tore the piece of paper he was carrying into four neat quarters and, with a smile on his face, placed then in the waste bin at the end of the passage. At reception, Chopin had been replaced by Handel's *Water Music*.

8 Part of a Quota

Despite the heavy snoring coming from the other three bunks and the bulb that burned constantly inside its mesh cage, I managed to sleep. It was the sleep of a drained man, but there was no escape from the horror of what lay ahead of me. It kept banging away like a headache, dulled a little by unconsciousness, yet too powerful to let go.

Self-awareness and the anticipation of extinction: that's what sets a man apart from other condemned creatures in the slaughterhouse. The pig might squeal with terror when it is at last confronted by the knife poised to slit its throat, but it won't spoil its sleep the night before by thinking about it.

The passage of days, nights, weeks, months – the difference between them – has lost its meaning for me. So much so that if I think about it at all, it's like speculating about a world outside my own experience, should there be such a place. And I wonder about that. Does anything exist anywhere else at all? Is everything not right here, where I am? Is not this the sum total of things? But whatever way I look at it, I want to stay alive.

The glare of the bulb – that seems real enough, not a piece of speculation. And the things that it shows me, they're real too. And how I cherish them – every one of them – fondling each in turn in my mind: the iron cell door with the hatch; the brick walls with their flaking paint and stains; the blackened panes behind the grill high up under the ceiling. How I cling to these things, loving them for simply telling me that I'm alive – that precious so-soon-to-be-lost-for-ever sense of my own existence, of being me and knowing that I'm me – that I exist, have being – am uniquely me and nobody else.

It can't be for very much longer. After all, the confession has been signed. And then there was my appearance before the tribunal. And what a let-down that was. They raced through my case as if it scarcely mattered. It was a slap in the face, not simply for me but for Maxim Antonich, my interrogator as well, when you think of the all the trouble that the pair of us took with that confession – to get it just right. How we'd sweated blood almost, polishing it until it positively shone! Not a blemish anywhere; not a word out of place. And how after that I'd rehearsed it so that I knew it perfectly – my part in that vast, ramified conspiracy, uncovered by the tireless vigilance of the Party, which may have seemed trivial but was crucial all the same. Oh yes, there wasn't the shadow of a doubt about it – not a scintilla. I was up to my neck in it: all that sabotage on behalf of the Trotskyist bloc, every bit as guilty as the worst of them. And even if I had never struck a blow myself, the intention was there, wasn't it – the spite, the class enmity, the deep-rooted malice – and anyway, who's to make a distinction between the thought and the deed in matters of this magnitude? A point Maxim Antonich made very clear to me. Once a bourgeois soul, always a bourgeois soul. Except we can't talk about souls anymore, can we? Not if we're materialists. There you are, that gives me away, doesn't it? A bourgeois reactionary talking about souls. Maxim Antonich was not slow to point that one out to me. And didn't I try to tell the court the same thing? And did they care? Not a bit of it! They scarcely bothered to listen. They didn't want to hear me make my confession and didn't even glance up at me from their papers the whole time I was there. One of them yawned – not just once, but repeatedly. That was the crowning insult. But it's all over and done with – if any of it ever happened anyway – outside my own head, that is. I seriously wonder about that. It seems quite possible that I dreamed it all. And the real world, the one and only one, is here, where I am, listening to the snores of my fellow-prisoners and examining the marks on the wall.

And why shouldn't this go on for ever? Just me and those things that tell me that I'm me? Why does it have to come to an end? And quite so soon too? I know it has to be soon. That's what they said. What is more,

Maxim Antonich said it as well, which means it must be true. Extinction! Ceasing to exist! Nothingness. That's what a death sentence means, thinking about it – that very thing. Knowing that all too soon I'm not going to be me any more – dwelling on the horror of it – something that there's no escape from – annihilation – that's what a death sentence means – the realisation that in a little while from now I won't exist. No more me …

What are these marks on the wall? Next to my face? Do they mean anything? They're squashed bedbugs, surely? And they're arranged in the form of a triangle – one with equal sides. Each bug squashed and carefully fitted into the side of an equilateral triangle! One … two … three … four … five … six. Six squashed bugs forming one side of the triangle – with the three corner ones serving twice. Someone must have done it with the likes of me, Yuri Petrovich, in mind. That's why it's where it is – right next to my face when I'm lying on my bunk. For me to notice and to puzzle over. Really quite neat in its way – and rather original. A visual statement of some kind, but cryptic. An encoded message, written in squashed bedbugs. An interesting idea, but it's a pity I can't read the code.

I need a drink. Quite badly. Now that's something that really does tell me that I exist – wanting to have a drink. It's so hot in here and I'm feeling thirsty – very thirsty. I'll ask the guard. There must be one, surely. I'm a condemned man, aren't I? There must be a guard somewhere in the vicinity of a condemned man, mustn't there? Me – a condemned man! That's one to think about! How people would gawp at me if they could see me right now – knowing that I am a condemned man! I probably would do exactly the same if I was in their position: stare till my eyes were popping out of my head – trying to imagine what it feels like to be a condemned man! Trying to read the mind of somebody who knows that he's shortly going to be put to death. I've always had my share of morbid curiosity. I'm just as much of a ghoul as the next man.

My socks have got holes in them, which the toes are sticking through. That's something I hadn't noticed until now when I put my feet on the floor to cross over to the door. But what do I do to draw the guard's attention, assuming that there is one out there? Bang on the hatch with my fist? I've nothing else to do it with. Bang, bang, bang! Grunts from the sleepers – pigs. One of them turns over but still none of them wakes up. Bang, bang, bang! More grunts – angry ones this time – muttering. Then a voice outside, hollow sounding, echoing from a distance down the length of the corridor, clearly annoyed. "What's all that fucking noise about?" Bang, bang, bang! "Shut up, you cunt!" Bang, bang, bang! I'm supposed to be a condemned man, aren't I? So why should I shut up? Why should I obey the fucking rules any more? So why should I fucking shut up? What have I got to lose? Dragging footsteps outside and sounds of stirring and a creaking bunk behind me in the cell. The hatch flies open – so suddenly that it takes me by surprise. "What's all that fucking noise about? There're people trying to sleep, you selfish cunt. Have you no consideration?"

"I'm thirsty. I want a drink."

"You do, do you? What kind of a drink?" There is a sneer in his voice. The brat can't be much more than eighteen years old judging by his spotty face and the pathetic attempt at a moustache. Less than half my age, anyway. And he speaks to me like that – but then he is talking to an enemy of the people, after all – vermin that has to be wiped out. It says something for him that he's even bothering to address me, I suppose. He's the future after all, isn't he? And that's what it's all about. The reason why I've got to die – to make way for him – so he'll live to a ripe old age and see his grandchildren grow up long after I've rotted back into the soil. But one day, he'll rot back into the soil as well and then we'll be quits. We'll be as dead as each other then.

"What kind of drink? Champagne or vodka?" Cheeky brat. I'd like to turn him over and give him a good spanking.

"Champagne, of course. I shouldn't have to tell you that, should I?"

The look of cold contempt is pathetic – so sad to see in one so young and naive. "Rat's piss for a bourgeois wrecker like you. But if you ask me nicely, I might bring you some water instead."

"Water then."

"Please. Weren't bourgeois cunts taught better manners than that? You know, little words like please and thank you?" Funny how fixated he seems to be with the word 'bourgeois', but that's the dialectic too, I suppose, as understood by the masses – of which, no doubt, he's a fair specimen – so I can't complain.

"Please." If I wasn't so thirsty I'd laugh in his face.

He shuffles off, dragging his feet lazily down the passage. And comes back with a battered aluminium mug of water, which he thrusts through the hatch. "Get your snout into that, you bourgeois pig."

I drink greedily but, before I've quite drained the cup, a wicked thought comes to me. As the youth puts his face back into the hatch to see if I've finished, I dash the last dribble of water into his eye – right into his cold, fishy-blue eye. "You're not a man," I say to him. "That attempt at growing a moustache wouldn't fool anyone and … and if I could lay my hands on you, I'd put you over my knee and spank you." I push the mug back at him.

With a startled look and without a word, he slams the hatch shut. Just for a moment, I have forgotten what it's like to be a condemned man who's shortly going to die.

I lie on my bunk, hands under my head, contemplating the ceiling. Moving my hands, opening and shutting my eyes – that's being alive – doing simple things like that. My companions turn over and resume their slumbers, which were hardly disturbed anyway. I'm glad I don't have to attempt to make conversation with them, for the time being at least. A thought comes into my mind: a trick played by Tsar Nicholas the First on Dostoyevski and the other members of the Petrashevsky circle. He had them placed in front of a firing squad, dressed in shrouds, and when death seemed only minutes away, they were reprieved. Could Josef Vissarionovich possibly be doing the same thing to me? And I won't have to die after all? Peter the Great played the same trick. And Josef Vissarionovich is rumoured to be a great admirer of him. So I've been told, anyway. But a fat chance: he's never even heard of me. I don't exist for him. I never have done. And now, of course, I never will.

So are they going to give me anything to eat? Don't they give a condemned man something good to eat before taking him out to die? A final treat? I even fancy a bowl of kasha. That would be a perfectly acceptable last meal. Babushka used to tell me when I was little to eat up my kasha so that I could grow up big and strong enough to be a soldier. I wonder if that brat of a guard eats his kasha? Perhaps his moustache would grow better if he did. Maybe I'm already a dead man, so to speak, and they won't waste precious resources on me. Not much point filling the tank with petrol if you are never going to drive the vehicle again, is there? It's funny how I can remember Babushka so well – that crumpled nose with the wart on the left nostril. She's the only one who stands out at all clearly. But that's the thing they say about dying, isn't it? Your early childhood comes flooding back to you at the end, pushing later memories aside. I've heard it said, too, that men who are about to be executed sometimes call out for their mothers. Will I do the same thing? If I do, I suppose it'll be for Babushka, not my mother whom I hardly knew. And aren't I just sliding into sentimentality? Not at all the way a revolutionary fighter should be thinking. But I can hardly call myself one of those any more, can I? A capitalist running dog, more like. That's what I am now. You ask Maxim Antonich. He'll explain to you exactly where I stand, in dialectical terms I mean – an insect to be crushed underfoot – wreckage, a mere splinter, tossed aside in the great surge of history. A kinder image perhaps – I like it better than the insect one anyway. But however you express it, the idea's really just the same. It's what the dialectic is all about, isn't it? That's how it works out in practise. So it's no good feeling sorry for myself. Because that's the way things are. If you don't believe me, just ask Maxim Antonich. He'll explain it to you far better than I ever could.

And you know, I love that man! I really do. I love him and only hope I'll see him one more time before the end comes. He's the only one I want to see. I don't care a fig about any of the others –not a fig. Just Babushka, of course, and she's been dead for so long that she's only a fading memory – a sweet one, certainly, but a bit like a scented greetings card. There I go, what can 'so long' possibly mean? She doesn't exist any more and that's the end of it, so where does the long time come into it? You may think it means something while you exist – are still inside time, so to speak – but that doesn't mean it really does, does it? It's like being afraid of death. Just because you hate the idea of dying doesn't mean you're not going to do it, does it? Wanting something badly doesn't mean that you have to have it.

That drink's made me want to pee. Now that's something I learned quickly enough in prison, sharing a cell with other people: to pee onto the side of the bowl rather than into the middle. It's quieter that way and nothing annoys his fellow prisoners more than a noisy pisser. And one who farts too, of course. I've learned all about that as well – but, come to

Part of a Quota 119

think of it, what's the use of that or indeed any kind of knowledge now? What's the point of building up a store of knowledge if all that happens to you is that you cease to exist?

That was a good pee. I feel better for it, and no one even noticed me doing it. I must say it's amazing how these fellows manage to sleep: peasants seem to be able to curl up and sleep anywhere – like the pigs I was thinking about earlier, which is all they are really. Pigs. Lenin thought as much, anyway. But I'm glad of it because it saves me having to try to talk to them. Are they condemned men as well, I wonder? They weren't awake when they put me in here with them so I haven't found out. I must say they're sleeping pretty soundly if they are. Which proves my point, doesn't it? And Lenin's too. Peasants are pigs.

Those squashed bedbugs. It would be nice to know what they mean before I die – to crack the code. If there is one to crack. Maybe Maxim Antonich might help me there if I asked him. He knows the answers to most things. He's certainly pretty hot on his dialectic. So why not at cracking codes too? I hope he comes.

It may be something quite basic really – a simple piece of philosophy: that we're no different from bedbugs in the end. Just bedbugs that can think. Is that the meaning of the equilateral triangle, I wonder? Now isn't that so typically Russian? Searching for a deeper meaning when there isn't one. Dammit, a prisoner squashed the bedbugs and fixed them in that position because he was bored. He'd nothing better to do. He wasn't trying to tell me or anyone else anything at all. He was merely killing time. If he'd had a pencil and paper he would have used them instead. Mind you, he didn't need those to have etched a poem on the wall if he'd really wanted to. Maybe he wasn't a poet but a mathematician? Though he hardly needed to be much of one to come up with an equilateral triangle. Anyway, he's given me something to think about besides my impending execution, whether he meant to or not. And possibly that's all he intended – if he wasn't just thinking about himself. I wonder what happened to him?

Footsteps are approaching along the corridor. Several pairs of them. Where are they going to stop? Right here? Outside my cell? Surely not. After all, there are lots of other cells along this corridor. I haven't counted them, of course, never even given it a thought as I've had other things on my mind. Anyway, there are lots. So the chances of them stopping outside mine are pretty slim. They're getting closer. And they have stopped. My God, it is outside my cell! Or is it the one next to it? It's hard to tell. Oh my God, that's the bolt being drawn – on my door!

Two guards, whom I've never seen before. One of them has cut his cheek shaving – a dark red clot on his left cheek. And the other has got skin that's almost yellow and dirty-looking blond hair to match, which he wears a bit too long for a prison guard. I wonder if anyone has spoken to him about that? How old is he? In his middle thirties?

"Yuri Petrovich?" I notice they don't call me comrade – no one has done that ... since when? I don't know. I sit up and say nothing. "Get down and put your shoes on." I swing my legs off the bunk and the need to find my shoes under the tier of bunks makes me think about shoes – small things – they're everything now. "Get a move on, we haven't got all day!" It's all right for you, isn't it? I find the shoes and push my feet inside them. There are no laces, of course. No laces in my shoes even when I'm about to die! And my toes poking through the holes in my socks are rubbing against the inside of the shoes. The guard with the cut on his cheek takes my arm and draws me out into the corridor. The pigs don't even stir. There are three other men. One of them is that brat of a guard. He would be in for the kill, wouldn't he? Well, I'll show him! That's something I can do. And at least I gave him one in the eye before he saw me shot. And there's an older man, some kind of an officer judging by the trimmings on his uniform, which is a bit threadbare, especially along the edge of his tunic. Shiny buttons though. And here's Maxim Antonich!

"Maxim Antonich, you've come to see me at last! I hoped you might. It's so good to see you! You taught me so much about myself! And where I fitted in. Into the dialectic, I mean. My place in history! You taught me well. Made it mean something to me! So say something to me now, Maxim Antonich! Speak to me. Just say something. This really is the end, isn't it?"

But he says nothing. Just looks at me with eyes that are dead and turns away, avoiding mine. Is that historically necessary too? The way it works in practise, so to speak? Is that a part of the dialectic too?

"Speak to me, Maxim Antonich. Just say something to me, Comrade – we're friends, aren't we? No, we can't possibly be that. Forgive me for presuming such a thing! It isn't what I mean at all. 'Friends' can't be the right word for our relationship, can it? But you are a great teacher all the same, Maxim Antonich, who explained to me things I had failed to understand on my own and I'm deeply grateful to you!"

No one speaks. An embarrassed silence – but then the officer with the shiny buttons says, "Let's go." Such an ordinary thing to say. So banal. We might be setting off to have a drink together. The man with the cut face and his comrade with the dirty blond hair each take me by an elbow while the brat with the fluffy upper lip prods me in the back. He likes doing that. He's revelling in it. Yet that's what's giving me courage – of a sort, anyway. But the terror of annihilation is welling up. And I can't keep it down. It's throbbing through my entire being. Extinction. Being dead. Not being alive. Not existing. I'm looking at the back of that officer's head under the blue-topped cap just in front of me. There's not a single hair showing under his cap. That's curious. Is he completely bald, I wonder? We're walking now. Maxim Antonich is behind me somewhere. Hanging back? Why doesn't he say something to me? What's the matter with him? He must have a good reason. He has a good reason for everything he says or does. So why has he come now if he doesn't want to speak to me?

We've reached the end of the corridor and are going down some steps. They're worn at the edge and quite dangerous – someone could have a nasty accident – so the two guards grip my elbows tighter – almost lifting me off my feet as we descend. Down, down we go. Past the end of another corridor and still down. A crisp echo of footsteps. The sick fear is rising. It's screaming inside my head. Yet I'm walking as if I'm dreaming. Everything is so close to me and utterly real – but so far away.

We are walking along another passage. Dim light bulbs and a cable running the length of the wall. The sound our feet make is almost rhythmic. Is it the last thing I'm ever going to see? I don't want to be dead! I want to be alive so much – Oh God, I do! But with that brat with the fluffy moustache gloating at my back, I'm not going to let them see it. That's the one thing left to me: not letting him see that I'm afraid. The officer is stopping and stepping to one side. We're not quite at the end of the corridor yet. Shouldn't we get there first? Reach the end at least. Are they going to cheat me out of that last tiny scrap of my existence? Oh why couldn't it have been just a tiny bit more? Why does it have to be quite so soon?

"Get down on your knees." But they're forcing me down anyway. Saying so, that is just a formality, a matter of procedure. Something hard and cold's touching the back of my neck. Oh God …Oh my God … Maxim Antonich … Can't you stop them doing this to me? I'm not saying it though. I'm showing that brat of a guard that I'm not a coward. But if I close my eyes now I'll never see anything again – not ever. They're gripping my arms so I'll never see my hands again! But don't call out. No, don't call out! Show that brat with the mangy moustache! What else is there?

The room was dark, the only light coming from the desk lamp and the screen in front of him. Tristram shook his head and rubbed his eyes, as if he was waking up, which, in a way, he was. He had lost all sense of time passing, locked as he had been into the mind of Yuri Petrovich in the last seconds of his existence, if indeed that is what it was. It was the centenary, certainly – a hundred years since Yuri Petrovich met his end in a prison in Novisibirsk. Or at least as near as it was possible to get. The year, 1938, was right anyway, and probably the month too. A hundred years ago. And Yuri Petrovich? Only a name in a yellowing dossier, later transferred onto a computer file in a regional police archive. One name in a very long list with a simple mark against it – a Russian letter R, standing for 'rasstrel' – shot – which had given Tristram his lead. But apart from that, why pick out Yuri Petrovich of all people for his first experiment with the empathy drug? After all, there were thousands – millions – of others just like him. Why Yuri, indeed? For precisely that reason – the randomness of it – because while his fate seemed plain enough, he was just a name – one among scores on that particular list – part of a quota … hundreds … thousands, even, if you added it to the other lists in that particular archive. And millions if you extended it nationwide and added every other list of the same kind drawn up in the former Soviet Union. So that was Yuri's claim to Tristram's attention as an historian writing on the centenary of Stalin's Great Purge, known to history as the Yezhovchina, named after Nikolai Yezhov, his soon-to-be-annihilated head opprichnik – he was merely a name, one of millions on a vast list. Yuri Petrovich. It comes off the tongue easily. Possibly, that's what had appealed to the researcher – the name has a certain resonance about it, lodging readily in the mind of a non-Russian. So Yuri Petrovich – a name on a list – part of a quota – existed once more

– in the mind of an historian this time – a hundred years after his extinction. In the mind of an historian – whose powers of empathy had been greatly enhanced by the aid of a new drug – he had come alive again and was re-living his hell – in a manner of speaking – but this time round, mercifully perhaps, he didn't know it ...

9   The Bedroom Window

I've no idea how long I've been asleep but, as I wake up, the sunlight is streaming through the open window. It was dark when I went to bed and I felt too tired to think about drawing the curtains, and in any case, I like to be woken by the sun; far better than having my slumbers shattered by an alarm clock and dragging myself up out of bed while it's still dark. That's one of the many little things I enjoy about being in Italy – not being obliged to get up early, but to take life at the pace that suits me. And just to lie there, drowsily contemplating the day ahead – one to be spent poking around old streets, taking in the odd church or gallery and drinking cups of espresso coffee when the mood takes me – that's bliss.

Simple pleasures, perhaps, but I've long since come to realise that the greatest satisfaction in life is found in simple things. I know it's a platitude, but it doesn't make it any less true. Or does the real pleasure lie in the anticipation of things to come rather than in the things themselves? It's a corny old question that I've asked myself so many times before and I'm sure a lot of other people have too.

For the moment, I just want to lie in my bed and think about the day ahead. But at least I should take a look at the view from the window. And isn't that the real magic of coming to a place like this? To arrive in the dark and to look out on that view, all pristine and fresh in the morning – like a child waking up on Christmas Day to a stocking full of presents …

And the great thing about it is that I don't have to get off my bed to do it. All I need to do is to throw back the sheet, crawl to the foot of the bed and haul myself up onto my elbows at the window. A small room in an

Italian pension has always been enough for me. Why should anyone need more than that? What additional luxuries could possibly cap the delight that's now in store for me?

It's a scene that I'm already familiar with because I've seen a picture of it before. So I instantly recognise the Temple of Hercules at Cora, not far from Rome. But this is better than any picture that I've ever seen and stronger, indeed, than any direct experience of nature itself that I can recall. Dare I use the word transcendental? I think it's what I mean, though I risk straying into cliché or platitude when I say things like that.

Everything I expect to see is there, of course, above all, those peculiar Doric columns, which are quite the wrong proportion for that order; they are long and thin when, to be in the true Doric style, they should be squat and thick. These ones look as if they ought to be Ionic or Corinthian. They still support an architrave and a pediment, but the roof of the temple has long since disappeared and vegetation is sprouting from the ridge of the pediment. A few slabs of marble still cling to its face, but otherwise it has been stripped down to the bare stone, which glows so softly, yet so sharply, in the morning sun. Every grain of it seems to have been picked out by the finest sable brush, so that if I stretched out my hand, I could feel the graininess for myself. But I know I can't do that because it's on the other side of the street. In spite of the detail's sharp focus, it's not hard on the eye – quite the opposite, in fact. Everything is crystalline yet gently luminous, restful, not strident …

The temple is an empty shell, a skeleton, and in the dust at its base are scattered the drums of other columns on which lizards bask, soaking up the warm sunshine …

Built onto the back of the temple is a tall brick building with a great doorway that looks like the main entrance to a church – which would make sense because pagan temples were very often turned into churches. And to the left of that is an assemblage of buttresses and penthouses with pantiled roofs, piled one above the other, which, like the side of a mountain, seem to climb right up into the sky. Their gloomy bulk contrasts starkly with the radiance of the neighbouring temple. And at the base of the pile, in the deepest shade, is a rustic gate of rough-hewn planks – the entrance, perhaps, to a stall for animals or, more likely, vagrants.

Further off to the right in my field of vision are more buildings, their crumbling plaster and exposed brickwork as clearly delineated as if I was standing just inches from them. And yet, like the grainy surface of the temple, the effect is not oppressive, but a harmonious fusion of close proximity and distance. I feel that I ought to be able to reach out and touch these things. I know I can't, but the sensation doesn't feel wrong. Everything has its proper proportion and spatial relationship with everything else, yet at the same time still seems to be within my reach.

On the broken roofs of the buildings, young trees are sprouting with angular, claw-like branches that seem to echo the forms of the bent old men who lean on sticks in the street below, providing the scene with a human scale and adding further to its air of slumberous antiquity ...

And now, looking more closely, I can make out other figures too, lurking in the shade on the left of the view. There's a young woman, for instance, statuesque and apparently immobile, glancing back over her shoulder at another pair of figures, a mother helping her infant to relieve himself against the base of the temple. Altogether, I count twelve people there, all coming into view as I study the scene, and each one so sharp that I wonder how I missed it in the first place. Their clothes seem old-fashioned – it's difficult to place them in a particular time – but somehow appropriate to the vision of picturesque decay that is laid out before me.

Then shadows advance, gliding over the sunlit surfaces while the sullen pile on the left remains unchanged. The clouds pass and are swiftly followed by others – billowing cumulus clouds, purple, indigo, almost black, fringed with brilliant pale gold, set against a backdrop of deepest ultramarine. In the shifting dappled light there is a ripple of a breeze, leaves rustle drily and the old men, who were as motionless as the basking lizards, stir into life and shuffle their feet in the dust. The clouds pile up and the temple glow fades. But between the now darkened buildings on the right, a flight of steps is suddenly picked out by a solitary beam of light. In a golden haze it ascends and vanishes behind a wall.

I make a resolution: when I'm feeling up to it, I shall climb those steps and see where they lead. I've always liked the excitement of turning corners and coming across things that I've never seen before. You don't have to go to the ends of the earth to enjoy the thrill of discovering new things. But, for the moment, I just want to go to sleep again …

*****

Connie and Toby were engaged in a melancholy but not disagreeable task – earmarking their share of the spoils from their uncle's house. He had died alone, but was luckier than some, dying on, if not in, his own bed and under his own roof. He had been found with his head resting against the foot of the bed where he seems to have been contemplating the picture on the wall in front of him when he breathed his last.

Uncle Edwin had not been rich, but his eye was good and, within his limited means, he had bought well, a great deal better, indeed, than many people who had a lot more money to play with than he did. He had some decent late eighteenth century furniture, mostly mahogany, and well-stocked bookshelves, but probably his pictures were his best things. Again, there was nothing desperately valuable, but there was an interesting landscape by a leading German modernist, Kurt Schwitters, which his parents had bought from the exiled artist in Norway shortly before the Second World War, and a genuine Hokosai print, which he had acquired for next to nothing in a job lot in Bournemouth. There were a number of good prints – several David Roberts views of Egyptian antiquities in his dining room, and one in a heavy Italian frame, which hung in the bedroom where his nephew and his niece were right now. It was on the wall at the foot of the bed where their uncle could see it when he woke up in the morning. If he left his curtains undrawn, the early sunlight would fall across it, though it did draw attention to the foxing that was sprinkled over its surface like a rash.

Now, in the bedroom, Connie and Toby looked at the picture, not uncritically.

"What do you think?" asked Connie, who was less sure of her opinions than her brother.

Toby did not answer at once, but screwed up his face in a frown as he examined the dingy print.

"Hmm," he said at length. "I'm not sure. It's a bit of a mess, isn't it?"

"But possibly rather good," ventured Connie. "And anyway, it's the kind of subject I rather like – change and decay – the melancholy business of time passing, that sort of thing." She went right up to the picture. "And look how these stooped old men seem to reinforce that idea."

Toby scrutinised the inscription in the corner. "Piranesi," he read. "Who else? It stands out a mile. The original drawing by the father and the engraved plate by the son, no doubt. Eighteenth century, of course, and a leaf from a folio, one of a collection of similar subjects. Not bad, but not a patch on one of his famous prisons. I'd really like to have one of those." He frowned at the picture. "A clean would improve things a bit."

"I'm not sure about that," replied Connie. "I rather like it the way it is. The picture itself is subject to the process that it represents. The effects of time passing. Its own condition rather reinforces that idea, don't you think? And there's something else I like about it."

"Go on." Toby didn't quite share his sister's romantic notion of allowing art objects to succumb to the same aging processes as the rest of nature.

"It's mysterious."

"Mysterious?" He looked again at the picture, wondering if he was missing something that his sister had seen, but at the same time rather doubting it.

"Yes," said Connie. "I like mysteries. Do you see those steps to the right of the picture? The way they're lit up by that shaft of sunlight when everything else around them is dark? They go somewhere. But who knows where? It's a mystery. What lies round that corner?"

"Another broken-down hovel perhaps. But who knows? Probably not even the artist."

"Do you think I sound pretentious when I say things like that?" asked Connie a little anxiously.

"Not really. Maybe a little romantically naive, but there's no harm in that. Better to be honest and say what you really think. Anyway, it's a perfectly decent Piranesi, though not one I'd give my right arm for, I confess."

"Can I have it then?"

"Sure. I won't start a war over it," said Toby. "I'm more interested in what's downstairs. But if it were mine, I'd have it cleaned."

10   Ice-Cold

No one had seen the old man for several days. Latterly, he had become something of a recluse, living alone in the big house on the Esplanade, which seemed odd because he had always been a family man and had a large flock of grandchildren. Moreover, he was known to have made a tidy fortune during a lifetime in the confectionery trade. A cleaning lady, Mrs Ackroyd, went in a couple of times a week and occasionally one of his daughters from the south would appear. Sometimes, Lorenzo might be seen taking a stroll along the seafront and into the centre of town where he would buy a paper and perhaps drop into a cafe for a cup of coffee. But for a man who had once been so gregarious, he had surprisingly little to say to anyone and never had any company.

He was still known as Lorenzo despite being the third generation of his family to have lived in Britain. His grandfather, Alfonso Arnolfini, had come originally from Salerno in the south of Italy, bringing his bride with him and, in the eighteen-nineties, had set up an ice cream parlour in Glasgow. She had borne him a son and three daughters and they had run the business together. The son, Lorenzo's father, had married into another Italian family who had also settled in Scotland, and they had duly produced three sons of which Lorenzo was the last. His oldest brother, Alfonso the Second, took on the family business while the next, Giovanni, had gone to America where another branch of the Arnolfinis was established in Chicago. Lorenzo, though restless and moderately ambitious, had always been his mother's favourite and had no desire to remove himself so far from the family nest. Instead, he took himself to Scarborough where one of his aunts was already living, married to an Englishman.

Ice cream might have been said to have been in the Arnolfini blood – if such a metaphor didn't sound too contrived. So selling it to holidaymakers seemed an obvious way for Lorenzo to make his way in the world. Yet it wasn't as straightforward as that. It was the thirties and much has been written since about the turf wars between the Sicilian and southern Italian families in Chicago and New York at that time. The Arnolfinis played their part in these too, albeit as humble spear-carriers, but what has been overlooked are the much smaller wars that were being fought at about the same time in the seaside towns up and down the coasts of Britain. For this was the era of new excitements like amusement parlours with slot machines and permanent fairgrounds, an era when even the legendary Billy Butlin, founder of the holiday camps, was alleged to have sallied forth with a cut-throat razor in his pocket and a gang of heavies to wreck a rival enterprise in the days before his name had become synonymous with wholesome family fun. And while the Chicago Arnolfinis took part in the great liquor wars, their cousin in the English seaside resort fought his own ice cream one.

Scarborough's main beach was the scene of an action, which was short, sharp and with all of the bitterness of a cold north-easterly gale on that bracing coastline. For several years, Rinaldo Belotti had plied his trade from a van under a brightly painted plaster ice cream cone with its contents rendered in red and white stripes, presumably to suggest some exotic fruit flavour. This had become his trademark. He held the prime site on the beach and did a roaring trade.

A van on the beach was where Lorenzo needed to start, but it was not where he intended to finish. In a nutshell, he had to get Rinaldo out and himself in, which was not so easy as Rinaldo had been going for several years and was a popular character with the holidaymakers. Like many of his race, he was especially good with children and had a melodious, Italian-accented patter, which fitted in well with donkey rides and Punch and Judy shows.

But patience was already the key to Lorenzo's character – unusually so for a young man still in his early twenties. He consulted his aunt first – without mentioning the matter to her stolid English husband – and then his brother, Alfonso, in Scotland where the Arnolfinis had already fought an ice cream war. Alfonso, perhaps drawing inspiration from the larger theatre in Chicago, knew what to do; Rinaldo's van was burned out one moonless night when Lorenzo was out of town. In addition, the wretched man himself had been snatched on his way home, held hooded until the small hours of the morning and then, with a razor thrust against his throat, forced to witness the destruction of his livelihood. If he gave any trouble he was told what was going to happen to his twin sons and the apple of his eye, little Concetta. Finally, he was dumped, bound and hooded once more on the cliffs outside town where he was found later the same morning.

Rinaldo took the hint and quit, but Lorenzo was careful not to step into his shoes too quickly. For a month or so, he kept his distance, lying low with Alfonso in Glasgow. Meanwhile, Aunt Julietta kept him up to date while her husband, who ran a garage, remained oblivious to the machinations of his Italian in-laws.

Once the Belottis had fled and when word reached him that the coast was clear, Lorenzo came forward and claimed the pitch that had once belonged to Rinaldo. He did it unobtrusively and very politely, and if any questions were asked, no one bothered about pursuing them very far.

Like his predecessor, he was a huge success on the beach, though his manner was more polished and less overtly "Italian'. He was blessed in those days with almost film star good looks and a slim figure. So while he was less jolly than Rinaldo, he was a greater hit with the girls, which suggested that an ice cream van on Scarborough beach was unlikely to be the summit of his ambitions. Lorenzo had his foot on the bottom rung of the ladder.

And it went terribly well. The van was maintained on the beach, but added to it was a soda fountain, which he called The Lido, then a larger cafe and then a small factory for the production of confectionery that, in due course, became a larger factory selling into the national market.

Lorenzo married shortly before the outbreak of the Second World War, just at the time he won a contract to supply the NAAFI with soon-to-be-scarce wartime luxuries for the troops. Despite – and probably because of – the rationing and austerity, he continued to prosper and was poised to take immediate advantage of the return to pre-war conditions in the fifties. Thus it went on.

And in other ways too, Lorenzo gained prominence in the community. He was elected to the town council and became an influential figure in its affairs, and the Rotary Club as well. With his wife Amelia he produced two sons and three daughters. His film star looks didn't last, of course, and he grew quite stout – he had a predilection for some of his own products – but he still had an eye for the girls, some of them a good deal younger than was considered proper for a man of his advancing years.

He had moved into the big, late Victorian house on the Esplanade where his children had grown up and from which nest they had eventually flown. And that was the sad part of it, for despite his reputation as a family man, not one of them had been prepared to step into his shoes. The daughters had all found husbands in the wider community, having been privately educated and gone to university. Two of them were married to barristers and the third, Leonora, to a painter living on the Isle of Wight. One boy, Alfredo, had decamped to the United States and worked as a scientist on the NASA space programme, while the other one, Jo, had set up his own tour company in London.

They had all come back for their mother's funeral in 1995, of course, but had promptly decamped again, leaving the old man alone once more. In an unnatural way, they had wanted to keep their distance.

So the House of Arnolfini looked as if it might have no successor – a melancholy outcome after a lifetime of toil. Perhaps it explained, in part at least, the old man's withdrawal into his own private world. Possibly, the mild scandal of his sexual proclivities – there had been a court case involving a fourteen-year-old nymphette when a neat piece of legal footwork had saved his bacon – had played its part too. Even young Jo had referred to his father rather loudly at the time as a dirty old man.

And now, when Mrs Ackroyd called at the big house in her usual way on a Monday morning, there was no response. Both the side door and the main front one were locked. Despite his dependence on her, the old man had never given her a key, so she had called the police who broke through the side door rather than damage the much finer front one.

But there was no sign of Mr Arnolfini upstairs or downstairs, or in the big neglected conservatory at the back, and the place seemed undisturbed. Nor was there any sign of a break-in. So had he slipped away unannounced without leaving a message of any kind for Mrs Ackroyd? She checked through his things and they all seemed to be in their usual places: his toiletries in the bathroom, his slippers by his bed. His coats and hats were where they normally were. If he had gone off he had done so without packing a bag. Then Mrs Ackroyd remembered the underground passage leading to the garden on the other side of the street.

Luke lay on his bed and recalled his grandfather's last words to him. Although he was well into his nineties, the old man had spoken passionately as if the wound was still fresh. He had been in a private ward in the hospital in Baltimore for a week before his grandson got round to visiting him. Despite the approach of death, his mind was perfectly clear. He knew his time was up but he seemed to be driven by a final surge of energy to complete his business on earth before he left it for good.

"You're the one, Luca," he said, seizing the young man's hand. He sat high against the pillows and his eyes shone with the intensity of his feelings.

"The one, Grandpa?" replied Luke almost languidly. "You make me sound like the Messiah when you say things like that."

"You're mean."

"Thank you, Grandpa, but I'm not sure how I'm meant to take that."

"The right way, I hope. It would break your mother's heart if I was to ask any of her other boys to do it." Luke's mother had always been his favourite child.

"Do what, Grandpa? You're being very mysterious."

"Something special – for me."

"Something special for you? Why? Because I'm mean? Because I'm the black sheep of the family, so if anything goes wrong I'll get the bullet while Mom's little lambs keep their fleecy white coats clean? Is that it?"

"There's more to it than that, Luca. It's a matter of honour," declared the old man, leaning forward from his pillow and tightening his hold on the young man's hand. There was a surprising strength in the grip of one who was supposed to be on his deathbed.

"That's a funny old word, Grandpa. Does it mean very much these days?"

"More than you think. It's carried in the blood – mine and the family's, yours too, Luca, if you knew it. But it's not much use without courage – and brains as well – if it's to amount to anything," went on the old man. "And that's where you come in, Luca. You've more of those two things than all the rest of them put together. Hell, you're the brightest of the bunch. That's what they put you inside for, isn't it?"

Luke pondered for a moment. "I hadn't thought of it quite like that, Grandpa," he replied, "but maybe you've got a point there. I do rather like sticking my neck out, walking a tightrope, whatever you like to call it. Is that what you're trying to tell me?"

"You're not afraid to do it – not like the others." The old man rested back on his pillows but the eyes in his shrunken cheeks remained fixed on his grandson's.

"So what's this all about then? Do I have to guess? A bit of history? One of your ancient Italian feuds still festering after all this time? Unfinished business from the heroic days of Prohibition?" asked Luke at length. "You're an old romantic, Grandpa. Or maybe it's more recent than that – but something that none of us have been told about?"

"Sure, it's a loose end I'd like tied up," said his grandfather. "Something that should have been taken care of a long time ago. It was my quarrel and if you don't think much of it, what the hell. It's no skin off my nose. I'm not complaining. But I thought maybe it was your kind of game, Luca. One that needs your kind of nerve."

Luke did not reply but rocked his head from side to side, weighing up what his grandfather had said.

The old man suddenly sat up and, clutching Luke, held him close. "Well? What do you say? Feel you can do it?"

He fell back on the pillow and closed eyes but quickly opened them again. "Well?" he repeated.

"Well what, Grandpa?"

"What do you say?"

"What am I meant to say? You haven't told me what you want me to do yet. And anyway, apart from testing my nerve or my manhood or whatever, is there anything else in it for me?"

The old man eyed him intently for a moment.

"Good question, Luca. A trip to England – and to Europe. Somewhere you've not been and I know you want to go."

"That sounds fine – if you're paying for it."

His grandfather clucked impatiently. "Of course I'm paying for it. And anyway, I'll be dead by then."

"Do you have to say things like that, Grandpa?"

The old man chuckled. "And someone else will be too if you don't screw up." Luke looked hard at his grandfather.

"Are you asking me to kill someone?"

"Call it giving a guy what's been coming to him for one hell of a long time."

Luke said nothing but gazed at the old man with an unfamiliar kind of admiration. He had never heard him talk this way before. He was the kind of guy who got all dewy-eyed when the kids opened their Christmas presents.

"Only you can rise to it, Luca. None of the others have got the balls."

"Speak on, Grandpa – if you're not too tired."

The old man struggled once more into a sitting position and Luke bent an ear to his lips.

"So I've got to kill a guy? But tell me one other thing, Grandpa. What did he do to you to make you so sore? After all, your life hasn't treated you so badly, has it?"

"I've worked like a black, that's why. None of you kids knows what that means. It all comes to you in a nice package – school, college, the lot. But it was because of that son-of-a-bitch that I had it all to do again. Right back from square one. But it was the manner of it. That's what makes me sore. You see, that guy threatened to kill your mother. That's what makes me sore."

"It's funny – this code of honour thing," mused the young man. "How it never quite seems to go away. I'm afraid it leaves me cold."

"Cold – I like that word, Luca. That's how it's got to be. Ice-cold. Forget about honour if you aren't bothered with the word. I am – maybe it's because I'm old-fashioned. You don't have to agree with me. Just treat it like a poker game and play it with a cool head. As I keep telling you, you're the only one in the family with the balls to go through with it."

He fished under his pillow and produced a thick envelope. "It's all in here. I've been doing my homework – or at least my friends have." He chuckled as he handed Luke the envelope. "You'll promise me you'll do it? Read it first and come back and tell me when you've done that. But don't leave it too long because I'll have moved on before the end of the month."

In fact, he moved on just two days later and Luke never spoke to him again. But he read everything in the envelope carefully.

He was the third of the four Signorelli boys and, as he had observed himself, the black sheep of the family. His two older brothers had been through business school and Ted, the youngest, was still at high school and thinking about university. Luke, however, had apparently blown it. It had been a break-in – but a crime of a high aesthetic order both in terms of its object and its execution. Despite its failure, Luke had been proud of it on each count. He had lifted a picture in a very polished operation, which was only wrecked in its aftermath by his accomplice before he had managed to offload the goods. The police had run them in almost immediately and Luke had served eighteen months in a gaol for young offenders.

Still, the blot on his record and his father's displeasure aside, he felt that it had been a good learning experience. Luke was ambitious and wanted to go places. He had an eye for beautiful things and a desire to learn more about them – something he combined with a fascination for intricate and perhaps dangerous games. Already, he saw himself as a being on a higher plane to whom the moral constraints that limited the behaviour of ordinary people did not apply. The beauty of an elaborate, cunningly contrived, hopefully watertight plot had all the attraction for him of an early Renaissance painting. He knew now, of course, not to take any green kids in with him – unless they could be ditched without any risk to himself. Luke had been proud of his plan. The lift itself had worked like a dream; it was just that little shit blabbing about it to his girlfriend afterwards.

But in all the family furore surrounding the case, his grandfather had been strangely quiet and had never once reproached him, except to say that that he shouldn't have trusted an idiot and got himself busted. And now, perusing the contents of the envelope, he saw something of the dead man in himself.

It was a very detailed piece of work, which he had clearly been engaged in for a long time but was nevertheless bang up to date. The target and his address were recorded as well as train and bus times from London to the town in question. Likewise, flights to and from the nearest regional airport and even a brochure of hotels and bed and breakfasts in the vicinity. There were details, too, of the intended victim's family and where they lived and a contact address in London for Luke when he first arrived in the country. Finally, there was a photograph of the back view of a heavy-looking guy sitting on a garden chair with a straw hat on his head. It didn't show his face but the information it contained was clear as far as it went. It appeared to have been a lifelong obsession with the old man, which had undergone regular updating. Laid out with a meticulous sense of detail, it was a kind of life's offering to posterity on his part.

But certain things were not there. Though the address was given there was no clear description of the building or means of access and no direct instruction as to how the thing might be done. Nor, apart from the photograph taken from behind, was there a detailed description of the intended victim. There were a few general suggestions about possible lines of approach but the actual execution of the plan and its fine-tuning were left to Luke. Except for one detail, which the old man insisted upon by underlining it in red. But for all his grandfather's intelligence work and obsessive preparation, this was to be the boy's own achievement. After all, the risks were to be his and so was the triumph. Implicit in the scheme was trust in the boy, of giving him his head. The old man had always understood young people and how to fire them up.

So Luke got off his bed and walked to the cemetery where his grandfather had lately been laid to rest.

"I'll buy it, Grandpa," he announced to the mound of freshly heaped earth.

The summer vacation was a good time. He could run the business together with a sightseeing trip – kill two birds with one stone, so to speak.

The old man had specified a small sum in his will for each of his grandchildren to make a small trip to Europe, so it was no problem for Luke to say that he was taking it up but preferred to go on his own, despite his mother's plea that two of the boys should go together. He wanted to devote his visit almost entirely to art and architecture, which he knew wouldn't suit his siblings, he said. So in July, he arrived by himself in London.

He stayed with the son of an old business acquaintance of his grandfather's who appeared not to be privy to any of the old man's personal affairs as far as he could tell. But, just to be safe, he maintained the plausible tale of only being a tourist, which, in a way, he was.

Luke was in no hurry. He intended to see as much as he could in the fortnight before he set to work. And he was careful not to rush off to his eventual destination straight from London because it was hardly the first call a young American was likely to make coming to Britain for the first time. No, he would do London and the South East and then take a train up to Edinburgh. York, on the return journey, would be a good jumping-off place for where he needed to be.

So he started with the usual tourist round – the historical sights of London where he mingled with the international throng. On the whole, Luke enjoyed himself – he liked history and was happy to get lost in the anonymity of the crowds. For the foreseeable future, at least, he preferred obscurity – it enabled him to practise the kind of skills he felt that he possessed. Fame – or notoriety perhaps – could wait. And with that long-term aim in view, he would keep a diary. It had its risks, of course, but then that was the kind of game he was playing and, like a good rock climber, he already felt that he knew how to weigh up the dangers.

He started the diary on day one of his visit and dutifully described his trips to the tourist sights of London. It was pretty pedestrian stuff until he visited the Chamber of Horrors at Madame Tussaud's.

"You can keep all your kings, queens and pop stars," Luke wrote, "a load of vague look-alikes, none of which fool me – just tacky rubbish. But the Chamber of Horrors is something different. It certainly sent no shivers down my spine but I've got my share of morbid curiosity the same as the next man and I confess I rather enjoyed looking at all those weirdos – they were just ordinary guys you wouldn't look at twice on the sidewalk. But then that's the point, isn't it? You wouldn't look at any of them twice. Yet just stop for a minute to consider the kind of things they've done. Some of them had the makings of great artists. I say the 'makings' because they all got caught. None of them got away with it in the end and that's what the game's about, isn't it? Or at least I think it is. You commit the worst crime in the book – again and again – as long as you feel that way, and yet no one manages to catch you. But I guess some of these guys needed to get caught in the end because it's the only way for their genius to be recognised. Take that Shipman guy, for instance, the doctor who murdered his patients. He handed it to the cops on a plate in the end with that forged will after he'd killed, what? Possibly hundreds – who will ever know how many? I wonder if I'll get to feel that way?"

And because his overriding passion was for the art of the Renaissance, Luke took himself off to the National Gallery the next day. Running his own gallery was an idea he was toying with – once he'd had the necessary grounding. Maybe it was an ingredient of his Italian blood, but he loved the pictures of the early Renaissance especially – the Botticellis and the Piero della Francescas. In a true sense, Luke was a Pre-Raphaelite.

"Now here's an interesting painter – Piero. Obsessed with geometry in his pictures. All that virtuoso use of perspectives. He just has to tell you how smart he is. And yet his pictures are mysterious too. A bit of a puzzle. I like that kind of artist, one who keeps you guessing …"

And then there was Luke's own name, Signorelli. Was he descended from the painter of those strangely disturbing frescoes of the Antichrist in the cathedral at Orvieto? Or was he no relation at all? No one in his family could tell him – the names of painters meant nothing to them. But they meant a lot to Luke. So once he had settled his grandfather's little bit of business he would move on to Italy. And then what might he be able to do with his name? No, he reflected, he wasn't going to be like Dr Shipman or any of those other guys in Madame Tussaud's. He was above that crude freak show kind of stuff. But Grandpa had got him to Europe, so he'd prove to him – wherever he was – that he'd got the balls to do what he'd asked, then move on to do the things he enjoyed most.

And there was the well-nigh irresistible fascination of it that couldn't be denied – the challenge of carrying out a properly planned murder, the ultimate felony, one that offered an aesthetic delight like no other, replete with the heady taste of forbidden fruit.

So after visiting the other leading galleries in London and a day spent almost entirely in the British Museum where he discovered the pleasures of Roman portrait sculpture for the first time, he took the train north to the Scottish capital.

And now Luke was impatient to get his grandfather's business over and done with. He hadn't the slightest intention of ducking out of it. Far from it. Deep down he knew that it was something that had to be done but, at the same time, he wanted to get on and see more of those wonderful things he was starting to find in museums and galleries. But yet, he told himself, how much more he would enjoy them once he had got that achievement under his belt.

So Luke arrived at Waverley Station in Edinburgh. He liked the Scottish capital better than the English one. It was quieter, if more dour, but he found the classical austerity of the New Town to his taste. Luke didn't like things that were overdressed. Nor did he need noise or clamour. He was fastidious about such things and while he enjoyed the anonymity of crowds, he did not crave human company. The rest of his family were gregarious, but he wasn't. The black sheep. He found a quiet bed and breakfast within easy reach of the most important places – the castle, the National Gallery of Scotland and the rest. But as the weather was warm and there was a full moon, he stayed out late and walked the deserted Georgian streets and squares in the moonlight. The effect would have been better still, he reflected, if the streetlights could have been turned off.

Luke devoted two whole pages of his diary to the pleasures of perambulation through classical streets under a full moon. It was an experience he was determined to repeat whenever he could, to make it a regular feature of his life. That was the real joy of night-time – being out all by yourself under the moon. "Quite the vampire," he concluded in his diary, "if that doesn't sound too crappy."

But he knew that he could not linger in Edinburgh. He must clear up Grandpa's business first and then take a plane to Italy – where real fulfillment lay.

He took the train to York and the next one to Scarborough. He knew nothing about the place except what his grandfather hold told him in his briefing notes, but he had already examined the street map and knew where the object of his quest was to be found – in a big house that fronted the Esplanade. He also had a list of hotels and bed and breakfasts and decided on one of the latter. Nothing too showy that might draw attention to himself, and anyway, Luke didn't need luxury. No, there were things that mattered more, that transcended mere physical gratification.

The bed and breakfast – The Flower in Hand – was in the old part of the town at the far end of the seafront, away from the swankier houses on the Esplanade. He felt that he had made a good choice because its landlady turned out to be a young and accomplished painter. A number of her works, mostly nostalgic pieces of old working class street life, hung on the breakfast room walls. Luke enjoyed the images of men in flat caps, women with turbans wrapped round their heads and boys in baggy short trousers. But in talking to Liz Peacocke about her pictures, he was careful not to own up to any connections with Scarborough. He just took the line that, after a hectic programme of sightseeing, he wanted a break in a typical seaside resort.

On his first morning, Luke set off to spy out the land. He took his time, ambling through the streets and down onto the promenade behind the beach where he noticed an ice cream van parked just below the wall. He made a note of it on his pad and strolled on. At the end, where the road turned to go up towards the Esplanade, there was an amusement arcade and he stuck his head inside before retreating quickly from it with distaste. Luke disliked the lurid flashing lights and raucous sounds of such places.

As he made his way over the Spa bridge and up towards the Esplanade with its elegant nineteenth century houses, he began to feel more at home with his surroundings. "Yes," he reflected, "if I'd made my pile out of flogging ice cream I might have chosen to live somewhere like this – with plenty of wall space to hang my pictures."

Luke had the number of the house and a general description of it but not much else. From his grandfather's letter, he knew that the occupant was probably living alone and was visited only occasionally by members of his family, none of whom lived in the locality any more. That was about it. All the same, it was impressive that the old man back in Baltimore had managed to assemble so much information. He had possessed hitherto unsuspected depths and Luke found himself wishing that they had known each other better. A pity, though, that he had been such a philistine – a baseball game had mattered more to him than a piece of music or a painting.

The house in question was a large brick building amply dressed with a carved lintel and jambs set into a generous porch with double Tuscan columns, which was reminiscent of a Roman triumphal arch. But for such a large, freestanding house, it seemed to have very little space of its own at the front. There was a low wall with a small paved court, a gate and then the wide Esplanade sidewalk. On the other side of the road were gardens, falling steeply towards the sea. Clearly, one of these belonged to the house in question.

All these details, including the style of the house and its mouldings, Luke jotted down on his pad. Then he crossed to the garden directly opposite, which was reached by a small path that skirted it, and peered over the iron fence. It was in a neglected state but had not yet gone completely to wrack and ruin though it looked well on the way. There was a small paved terrace at the top behind which an ornate iron gate marked the entrance to what must have been a passage running under the street to the house on the other side. From the terrace, there was a clear view of the sea. Weeds grew in the gravel path that surrounded a lawn, badly in need of cutting. The rose bushes were straggly and the privet, which grew against the railings at the bottom, was in the same condition. On the terrace was a folding garden chair and a table with a wine bottle and an empty glass beside it.

Luke glanced around – he did not want to be seen to be loitering, especially by anyone in the house. There was nobody watching him from the windows that he could see, but there was the occasional passerby on the sidewalk. So he strolled on a bit further down the path beside the garden and paused to look out to sea. Then he wandered back the way he had come and glanced into the garden again. During the couple of minutes he had been away, someone had appeared and was sitting at the table. Clearly, the man had entered the garden by the underground passage. A second bottle of wine had joined the other one.

Luke realised at once from where the photograph in his file had been taken – from the sidewalk where he was standing right now. And it was the same man as the one in the picture. He sat with the same slumped posture, his broad buttocks spilling over the sides of the garden seat, and a straw hat jammed untidily on his head.

"That's my man," Luke told himself. He glanced over his shoulder to make sure that he wasn't

being observed in his own turn. "Someone as fat as that can't put up much of a fight but, on the other hand, with all that blubber …"

As soon as the word blubber entered Luke's mind, he thought of a seal and, for a second, he felt a stab of pity for the man. Luke quite liked seals.

It was sufficient to be getting on with. He jotted down a few more quick notes on his pad and wandered back the way he had come, taking in the view across the bay as he went.

It would need some preparation, but he was anxious not to take too long about it. Money was no object; he was just keen to get off to Italy.

So the guy liked sitting in his garden, swilling wine – when the weather permitted, of course. He was certainly no gardener. Why live in a decent house with a garden, Luke wondered, if you just let it run down like that? Better to live in trailer park. That sort of guy doesn't deserve to live – certainly not in a place like that.

If he was sozzled, he probably wouldn't put up much of a fight, but the timing had to be right. There was obviously a way into the house from under the street and presumably, as the evening drew on, he would retire indoors. That was the time to take him – when he was half-cut and on his way back into the house. He would have to follow him quickly, though, before he had time to lock the gate. Or should he sneak in ahead of him and wait for his return? That would be better – to sneak in behind his back, preferably when he was well into his second bottle …

And silence was all-important. He mustn't be heard from the street. No sounds of a noisy death reaching the ears of people passing above …

It was going to need at least one preparatory visit to confirm the guy's habits – or at least as much of them as he needed to know for his purpose. And, of course, he would have to think of the actual means of dispatch … and there was his grandfather's special stipulation – that was an important detail that Luke himself rather liked. It provided the cherry that topped the icing on the cake, so to speak. Grandpa may have been an old philistine who preferred baseball to art, but that showed a bit of flair, at least. But careful planning – that was vital. He would have to get it down on paper and, of course, write it up later in his diary.

"The key is the garden," he wrote in his notes, which he would later include with his account. "I have to get in without the guy seeing me and into the house ahead of him and then take him from the rear. But I've not got to be seen by anyone entering the garden and it must be done behind his back. He must never see me."

The means of dispatching his victim were not a problem for Luke. "There must be no mess – except for the extra thing Grandpa asked me to do. But no blood. There's no need for that. A spanner wrapped in a pair of socks and a well-worn leather belt. They will be sufficient. And a handkerchief to stuff down the man's throat in case the spanner doesn't do the trick right away."

But, of course, it was necessary to check out the place and the guy's movements one more time before he acted. And he needed a warm evening too. So the one following his first quick survey he went back. There had been a sharp breeze off the sea all day and it was a little cloudy, but it had settled down by five o'clock.

The garden was sheltered and, sure enough, at five o'clock the man was already there. Looking quickly about to make sure that no one was watching him, Luke checked the railings. They were no problem, though silence was essential. The man was sitting slumped in his chair as he had been on the previous occasion. There were two bottles on the table – his evening tipple, it seemed – and by listening, Luke was able to pick up the sound of snoring. That was a good sign – it would make things a hell of a lot easier if he was asleep when he needed to get into the house. And then there was the matter of making his escape. He understood that he was alone in the house, but what would happen if someone called and didn't get an answer? Would they be suspicious and raise the alarm? Luke didn't want to leave too quickly. He preferred to go back through the garden and it would be better to do it after dark.

All this was the work of a minute and he was off again before anyone approached him. He went to the middle of town where, having ordered a large cup of coffee in a cafe, he jotted down his conclusions on his pad. Tomorrow night then, assuming that the weather held.

But it didn't. It bucketed all day and Luke had to put it off. Instead, he passed the time reading a paperback about Michelangelo that he had bought in the National Gallery in London. He wasn't quite sure about him; his figures were rather over-muscled for his own taste. But the link with Signorelli was clear enough. And it would be quite something if his own ancestor – if such proved to be the case – was the inspiration of one of the greatest figures in the history of European art. He needed to find out more … in Italy.

The following day dawned fine and when Luke went out he knew that the time had come. It felt fresh after all the rain of yesterday but there was no movement in the air. He had several things to do, such as buying a spanner. He realised the need for caution. It was better to buy it in a large crowded store rather than in a smaller shop where he might be remembered, especially as he spoke with an American accent. So Luke went to a large emporium in the middle of town where he selected an adjustable spanner from a shelf of household tools and took it back to his room where he wrapped it in a pair of socks before placing it in a plastic carrier bag. He also put in a handkerchief for stuffing into his victim's mouth, but hoped it wouldn't come to that. Grandpa's special stipulation would have to wait.

"I'm not sure about Michelangelo. There's something a bit gross. He does rather overdo it with all those bursting muscles and violent postures. The cardinal who complained that his *Last Judgement* looked like a men's bathhouse had a point. But art is like anything else, isn't it? It doesn't stand still. You can't live in a perpetual springtime, can you?" Luke wrote it in his diary and felt that he had just said something rather good. He wasn't going to fall into the trap of admiring one of the "great" figures simply because he was expected to.

As well as the old guy, Luke had time to kill. So he took himself out to the Spa concert hall below the Esplanade where he sat down in a cafe to read his notes. Was there anything that he hadn't thought of? He wondered about his shoes and the possibility of footprints, but he had on a standard pair of mass-produced trainers and he would try to avoid stepping in any flowerbeds. And finger prints? That could be a problem, but a remote one. He was on police files back home in the States – if anyone should even make the connection. But better to be safe than sorry. He would buy a pair of rubber washing-up gloves. And what about his departure from Scarborough? He had deliberately left it open, but it might arouse suspicion if he disappeared too quickly after the deed. With any luck, it wouldn't be discovered until he was well clear of the town if the man really was alone in the house.

"I hope Grandpa was right about that. How the hell did he know all this stuff? Is there someone around here who might have an idea of what I'm up to? Who might be keeping an eye on me, for Christ's sake! He was a dark horse was Grandpa."

But Luke knew that he had to remain cool and leave a day later, preferably by train or a night bus to London. He would arrange his flight to Italy when he got there.

So after he had bought the rubber gloves, he took himself back to his room and put them in the bag with the other items. Two more things were necessary, but would have to be bought as late as possible.

At four-thirty, Luke went out and took a stroll up the Esplanade and down the path that passed the garden. Sure enough, the guy was there, slumped as usual with his two bottles. Luke turned quickly on his heel and returned to the middle of town. In a supermarket, he bought a carton of raspberry ripple ice cream. Then he made for the beach and, at the van, which he had previously noted by the sea wall, he treated himself to a plain vanilla ice in a cone. But he was careful to eat only the ice cream and not to bite into the cone. Instead, when he had sucked out the last of its contents and licked the rim, he wrapped it carefully in a paper napkin and placed it in his carrier bag. Then he strolled back to the Esplanade. He was keen to get there quickly but knew that he must not draw attention to himself. The dark glasses that he had put on made him feel more secure; he was afraid that his eyes might betray him if nothing else did.

A glance into the garden told him what he wanted to know. The victim was exactly as he had left him but if anything, had slumped further down into his seat. A good sign – the guy was probably fast asleep.

But there were a number of people on the street and it took several perambulations before Luke felt that the way was sufficiently clear to climb over the railings. At the critical moment, he snagged the bottom of his trousers on a spike.

"Shit," he said under his breath, "shorts would have been better."

But his luck had held. He made a soft landing while the old man still hadn't stirred but remained perfectly still. The gate at the entrance to the passage remained wide open.

For a moment, Luke felt that it was going to be too easy. He slipped into a pleasantly tiled subterranean passage at the end of which was a flight of steps leading up into the house. Quietly, he went up to the top where he waited out of sight.

He waited, but the old man was in no hurry to come back in. Luke, meanwhile, had put on the rubber kitchen gloves and laid out the spanner in its wrapping of socks, the belt and gag in readiness. He was concerned only about the carton of raspberry ripple ice cream, which would be turning to liquid by now.

He waited, and still the old man made no appearance. Luke checked his watch. It was after half past five. He decided to tiptoe back to the garden and take a look.

Gingerly, he advanced up the passage, keeping against the wall and, as far as possible, in the shade. When he reached the end, he crouched down and peered in the direction of the old man. He was exactly as he had last seen him, still slumped in his chair with his back to the passage. His head had fallen forward onto his chest. Luke listened for the old man's breathing, possibly the sound of snoring, but he could hear nothing. He was too damned still.

Crossing the terrace with the stealth of a cat, Luke approached his prey who was sitting with his arms dangling loosely over the arms of the chair with his chin resting on his chest, propped up, it seemed, by his considerable paunch. Very cautiously, Luke put out a hand and touched him on the shoulder.

There was no movement – not the flicker of an eye, not a grunt, nothing. "Christ!" Luke exclaimed. "The bugger's dead."

Relief and regret mingled in his brain. Relief that he had been spared from committing a pretty ugly crime, but regret too that he had somehow let his grandfather down and hadn't proved himself in the way that had been expected of him. "If only it hadn't rained yesterday …"

Luke glanced over the fence and up towards the street. He wasn't being watched. But what was he to do now? It was perfectly clear to him that he owed something to his grandfather. Was it this honour thing after all? Hardly. But he had given his word over his grave and Luke didn't like breaking a promise. And then there was that final touch that meant so much to Grandpa – the thing that he had underlined in red and which Luke himself admired for its unexpected sense of style. He simply had to go through with that.

There was no time to waste, so, tilting the chair back, he start to drag it with the body still in it over the terrace towards the entrance to the passage. He was aware of the scraping noise it made on the stone slabs and it was slow work because the cadaver was heavy. So Luke decided to abandon the chair and pulled it out from under the dead man. He took hold of him by his shoulders instead and gradually eased him into the passage where he stopped to draw breath.

"The slob," he muttered. "Why do people allow themselves to get into this condition?"

But by now there was no great rush and he could take his time. So he laid the body out carefully on the passage floor, folded the hands across the mountain of a stomach and closed the eyes. He had never laid out a corpse before but the actions seemed to come quite naturally to him.

And now for the finishing touch. That, at least, he could do for Grandpa. He went to the stairs where he had left his equipment and returned with it to the dead man. Then he arranged it in an arc round his head – the belt, neatly coiled, likewise the gag, and the spanner he placed on top of its former wrapping of socks from which he had been careful to unpick the maker's label. Finally, he took the ice cream cone from the plastic bag and opened the carton of raspberry ripple. It was a runny mess, the colours fusing to make it look pink. But he scooped out a dollop with a plastic spoon, which he had remembered to take from the cafe where he had drunk coffee earlier in the day, and started to fill up the cone.

Once he had filled it to the brim, he deftly turned it over and jammed it onto the dead man's nose. The melted ice cream ran down his cheeks as Luke stood back to eye the effect critically. And instantly, he saw that his grandfather had been right. The effect was both meaningful and grotesque, for the dead man with his false nose and streaked face resembled a bloated clown, like something out of the *Comedia de l "Arte*.

"That's the best I can do, Grandpa, but it's a nice touch and I congratulate you," Luke whispered before he picked up the plastic bag and stuffed it in his pocket, then slipped out into the garden and quickly climbed over the fence away from the street, where he took off the rubber kitchen gloves.

And so Luke left Lorenzo to be discovered by Mrs Ackroyd three days later. After spending one more day in Scarborough, he took the night coach to London and within the week he was in Italy.

But he was in for a big disappointment when he got to Orvieto to see the Signorelli frescoes of the Antichrist. The way to them was barred. They were being restored and, despite producing his passport with the same name as the artist on it, the security guard was unrelenting and refused to let him through the plastic drapes to see them.

And then, for the first time since leaving the United States, Luke lost his cool. "Philistine," he yelled at the guard. "I've come all this fucking way for nothing!"

He just wished that he'd known how to say it in Italian.

11 The Symposium

Nicko unlocked the door of the flat and quickly crossed the hall to switch off the burglar alarm.

"Quite safe now," he called back to Viktor who was already crossing the threshold and casting an eye about him.

"Casing the joint?" joked Nicko. "Do you know what that means?"

"Sure, I know," replied Viktor. "I was just checking for bugs." He spoke with an accent, which was a pleasantly melodious blend of standard received English and Russian.

Olive skinned and rather thickset with dark wavy hair, Viktor Ilyich Nikishov was what is described as a New Russian. His family had made a fortune from the wreck of communism in the former Soviet Union and, out of the proceeds, had sent him to a leading English public school, which was where he had met his chum Nicko. Now, having both left school together in the summer, they had time on their hands before moving on to university after the obligatory gap year.

Nicko liked to think that he was Russian too – he even talked about his 'Russian soul' – but of quite a different vintage to Viktor. In reality, he was English, despite his family name of Orloff. His great-grandfather was, indeed, a Russian count of that name who had fled to England in the early twenties, having fought in Wrangel's White Army against the Bolsheviks. Fluent in French and English and with a good number of well-placed friends in Paris and London, the count had fared better than many of his fellow exiles at that time. A sound classical scholar, he had started life again as a humble schoolmaster teaching small boys Latin, but not for long. He had fairly swiftly moved up onto a higher plane where he had found an English wife, as did his son and grandson. By the time Nicko was born, the Orloffs were living in Sunningdale, and Nicko had gone from a fashionable preparatory school to a public school in the Home Counties. But, despite his mildly exotic surname, he looked as Anglo-Saxon as they come.

And it was at his public school that he had met Viktor, who had arrived there straight from Russia. Ironically, it might have been Nicko's golden-haired, blue-eyed Englishness that had drawn Viktor to him in the first place, for, like a lot of Russians, he carried in his head a stereotype of Englishness – which he identified with the ideal of the perfect gentleman – and Nicko fitted.

Nicko laughed at Viktor's remark. "Wait till you see the rest of the place," he said, throwing open a door. "In here, for instance."

It was a small room, two walls of which were taken up by books. There was a heavy Victorian writing table over by the window and a well-worn Turkish carpet on the floor. But it was the shelves that lined the remaining walls that commanded the attention of any discerning visitor. For here was part of Uncle Frank's collection of fifth century BC Athenian red figure pottery. The pieces were carefully spaced and Nicko turned on a light to illuminate them.

"Wow," said Viktor, who was quickly learning to appreciate such things. "But isn't it asking for trouble? I mean going away and leaving them standing on open shelves like this? Anyone could walk in and help themselves. That alarm wouldn't be too difficult to fix."

Nicko laughed. "That's Uncle Frank for you," he said. "But you don't have to tell any of your friends in the Petersburg Mafia."

Viktor smiled. "Tell me more about Uncle Frank."

"He's not my real Uncle. Father's old university tutor and my godfather. A retired professor of classical archaeology at Oxford, to be precise."

There was a sweetish smell of pipe tobacco in the room, which supported that description.

"Married?" enquired Viktor.

"What? Uncle Frank? No, of course not," said Nicko. "A confirmed bachelor."

The two young men looked at each other and smiled.

"You amaze me, Viktor," said Nicko to his friend.

"Amaze you? Why?"

"How quickly you've latched onto the nuances of English life."

"Ludi, ludi," replied Viktor in Russian with a shrug. "People are people. Much the same wherever you go."

He crossed the room and took a small vase from the shelf that was different from the others, being painted white.

"A lykythos. It was placed in the grave with the dead," explained Nicko. "That's why it's that colour. But be careful with it, for Christ's sake."

Viktor pretended to drop it.

"For God's sake," protested his friend. "He'd have my head on a platter if that got broken."

Viktor eyed Nicko's golden locks with a critical frown. "Somehow I think not in your case," he said. "He probably prefers it where it is." He replaced the vase carefully and ran a finger along the shelf. "It could do with a dust."

"As you may have guessed, Uncle Frank isn't very worldly," Nicko told him.

"But not very Platonic either," replied Viktor.

They both laughed, thinking something clever had been said.

"You're such a bloody cynic," said Nicko, "You always think the worst of people."

"What do you expect – where I've come from?" replied Viktor.

It was the middle of the afternoon on an early autumn day in Chelsea, and Nicko left the shelf lights on when they went out of Uncle Frank's study and took his friend into the other rooms of the flat, which weren't large but, like the study, rather faded. They smelled musty. The place had been done out in a neo-classical style – terracotta and ochre being its predominate tones – and the washed-out effect of the walls set the antiquities off well. Indeed, the threadbare quality might have been contrived because everything came together so perfectly. It was as if the ancient artifacts had been manufactured with the set purpose of coming to rest on the shelves of Uncle Frank's flat.

"How long's your uncle away for?" Viktor enquired.

"Another three weeks. He usually goes to the south of Italy or Sicily about this time – after the main tourist rush has subsided."

"And he always lets you have the run of the place?"

"I keep an eye on things."

"If I had this little treasure house I wouldn't go off for a month and leave it in the care of someone like you. That door and alarm look a bit too easy." Viktor shook his head.

In the drawing room was the pièce de résistance of the collection. It stood by itself on a console table in the Empire style opposite the Adams fireplace.

"That is what is known as a krater," explained Nicko. "It held wine mixed with water."

"Why spoil the wine by mixing it with water?" queried Viktor.

"It was the way the Greeks seemed to like it," said Nicko. "No doubt they made it strong enough to loosen their tongues without letting them get too drunk. Think of those dazzling symposia."

"Symposia?"

"Supper parties. Strictly men-only affairs. You've heard of Plato's dialogues, haven't you? I should get Uncle Frank to tell you about them sometime."

Viktor frowned, unconvinced.

The krater was a magnificent piece, impressive to the eyes of even the most untutored layman. And Viktor, who was making rapid progress in such matters, was accordingly impressed. It was tall, almost the size of a household bucket and shaped like an inverted bell with upturned handles at the shoulder above its base. There was a broad frieze of figures running round the main body of the vessel. The outlines of their muscles and folds of their garments were applied with a vibrant delicacy on the red clay ground, while the blackness against which they acted out their drama added further to the dynamism of the scene.

"Now you can see why the Greeks were so special," declared Nicko. "No one else could touch them for their handling of the human form and for the sheer vitality of their art. I'm not sure anyone can, even now."

"What's it meant to be?" asked Viktor. He squinted at the back of the vase but did not touch it.

"The death of Agamemnon," explained Nicko. "Murdered by his wife Clytemnestra when he had only just got back from the Trojan War. Strictly speaking, he ought to be in the bath when she kills him with an axe."

But in this version, the King was falling backwards in a chair, as an armed warrior – presumably the Queen's lover – wielding a sword grabbed his forelock, urged on by the lady herself armed with a short double-headed axe. Agitated household slaves waved their arms on either side. "Uncle Frank tells me that it was done by the Dokimasia Painter – whoever he was," added Nicko. "He did tell me how he knows, but I'm afraid I can't remember exactly. There are little stylistic quirks that the experts can pick out."

"My God," said Viktor. His attention turned to a group of objects the size and shape of shallow soup bowls. "And these?" He picked one up.

"Please, Vik," pleaded his friend.

Viktor went through the pantomime again of pretending to drop it. "This one's too hot to hold," he joked.

And when he replaced it on its table, the meaning of his remark became apparent. But for Nicko, who was familiar with the object, it required no elucidation.

"A drinking cup," he said. "You have to remember this would be used at a blokes-only dinner party. That's what a symposium was."

An older, bearded man was penetrating a naked youth, who was bent double, from behind. The composition was surrounded by a 'Greek key' frieze, which neatly contained it within its circumference. Both the handles of the piece were intact and it seemed to be in perfect condition.

"This surely tells us something about your Uncle Frank," said Viktor who, in his blunt New Russian fashion, felt no compunction about being so direct with his friend.

"You can draw your own conclusions," replied Nicko tartly, "but it wouldn't surprise me if Uncle Frank is simply a harmless old celibate. His kind very often are. And is that such a bad thing?"

The last remark came as a challenge to Viktor who Nicko felt was pushing his insinuations about his godfather a little too far. Indeed, his friend's vehemence came as a surprise to the Russian boy, especially after he had seemed to collude with him in the earlier innuendo about Uncle Frank's sexual preferences. Despite his being perfectly au fait with such matters, there was something sweetly old-fashioned about Nicko who preferred not to probe too deeply into the inner urges of the people who were close to him.

They looked over the rest of the flat, even into Uncle Frank's rather Spartan bedroom with its single bed and cane-seated chair, which took the place of a bedside table.

"Not exactly a bordello," observed Viktor, trying to make amends for what he had implied earlier about its owner.

"The bedroom of a sober and rather shy university don, if you ask me – and therefore more like a monk's cell," Nicko declared. "You must have people like Uncle Frank in Russia, surely. As you said yourself, people are much the same wherever you are."

"Kaneshna," returned Viktor. "Of course." He smiled at Nicko, almost archly. His friend liked it when he used Russian words.

They went back to the hall. "Now what?" said Viktor.

"Now what?" repeated Nicko, slightly at a loss, having now shown his chum every room in Uncle Frank's flat.

"I've got an idea – if Uncle Frank doesn't mind."

Nicko looked at Viktor dubiously.

"Only if he doesn't mind," insisted Viktor.

"How do we find that out? Ring him at his hotel?"

"Not necessary," said Viktor. "I'm sure he doesn't mind. He sounds a very understanding sort of chap, tolerant of young people, that kind of thing."

"What are you getting at, Vik?" retorted his friend, who occasionally found the other's prevarication tiresome. "Stop beating about the bush."

Viktor muttered the phrase 'beating about the bush' in a low voice as if he was trying to store up a useful English expression for the future.

"I'm sure your uncle wouldn't mind if we borrowed his flat for our own little symposium," he said. "He would probably understand that perfectly well. Though we don't have to go quite as far as those two guys on the drinking cup," he added.

Nicko still looked doubtful. "We'd have to be bloody careful to we didn't do any damage."

"That goes without saying," replied Viktor. "But something simple – drinks and snacks in the Russian style with lots of good talk – also in the Russian style – and surrounded by all these wonderful things."

"And drunkenness in the Russian style with its unfortunate consequences," pointed out Nicko. "I don't like it, Vik. It won't wash."

His friend repeated 'it won't wash' under his breath.

"I wish you wouldn't keep doing that, Vik."

"Doing what?"

"Repeating things I've just said. You turn our conversations into English lessons."

Viktor laughed. "I'm sorry, Nicko. But to go back to what we were saying. With such beauty all around us we cannot allow anything so squalid as a Russian orgy to take place in Uncle Frank's flat."

"Don't be so sure," replied Nicko. "You know the story of Peter the Great's visit to London, don't you?"

"Kaneshna," said Viktor. "But if it makes you feel easier about it we can use the kitchen. Simply to know that there is all this history and art so close at hand would be sufficient."

"But not too close at hand."

"The kitchen would be ideal. That, after all, is the place where Russia's intellectuals have been meeting to share the mind's forbidden fruits for the past seventy or more years. And Nicko, we're both Russians, aren't we? Admittedly from different sides of the great revolutionary divide, but together once again and with so much to talk about. And look what else you and I have got in common: that sacred English thing – what do you call it – our alma mater near Godalming, the Old School. That factory of gentlemen, the English public school."

Nicko smiled. "You talk an awful lot of shit, Viktor."

"Seventy years," mused Viktor. "More than seventy years – that's what it's been. I know we've talked a lot already but there's still so much, and we've hardly scratched the surface of it. We could go to a pub or back to your folk's place in Sunningdale, but hell, why not here in Uncle Frank's kitchen? We will call it a symposium. It doesn't have to be a Platonic dialogue, but it'll be a symposium just the same. I'm sure your uncle would approve of that. Two intellectual young men talking seriously in his kitchen. The ambience is ideal. Do I sound a little naïve?" he added with a trace of self-mockery.

"I'll buy it," said Nicko. "Provided we don't touch anything that matters."

Then Viktor did something very Russian, the kind of thing Nicko enjoyed. He hugged his chum and planted a kiss on each of his cheeks.

"Sit down, Nicko," he ordered. "Or just wander about, enjoying the treasures. This one's on me. I don't want to patronize you, but my dad could buy one of your English football clubs any time he liked. But you – with the help of your Uncle Frank – provide – what do I call it – the class – the thing that we New Russians most badly need at this point in our history."

"You're a snob," said Nicko.

"Perhaps I am," replied Viktor. "But no more than Tsar Peter was. I won't be long."

He slipped out and Nicko could hear the lift descending to the ground floor. Going round the rooms, he picked up and examined some of the smaller objects – as he had done many times before: the Roman oil lamps, a moulded ceramic Greek figurine – a temple offering, not rare and rather crude, but interesting, nevertheless, for what it said about the small change of life in the ancient world. There was even a lamp done in the form of a gladiator's helmet – the Roman equivalent of modern seaside kitsch. In a way, these mundane objects brought him into closer sympathy with the ancient world than the grander works did.

Then it occurred to Nicko that he ought to do something about setting up the kitchen in readiness for the forthcoming symposium in the Russian manner. He had better get it done before Viktor returned and started to get ideas about shifting the venue to a more exalted setting. Fishing around inside the kitchen cupboards, he found Uncle Frank's cheaper glasses and a selection of plates and bowls. These he set out on the kitchen table with cutlery from the drawer by the sink. Having completed the task to his satisfaction, he retreated to his godfather's study to look over his books.

Three quarters of an hour later the doorbell rang, announcing the return of Viktor.

He carried three bulging supermarket carrier bags, which he dumped on the kitchen dresser. "Christ, you must have bought the shop," his friend expostulated.

"Not quite," said Viktor, "but I did my best."

There were four bottles of champagne, an equal number of claret and vodka – the proper Russian stuff, Nicko noted – as well as a mountain of cold snacks: salami sausage, rollmop herrings – indeed, a whole range of fishy things – black rye bread, butter and olives. Then Viktor rummaged in his coat pockets and produced four jars: two of black caviar and two of red.

"That must have cost you something," exclaimed Nicko. "Where did you find it?"

"I have my ways," replied the other.

"But there's so much. I thought this wasn't meant to be an orgy."

"It's a symposium," Viktor corrected him. "Is the freezer switched on?"

Nicko checked and Viktor placed the vodka inside and the champagne in the main fridge compartment. "We'll have to give the vodka plenty of time, but we can start on the champagne before that."

The spread covered the kitchen table and the adjacent dresser. Nicko shook his head. "My God, Vik."

"Why 'my God'?"

"Are you quite sure I can't chip in?"

"Quite sure. You have provided Uncle Frank and his priceless collection of Greek vases. So surely I can lay on a little caviar, can't I? And talking of which, I really like the red stuff better than the black. I know I shouldn't, but it's a fact. Let's kick off – yes? – with the wine. We'll have to give the champagne a bit longer. Corkscrew?"

He uncorked a bottle of wine and filled their glasses.

"I hope there'll be enough," he said anxiously.

"More than," responded his friend.

The symposium began.

"What are we going to talk about?" said Viktor. "Think of something suitable."

"A Russian topic. You."

"Me?"

"You," repeated Nicko. "Who you really are. What your people got up to and why you're here right now. I know some of it, of course, but it's a bit too vague and somehow not in focus. Kind of shadowy."

Viktor smiled. "You mean shadowy or shady?"

"Very good. You've come a long way."

"Your ancestors were aristocrats?"

Nicko nodded. "You know that."

"Big ones, I mean? You know, like the Sheremetevs? Vast estates and armies of serfs?"

"Not as big as all that. But a couple of sizeable estates and, sure, they had plenty of serfs. But why are you asking me all this again, Vik? We've been over it so many times. And you don't have to tell me that your great-great – however many greats – grandfather was a serf shovelling pig shit while mine was blowing a fortune at the gaming tables of St Petersburg and shagging the Empress of all the Russians at the same time."

"Both at once?"

"Fuck off. You know what I mean."

Viktor grinned broadly and lifted his glass. "Nasdorovia," he announced. Nicko repeated the Russian toast.

"That champagne won't be ready yet. We'll get on with the wine in the meantime," said Viktor. "He lifted a piece of salami sausage on his fork. "No," he went on, "you'd really like to know more about my family, wouldn't you?"

"I would," said Nicko. "What you've told me already has merely whetted my appetite – high ranking members of the Communist Party and asset strippers when the time came."

"In a nutshell. Is that right?"

"What?"

"'In a nutshell'? Did I use it correctly?"

"Perfectly, but remember this isn't an English lesson. It's a symposium. You said so yourself."

"Every conversation with you is an English lesson."

"You can speak the language perfectly well. You don't need me to teach you. So fuck off."

"Well, that's about the most English word you could have used. Come on, Nicko, tuck in. And mind, I did say tuck, not fuck."

"Very droll."

They drained their glasses and Viktor put the half-finished wine on one side and took one of the bottles of champagne from the fridge. "Fresh glasses?"

Nicko rummaged in the cupboard and found fresh glasses.

The cork popped and the bubbly frothed onto the table. A Russian toast followed and Viktor smacked his lips.

"And now for the caviar," he said. A tin opener was produced and also some ice to provide a bed for the delicacy. "It was nice of your uncle not to turn off the fridge before he went away. He must have known we were going to hold a symposium in his flat."

Nicko took a generous spoonful of the caviar. He wasn't sure whether he really liked it or not but helped himself to a second one, partly to convince himself that he did. "You've never really told me," he resumed, "but what exactly did your family get up to? Good communists once upon a time, and then they end up by sending you to an English public school – buying into the very thing they were dedicated to smashing, into social division and class privilege."

"Come on, Nicko, we've been through all of that before."

"But that's not all, is it? You know perfectly well the kind of things that went on in Russia for the best part of the last century. What part did your folks play in all of that? In Stalin's time, for instance?"

Viktor laughed. "Your family had serfs, right?"

"Right."

"Well, so did mine, in a manner of speaking. Did I say that correctly?" He took a mouthful of caviar, the red stuff this time. "Perhaps we should keep that to have with the vodka. That's the proper time to eat slimy, fishy things."

Nicko looked hard at his friend.

"Russia is Russia," explained Viktor airily. "Its essence doesn't change. Sorry if that's – what do you call it – a platitude? But it's true. Did we ever talk about Dalstroi?"

"Dalstroi? No, I don't think so. What is it?"

"The Gulag," said Viktor. "You know what that was surely?"

"Kaneshna."

Viktor smiled. "Well, Dalstroi – or, to give its proper title, the Dalstroi Trust – was a part of the Gulag. It ran its operations in Kolyma – in eastern Siberia."

"Go on."

Viktor topped up their glasses with more champagne and insisted on another toast.

"Kolyma," he said, "in the east of Siberia, and the port of Magadan. That's where my great- grandfather, Nikishov, ruled. And I mean ruled. General of the NKVD and the boss. Tsar Josef was far away in Moscow. Dalyeko, dalyeko – far, far away." He intoned the words of the soulful Russian song.

"The Tsar being Stalin?"

"As I said. Josef Vissarionovich. And a terrible one too – every bit as bloody as Ivan IV but with a much longer reach. What did people say? Ghengis Khan with a telephone. And Kolyma was run by the Dalstroi Trust as part of the Gulag – its most profitable part. Gold, you see. Mined by zeks, the prisoners who, in a nutshell – yes? – were Great-grandpa's serfs. Like you Orloffs, he was service nobility. Is that right?"

Nicko nodded "Quite likely."

"Communism or tsarism – it comes to the same thing. We're talking about Russia, after all. And what the Tsar gave he could just as easily take away. Come on, Nicko, eat up – there's a mountain of food to get through. 'In the North there is a mountain, covered o'er with frozen corpses, where the wild winds blow. Mother dear, you'll never know where your son lies buried.' A Gulag poem, an English translation from the Russian – sadly not my own. That's Kolyma for you. But it's only part of the story. There was gold, Nicko, gold – and it needed slaves to dig it out. Anyway, how do English people say it? Dig in? Eat up."

He filled their glasses with the remains of the bottle of champagne, letting it spill over onto the table.

"Tell me about Great-grandpa Nikishov then." said Nicko, having swallowed his champagne in a single draught.

Viktor nodded. "Every bit as exotic as any of your Orloffs, I'm quite sure," he replied.

"Why haven't you told me about him before?" queried Nicko. "You're not making this up by any chance, are you?"

Viktor looked hurt and put his hand on his heart.

"It needed the right occasion," he explained. "That's something you English are supposed to have, isn't it? A sense of occasion. You see, Great-grandpa had blood on his hands – and plenty of it, no doubt. After all, he was a chum of Beria and a senior figure in the NKVD who managed to survive the Purges – which meant only one thing. He must have put an awful lot of other people in the shit to keep out of it himself. He had to. And, for him, it worked. Like a cat – how do I say it? He always landed on his feet. He had nine lives and didn't run out of them."

"I think I can understand," said Nicko. "Remember, I'm a Russian too."

"Kaneshna, Nicko. Ya zabul. I forgot. How could I have done? Your Russian soul."

"Fuck off, Vik. Just tell me about Great-grandpa Nikishov."

"Where to begin? His limousines? His private army of security guards? And the dacha with the wonderful view of the Pacific? That vodka might be just about drinkable."

Viktor opened the freezer, felt one of the bottles and frowned.

"Not yet. Still a bit warm." He took two glasses and placed them in the freezer beside the vodka. "We nearly forgot to frost the glasses." He uncorked a second bottle of champagne. "Great-grandpa Nikishov?"

"The dacha overlooking the Pacific."

"Yes, the dacha. Some dacha – more like a palace, though I dare say you Orloffs might think it …a bit over the top? Does that sound right?"

"Perfectly," said Nicko. "Get on with it."

"Fitted oriental carpets everywhere, bearskins, crystal chandeliers – and a luxurious dining room where he entertained with his wife … roast bear, Caucasian wines, fruits and berries flown in from the South … fresh tomatoes and cucumbers grown in his private greenhouses …"

"A true boyar," supplied Nicko.

"Or a Roman who had been appointed governor of a newly conquered barbarous province …and vegetables quite foreign to the north, grown for him in special hothouses and orangeries …"

A dreamy look had come into Viktor's eyes and he plied the champagne bottle once more.

"Steady on," Nicko said.

"Fuck off. Remember my name's Nikishov as well."

"That's what I'm rather afraid of."

"Did the Orloffs have an orchestra?" asked Viktor.

"They may have done. No one's ever mentioned it."

"Well, Great-grandpa had one. A serf orchestra. Or, to be strictly accurate, a zek one – musicians who were prisoners in the Gulag. It amounts to the same thing. And they were just grateful to be kept out of the mines."

They finished the bottle of champagne. A wistful expression suffused Viktor's face. "I wonder if that vodka's drinkable yet? To hell." He took a bottle and the two glasses out of the freezer. As he poured it, the vodka overflowed onto the table.

"Steady on," said Nicko. "It's good stuff. Don't waste it."

Viktor sipped his glass. "Not as cold as it should be, but what the hell?" He threw the rest back.

Nicko sipped his more cautiously, though he too was feeling the effects of the champagne. Viktor plunged into what was left of the caviar.

"I suppose Great-grandpa Nikishov had as much of that as he wanted," said Nicko.

"Kaneshna. And carpenters to make his furniture …"

"Cabinet makers."

"Cabinet makers … and fashion designers to dress his wife. He had some of the best …"

"Were there still such people in Russia then? Very bourgeois." Nicko was beginning to slur his words.

"Kaneshna. And doctors … the very best … specialists from Moscow and Petersburg – or whatever it was called then …"

"Leningrad."

"Leningrad."

"Fuck Lenin," announced Nicko.

"Fuck him," replied Viktor, who was onto his second glass of vodka while Nicko was following manfully in his wake.

"And the theatre," resumed Viktor. "Did I mention the theatre?"

"No."

"Oh, there was a theatre. With a front like a Greek temple … Uncle Frank would have liked it …in the park … a short walk from his main residence … and serf actors. Did the Orloffs have any of those?"

"Actors? I don't know … maybe. Quite probably … no, I'm sure they did …" Despite his increasingly befuddled wits, Nicko felt he needed to uphold the reputation of the Orloffs in the face of this Soviet upstart.

"The finest company of actors east of the Urals," went on Viktor. "They did all the great Russian classics. And your Shakespeare too."

"Shakespeare? In English?"

"In Russian."

"Not the same thing."

"Like Pushkin in English," rejoined Viktor.

"True," said Nicko. "Which Shakespeare play did the Boyar Nikishov like best?"

"Macbeth."

"He would," said Nicko. "It's my favourite too."

Viktor replenished the glasses, spilling the vodka liberally across the table. Nicko ran a finger through the stream and licked it while Viktor opened a tin of red caviar and spooned half of its contents into his mouth. He handed the rest to his friend who did likewise.

The vodka bottle was empty and the last tin of caviar broached. For a moment, neither of them said anything but Nicko was aware that there were still questions to be asked about Great-grandpa Nikishov. What had happened to him after the party was over, for instance? Viktor had said that he'd had nine lives and hadn't run through them. He didn't like the sound of the man one little bit and resented the implication that he was the equal of an Orloff. But, if what his friend had been telling him was true, he had a point. After all, he liked to think that his Orloff ancestors had been larger-than-life Russians as well. According to Nicko's canon, all true Russians were larger than life …

But now his brain was becoming fuddled and, though clever-sounding things were pressing to be uttered, he was aware that he could not follow the thread of a logical line of questioning any longer. Nicko was only eighteen, after all, and not nearly as good at holding his drink as he imagined.

And the same was true of his more worldly Russian friend. The symposium was fast disintegrating into a series of bombastic toasts and silly giggles. But there was no question of letting up. They were both young enough not to think that they ought to draw the line and call a halt …

"And the football team?" mumbled Viktor. "Did I tell you about that? Stars from all the best Russian sides. Serfs too. So when my dad buys Arsenal … How do I say it?"

"Fuck it, Vik. Don't even try," said Nicko in a slurred voice.

One bottle of vodka remained, one of champagne and two of wine. "Watering the wine …"

"Whayousay? Watering the wine?" mumbled Nicko, whose head was now pillowed on his folded arms among the debris of the feast.

"This is a symposium, isn't it? We'll water the fucking wine."

"Water the fucking wine."

"That's what the Greeks did, isn't it?"

"That's what the Greeks did."

Viktor lurched to his feet. "Water the wine … water the fucking wine …" Then he starting to say something in Russian, which, even if he had been sober, Nicko, despite his Russian soul, would never have understood.

"There's only one way to water wine," said Viktor. "The Russian way."

"The Russian way," murmured Nicko from the surface of the table.

"Great-grandpa Nikishov's way."

"The Orloffs' way."

Viktor lurched out of the kitchen, pausing only to steady himself in the doorway. Meanwhile, Nicko closed his eyes, leaving the alcohol to take a complete hold.

His eyes were fast shut when Viktor returned, carrying the Attic krater by one of its handles. He plonked it on the table among the detritus. Then, opening the freezer, he took out one of the remaining bottles of vodka and, ripping off the metal cap, poured its contents into the ancient vessel. A bottle of wine followed and then the last of the champagne.

Nicko had started to snore and Viktor looked blearily round the kitchen before lurching out once more. This time he returned with two of the drinking bowls – one depicting the scene of sodomy and the second of Oedipus and the Sphinx. He dipped the former into the krater and pushed it towards his friend, giving him a sharp nudge at the same time.

"Wake up, Nicko," he mumbled. "Time to drink to Uncle Frank."

Nicko stirred and opened an eye. "Uncle Frank?"

"Drink up, Nicko."

"To Uncle Frank then … the old bugger."

Nicko blinked at the cup but did not seem to register anything wrong about it. He held it to his lips and slurped two big mouthfuls of the liquid before resting his head again on the table. His companion dipped the Oedipus bowl in the krater and poured its contents down his own throat.

"Uncle Frank … the old bugger. Your turn, Nicko."

"Oh shit," muttered the other. "Oh shit."

"That's not a toast," his friend said In Russian. "Come on, Nikoshka," he said, this time in English. "You're an Orloff."

"An Orloff," exclaimed Nicko, suddenly seeming to wake up. "Yes I am. A fucking Orloff."

"Not a fucking one, Nikoshka, just an Orloff."

"And certainly not a fucking Nik …Nikishov."

"Not a fucking one of them either, Nikoshka," said his friend.

"If I say fucking, I mean fucking," blazed Nicko. He sat up, swallowed the ferocious liquid in his bowl and dashed it to the floor where it shattered on the tiles.

"Oh my God," murmured Viktor. "Oh my God." But he followed suit and, draining his bowl, dashed it to the floor as well.

Nicko, meanwhile, had staggered to his feet. 'To Russia," he shouted, "to poor fucking Mother Russia."

He looked round in a confused way for his cup, unaware, it seemed, that it lay in fragments on the floor. Then lifting the krater, he raised it to his lips ...

In the early morning, the two young men fled from the scene of destruction, leaving the krater and cups lying in ruins on the kitchen floor.

And Nicko spent his gap year in St Petersburg with his friend, helping him to open a small antique dealing business on the Nevsky Prospekt. It was a sideline, which Viktor felt might go somewhere, especially with the back-up of Nicko's English public school manners and Russian soul to help him.

12   The Menin Gate

It was on the Piccadilly Line, while travelling between South Kensington and Knightsbridge, that a strange thing happened to Martyn Sharpe. He was admiring his own reflection in the darkened window opposite and wondering if other people were as impressed by his youthful good looks as he was, when he suddenly found himself looking at a different face. He glanced around but it belonged to no one else in the half-empty carriage.

Returning his gaze was a young man of about the same age as Martyn – slightly younger, perhaps – with closely cropped, dark red hair and a wispy moustache – a young man's first essay at facial adornment. Then Martyn noticed the khaki serge military tunic. The soldier's lips appeared to be moving. He was looking directly at Martyn, his eyes meeting his, but without any of the reciprocating movements of a proper reflection.

Oddly enough, Martyn did not feel particularly surprised – possibly because he had just returned from a visit to the First World War battlefields and cemeteries of Flanders and his mind was still full of the impressions it had received there. So if, in a moment of idle reverie, this image of a young British soldier of that time had floated to its surface, it seemed quite natural. Except that the image was obviously not inside his head. What's more, the young man seemed anxious to make himself known to him.

And yet, in a way that he couldn't put a finger on, Martyn felt that it was perfectly reasonable that he should be looking at this face that returned his gaze from the glass instead of the one he was used to. It was as if no natural law was being violated, so he slipped across the carriage to the seat opposite and, glancing about to make sure that he was unobserved, he tried to hear what the soldier was saying to him.

But this proved impossible because the window was set back from the seat by a shelf about six inches wide and he could not hear anything unless he knelt on the seat and pressed his ear to the glass, so he pointed to his ear and shook his head just as the train swept into the light of Knightsbridge station.

Strange as the experience had been, Martyn did not feel uneasy about it. He had seen that face before somewhere. It was familiar to him yet he could not place it. Had he seen it in a dream? He simply could not say.

So when he got off at King's Cross, Martyn headed straight for the gents, partly because he needed to relieve himself and partly because he realised that a mirror was necessary if he was to make contact with the young soldier again. The idea of meeting up with a soldier in a public lavatory struck Martyn as a bit droll, but he really did need to know what he had been trying to say to him.

Fortunately, it was not a busy time of day and the washroom of the gents was empty except for one other person when Martyn entered. The man was drying his hands and then went through the turnstile, leaving Martyn by himself, though he could hear sounds coming from one of the cubicles. After answering nature's call, he crossed to the line of hand basins.

Sure enough, the young soldier was there in the mirror where his own reflection ought to have been. Martyn could see him clearly this time – the wispy moustache – more down than bristle – and the sprinkling of adolescent pimples on his cheeks. Martyn raised his eyebrows, silently inviting him to speak.

"Hullo, Mart," he said.

"You know my name?"

"It would be odd if I didn't."

"Yes, I suppose it would." Martyn caught himself saying it and somehow it seemed the obvious thing to say.

"Martyn spelt with a y and not an i."

"And what's your name?"

"Cade – Jack Cade." It was a North Riding voice, a mellow-sounding burr.

"The same as the medieval rebel?"

"The same." He smiled weakly. It was a tired old joke he had learned to live with.

"Somehow I felt it ought to be the moment I saw you," said Martyn.

"Why? Do I look like one?"

"A rebel? Hardly," said Martyn. "It's just that I've seen your name recently. On the memorial at the Menin Gate in Ypres, as a matter of fact. And, of course, it stood out. It was J.C.Cade."

"That sounds like me. You say a memorial at Ypres?"

"At the Menin Gate – a memorial for the ones they never found."

Just at that moment there was a sound of flushing in one of the cubicles behind Martyn.

"Hang on a minute," he told the other. "I'm in a public convenience and someone's about to come out of one of the cubicles."

The soldier grinned back at him.

An elderly man emerged from the cubicle and washed his hands in a basin close to Martyn. He appeared to notice nothing unusual. At the same time a second man came through the turnstile and entered another cubicle. Martyn went through the motions of washing his own hands.

The elderly man departed and Martyn was about to speak to Jack once more when a long-drawn-out fart sounded from the newly occupied cubicle. It died away in a splutter, followed by an embarrassed sigh and an impatient click of the tongue as if its perpetrator was only too aware that the humiliating sound he was making could be overheard.

"Reveille," declared Jack and, curiously, Martyn had wanted to say exactly the same thing.

"Loud and clear," he said instead.

The two young men sniggered like a pair of schoolboys.

"You were telling me something about my name," pursued the soldier once they had sobered up. "Before we were so rudely interrupted."

"Yes," said Martyn. "I was saying that it's on the Menin Gate and it stuck out. That's where all the names of the soldiers are whose bodies were never found."

The other nodded. "That would fit," he said.

"When did you ...?" asked Martyn hesitantly.

"When did I die? Oh, I can answer that, though not the exact day. It was in the autumn of 1917. In November."

"Passchendaele?"

"That name rings a big bell. But tell me, Mart, what happened after that?"

"Of course, you didn't live to hear the end of it, did you? Well, we won – in the end – a year later. But it's a long story. I'll tell you another time, if you like. It's a bit of a hobby of mine."

"A hobby?" For a moment the soldier looked baffled, then he laughed.

"Sorry – that doesn't sound quite right, does it? But look, old boy, I can't talk to you here. It's a bit public."

Martyn had heard the rustling of lavatory paper behind him, then the sound of flushing after which a man emerged to wash his hands. Red-faced and embarrassed at being overheard by this young man who was still hanging about, he glared at Martyn.

"Are you still here?" he said.

"It looks like it, doesn't it?" Martyn gazed at Jack in the mirror.

"So what are you waiting for then?" the man persisted.

"For you to go away."

The man gave Martyn a filthy look. "Your sort disgusts me," he hissed and stumped off.

"I must go now, "Martyn said to Jack. "I'll get myself arrested if I stay here much longer. Loitering with intent – if that means anything to you."

Jack laughed. "I think I can guess."

"We'll talk later."

Martyn was looking at his usual features once more. But once home again in York, it was much easier. Normally, he shared his flat with a girlfriend, Meg, a student studying modern languages, whom he had just left in France where she was to do a term at the University of Tours, so he had the place to himself for the time being. He was a post-graduate historian, embarked on a master's degree, and a dialogue with Jack suited him perfectly – he could put the soldier straight on all he had missed by dying so young, while there was so much of the everyday detail of a soldier's life on the Western Front in 1917 that he would learn from him in return.

He talked to Jack in the morning just after he had got up or before going to bed by means of the bathroom mirror. Nothing was arranged between them, it simply worked out that way.

And yet, despite words being exchanged between them, it did not feel like a dialogue, for Martyn found himself anticipating the things that Jack was telling him, as if they were already inside his head, and he was stirring something deep-seated that he was familiar with. But it only felt that way while they were talking to each other and at no other time. "Of course," he would say to himself, "that's just how it was. How did I forget it?"

And he filled Jack in on the history of the twentieth century in the years that followed his death in 1917: the eventual outcome of the war, the course of the Russian Revolution following the Bolsheviks" seizure of power, the rise of Hitler, the Second World War, the atomic bomb, all the important things, as he saw them, up to the end of the twentieth century.

The young soldier's thirst for historical information seemed insatiable and, as Martyn was an historian, he rose to the challenge with relish. After all, it must be the bitterest of ironies to lose your life fighting in a war and never to know how the very thing you were engaged in turned out. So it was a labour of love and a good discipline for himself too – marshalling all the information and answering Jack's questions.

But he wanted to know more about Jack and vice-versa. They spent a lot of time talking about themselves, though it was only after several meetings that Martyn felt able to ask the question that was most pressing on his mind.

"When it happened, Jack, what did it feel like? What did you think of?"

"What? Dying, you mean?" Jack gave him a long, searching look, straight in the eye, almost as if to say, "do you really not know?"

Martyn waited patiently for his answer. He knew it wasn't easy. "Tell me only if you feel you can, Jack. What's it like to die? I'll understand if you can't tell me."

The same quizzical look from the soldier.

"Mud," he said at length. "Mud – that's what did for me – and sheer bloody exhaustion and the dark. If it hadn't been so bloody dark I might have been saved. A filthy night in November, driving rain and a bitter east wind. We were actually coming out of the line when it happened. Actually pulling out. The place was just a swamp with duckboards crossing it, and piles of churned-up earth sticking up here and there like small islands, and the odd shattered stump of a tree. There was a bit of shellfire, nothing out of the normal – and most of the shells were plopping into the mud where they couldn't do us much harm. Their explosions were swallowed up. That was the bloody silly thing about it, we'd seen much worse. Anyway, as luck would have it, one landed almost on top of us where we were crossing on a duckboard. I remember the sound it made and losing my balance and going in at the same time. I was the last in line and the others must have run for cover at the end of the walkway. I don't know because I was too bloody weighed down and fagged to take much notice. And it was dark. Anyway, I called out, but nobody answered. The shells were starting to come over thick and fast by now, because the last thing I remember as my head went under were the plumes rising out of the mud. Of course, I struggled, but only went in deeper …and I don't have to tell you, Mart, I wasn't the strongest man in the platoon, a bit weedy, as a matter of fact … deeper and deeper … like sinking into cold, black jam … sort of sticky … and the thought … that this is the actual business of dying … this is really it and it's happening … to me … the choking … and the terror, and at the same time the all-too conscious thought that this is what a hanged man must feel dangling on the end of a rope … I even thought that, as well … all these things thrown together, but pure funk … I wanted to call out for Mum but, of course, I couldn't … I was being choked with the mud and couldn't breathe … and then … then … somehow, none of it mattered … and I wasn't cold any more, but warm … rather like being tucked up in bed and about to set off to the Land of Nod … if that doesn't sound too soft, but that's just how it felt … and the pain of not being able to breathe had gone. But who can ever remember the exact second of falling asleep, Mart? And now I'm nattering to you … like all of us, I'd thought a lot about dying – what it actually would be like and so on – but with me, there was no screaming death agony … no terrible wound or lacerating pain … there was even a little time to think about it."

He stopped and Martyn said nothing. He simply knew … knew that's exactly what it had been like, but who can recall the second of falling asleep?

"There are some things I regret, Mart," went on the young soldier after a pause. "For instance, I never broke my duck. I died a virgin. I'm not ashamed of it – so many of us did – but all the same, I feel unfinished …

and carrying on with my education and a wife and children to bore with stories about the war. I thought a lot about all of that ... I've told you about dying, Mart, so can you tell me about loving? I'd feel more complete if you could."

Martyn did his best – not that he had a great fund of experience to draw on, but it seemed enough and he touched on the most intimate things – things he would never have told his closest friend. But with Jack, he felt he was not giving anything away. The young soldier listened and never broke in once.

But, of course, there was a limit to what could be said at one time and, after a while, they changed the subject.

"Tell me, Mart," Jack said, "There's something else I'd like to know. Not that it's very important – just idle curiosity, really."

"What's that, Jack?"

"My body. What happened to it? You wouldn't have any idea, would you?"

"As I said, they never found it. That's why your name's on the Menin Gate."

"So it's still out there ...under all that mud?" Jack laughed.

"Very likely, but it's not a swamp any more, Jack. A field with cows grazing in it, I expect."

"I rather like that," mused Jack. " Not that it really matters, of course. It's just a nice idea."

They smiled at each other and, for a moment, did not speak.

"Thanks, Mart," said Jack, "for putting me in the picture, about making love, I mean."

"I'm afraid nothing I can say is a patch on the real thing."

"It's better than dying," replied the other, "though you may be lucky and not have time to think about it when it happens to you, but I won't bore you with any more of that."

"You haven't bored me at all, Jack. But, in a way, it seemed as if you were telling me something I knew already."

"And later on you can tell me all about having a family and growing old – because that's something I don't know already." Jack shrugged and smiled.

Martyn found himself looking at the other face – the one he was more familiar with – but really, it made no difference which one it was.

13   Mr Smedley

"Julie-A? Jamie here. I've found something that might interest you."

"Really? What is it?"

"Come and see for yourself."

"Won't you tell me now?"

"Nope. I'm afraid not. You have to see it for yourself."

"Swine." Julianne put the phone down.

That was cousin Jamie all over: dangling a tempting little morsel in front of your nose, then whipping it away again. He was opening an Italian bar at the bottom of Huntriss Row in what had once been Great Aunt Constance's millinery shop, while Julianne, a student reading Law at Durham University, was spending the first couple of weeks of her long vacation at home in Scarborough. So, with time on her hands and her curiosity aroused, she set off on the ten minute walk from the Gabrielle Hotel, which her family owned in Belvedere Road, to the middle of town. Her route took her by way of the Esplanade, over the Spa Bridge to where Huntriss Row joined Harbour Square.

Jamie was standing amidst the clutter and confusion of a complete makeover. The shop had been gutted. Since the fifties, it had belonged to a dealer in leather and sports goods and as Wyndham's it had become a fixed point on the Scarborough scene. There were not so many people left now who could remember a time before that. As Middleton's Millinery, its heyday had been in the years before the Second World War and it had lasted into the fifties when it had doubled as a fancy dress and theatrical costumier's under Mr Smedley, Aunt Constance's successor.

Aunt Constance was not Julianne's own great-aunt, but her father's, so they had never met, though she had heard a good deal about her. Among her run-of-the-mill Middleton and Cox forebears, Aunt Constance stood out as someone exceptional.

And now here was Jamie, Julianne's cousin on her mother's side, opening his cafe in the very same premises. After the lengthy interregnum of Wyndham's, it seemed a happy chance that he of all people should be taking the place over.

"My God, Jamie," exclaimed Julianne as she gazed about her, "are you ever going to get it straight?"

Jamie just smiled at her in that mildly indulgent, knowing kind of way of his.

"Aunt Constance would be turning in her grave if she could see all this mess."

"Just wait till it's finished. She's going to love it."

"I'm not so sure about that, though she was supposed to be a great fan of Italy, so Dad says. And anyway, what makes you say 'going to'?"

"Did you know the place was haunted?"

"Haunted? What, by Aunt Constance? Christ, Jamie, you didn't drag me all the way over to tell me that, did you?"

"In a manner of speaking." Jamie pointed at the ceiling and Julianne glanced at the naked light bulb. "Come with me."

He led the way to the back of the premises, stepping round sections of board, timber lathes and the other raw materials of the conversion. They went through a small room at the back into a little passage and onto a rickety staircase.

"Gosh, Jamie, this is exciting!" cooed Julianne sarcastically.

Jamie said nothing but continued on up from the first floor to the attic level. "Mind your head," he ordered her as they entered a low room with a black-leaded fireplace and a lot of old cardboard boxes. There appeared to be nothing else in the room and the roof skylight was thick with grime.

"Is this where you saw the ghost?" said Julianne.

"In a manner of speaking."

"Where is it now? Or I suppose I should say 'she'?"

Jamie chuckled – he enjoyed his cousin's banter.

"I must say, if I was Aunt Constance I wouldn't swop Italy for a tip like this."

Jamie answered by pulling aside a large piece of plywood to reveal a low cupboard set into a recess to the right of the fireplace. Julianne's eyes glinted with mock excitement. "The secret place. Gosh, Jamie, this is getting more like an Enid Blyton adventure story with every passing minute. It's more than I can take."

Jamie pulled at the cupboard door, which scraped painfully against the floor, as it wasn't used to being opened. There were shelves inside, which appeared to be empty, and there was a more generous space between the bottom one and the floor.

"Well?" said Julianne. "Is Aunt Constance in there?"

Without answering, Jamie reached into the cupboard, which appeared to go back a long way. He pulled out an object and placed it in front of Julianne before returning to remove a second one. Altogether, eight of them were lined up on the floor.

"Wow! These are fantastic," exclaimed Julianne.

What stood before her was a row of milliner's busts – the kind of thing that was used to display hats in a shop window. But these were no bland stereotypes, for each one was individual and appeared to be the likeness of a particular person. They were modelled – sculpted more like – in plaster, including the hair, which had been rendered in the styles of the thirties and forties. Despite a fairly generous coating of dust, Julianne could see that the features had been touched up with considerable delicacy.

"And these have been here ever since Aunt Constance's time?"

"It looks like it," said Jamie. "Wyndham's never seem to have found them. The plywood looks as if it was in place before they moved in. And they'd been pushed right to the back of the cupboard."

"These are real people," said Julianne. "It's creepy."

"You see what I mean by the place being haunted?"

"A real artist made these," went on Julianne. "There's a lot more to them than showing off hats. You could display them in your new bar."

"Except they don't belong to me," Jamie pointed out. "If anyone, they belong to you or your dad, as Aunt Constance's nearest kin."

"I wonder who they are and who made them," mused Julianne. "Maybe she did them herself."

"Apart from making hats, was she an artist?"

"I've no idea. Artistic certainly. Dad might know."

She picked up one of the busts. It was of a dark-haired girl, her hair in the style of the late forties and her lips the deep, clearly defined red of that time.

"She reminds me of a cover girl from one of those old magazines of the post-war era," said Jamie. "You know, *Picture Post* or *Illustrated*."

"She's still fresh," Julianne replied, running a finger down the slightly tilted nose. "If that's the right word."

She placed the bust on the floor and picked up another. "What do you make of this one?" Jamie looked at it thoughtfully. "Hmm."

It was of an older woman, well over forty by the look of her. Julianne cast her eye swiftly along the row of remaining busts. They were all of younger women.

"I can't swear to it without looking at a photograph, but I have a sort of hunch that this could be the Great Lady herself. Maybe you're right, Jamie. She has come back to haunt the place."

"There you are. What did I tell you?"

Julianne replied by sticking her tongue out at him – a trick of hers that Jamie enjoyed. She placed the bust on the little mantleshelf over the fireplace.

"Careful," Jamie warned her.

For a moment, neither of them spoke, but examined the object in silence. Then they turned their attention to the others.

Julianne shuddered slightly. "You know something? What they remind me of?"

"Go on. We'll see if we agree."

"Madame Tussaud's. Those guillotined heads."

"Trust you to come up with something morbid like that, Julie-A." Jamie eyed the busts critically. "I can't say I agree with you. They look too lively to me. Guillotined heads would look well and truly dead."

Each head was undeniably pretty and a smile seemed to be hovering on their lips, which gave them an added charm. Whoever had created them was no mean artist. They looked at each of them carefully in turn before putting them back in the cupboard.

"Constance never married," said Julianne. "I wonder …"

Jamie laughed. "It's a thought. But trust you to think along those lines."

Julianne replied by punching him.

"I'll ask Dad," said Julianne. "He must know something about her. I do know though that she was crazy about Italy."

Julianne did ask her father and he came to inspect the discovery for himself.

"This is quite like opening the tomb of Tutankhamen," he observed as Jamie reached into the cupboard to draw the treasures out. He looked at them all carefully but it didn't take him long to make up his mind about the older woman. "I only knew her in later life, but that's Aunt Constance all right. It's a pretty good likeness as a matter of fact."

"So the others could be pretty good likenesses as well?" ventured Julianne.

"Quite possibly."

"She was artistic," went on his daughter. "Did she make them herself?"

Her father shrugged. "I've never heard of her doing that sort of thing. I understood it was just hats. Oh, and some watercolours. But she certainly had a love affair with Italy."

"Was it the only one she had?" put in Jamie. "After all, she never married."

"I can't answer that one, I'm afraid," said Mr Middleton. "It was one of those things that simply wasn't talked about. You know what people were like then. I had an uncle," he went on, "You remember Uncle Edgar, don't you? A bachelor who spent most of his life in India. And I remember my parents being genuinely shocked when I once suggested that he might have sown his wild oats out there. 'Oh? Were there any?' my father replied in a frosty tone. But when I talked to Uncle Edgar at the beginning of his last illness he started to tell me all about the brothels that he and his chums used to frequent on the Hoogli. He'd never said a thing about them to anyone before. So who knows what Aunt Constance got up to – bearing in mind she belonged to a generation before Uncle Edgar – and was a woman."

For a moment, they gazed at the busts in slightly bemused admiration. "Miss Hicks," Mr Middleton said suddenly.

"Who's Miss Hicks, for Christ's sake?" said his daughter.

"Did I never tell you about Miss Hicks? Surely I've told you about Miss Hicks. Do you know Miss Hicks, Jamie?"

"Not from Adam. Or Eve for that matter."

"Miss Hicks worked for Aunt Constance – sewing, that kind of thing – and continued with Smedley when he took over the business after Constance died."

"And she's still alive?" said Julianne.

"She was when I last heard of her. Living in Osgodby. She might be able to enlighten us."

They were all beginning to feel the excitement of the chase and it was no great problem locating Miss Hicks, who was a pensioner living in a bungalow in Seafield Avenue in Osgodby on the south side of town.

Her house consisted of five small rooms leading directly off each other and, back in the thirties, it had been an unpretentious holiday home a short walk from the sea. Miss Hicks, though well over eighty, was as compact and neat as her little house, the shelf space and walls of which were filled with memorabilia. Glancing round the sitting room and looking at the old lady sitting up straight and alert in front of her, Julianne had the feeling that she ought to have been a character in a detective story. What with cupboards in old attics revealing their secrets after many years and bohemian Aunt Constance living a dream of Italy, the situation already had something of that quality about it. She could see Miss Hicks in the role of a retired theatre dresser with her head stuffed full of memories of the thespian greats she had once serviced.

"It was a terrible shock when Miss Middleton passed away in Italy," said Miss Hicks, speaking in a genteel voice with the merest trace of a North Riding accent. "You know, I can still feel it – as if it were yesterday. It came right out of the blue. Your people must have felt the same or even worse about it," she said to Julianne's father. "In fact, I know they did."

"I was really too young to remember much about it."

"I remember you very well – a good-looking young man you were too, in your burgundy blazer and grey flannel short trousers," reminisced Miss Hicks. She gave a little sigh.

"You know that Jamie Bartlett, Julianne's cousin, has taken the place over now that Wyndham's have closed?" said Mr Middleton. "This is Jamie, by the way."

"How do you do, Jamie? This is good news. It's nice to think of it coming back into the family after all these years, though of course, you aren't a Middleton. Your great-aunt was such a lively person – so full of beans," went on Miss Hicks, addressing Mr Middleton directly once more. "And it came as such a shock her going like that. That dreadful accident. But I don't suppose she knew much about it when it happened. And it was in Italy, which she adored and, of course, she was getting on by then. That must be a consolation of a sort." A bigger sigh this time.

She's too good to be true, thought Julianne. The perfect embodiment of the loyal factotum of someone like Aunt Constance. And I loved the bit about Dad in his burgundy blazer and grey flannel shorts.

"But Mr Smedley was marvellous," went on Miss Hicks. "Quite marvellous. He arranged everything. Such a dependable sort of man."

"Mr Smedley?" said Julianne. "You mean the man who took over from her?"

"Oh yes. He'd worked for Miss Middleton for a long time before that. They were boon companions. She hardly went anywhere – especially abroad – without him," explained Miss Hicks.

"Interesting," said Julianne. "You see, we've just found something rather curious in the attic of the shop."

"Oh?" Miss Hicks looked at her sideways with her bright little eye.

"Some heads."

"Heads! Good gracious!" exclaimed the old lady with a nervous giggle. "I hope they're not real ones."

"Nothing as exciting as that, Miss Hicks," said Julianne's father, "but jolly curious all the same. We wondered if you could cast some light on it."

"Plaster heads," supplied Julianne. "The sort of things that were used for displaying hats. But these ones are a bit special."

"And they're still there after all these years. Well, well." Another sigh from the old lady.

How wistful it all sounds, thought Julianne.

"Exactly so," said Jamie in response to Miss Hicks. "At the back of a cupboard that had been boarded up in the attic. Clearly, Wyndham's never even knew they were there."

"And beautifully modelled," Julianne supplied.

"That sounds like Mr Smedley's work," said Miss Hicks. "He was a very artistic man. That's really what he should have been. An artist." This time she didn't sigh but pointed to a photograph over the little bookshelf. "That's Mr Smedley. Look at his hands. He had such beautiful hands. An artist's hands."

They peered at the picture. It was taken in Venice with its subject standing on a bridge overlooking a canal. To modern eyes, he seemed oddly buttoned up, though judging by the cut of his clothes it looked as if the photograph had been taken shortly before the Second World War. He wore what looked like a pale grey flannel suit with all three jacket buttons done up, a bow tie and a stiff collar. The wide-brimmed hat, however, had a touch of loucheness about it, derived possibly from the contemporary cinema, like his pencil moustache. The carefully arranged handkerchief in the breast pocket, on the other hand, added rather a fussy note, at odds somehow with the bow tie and broad hat brim. It was as if his mother had arranged it that way for him after she had buttoned up his jacket, before packing him off to school. Yet a milliner's assistant from Scarborough would hardly be the first thing that sprang to the mind of anyone looking at a photograph of Mr Smedley.

"Miss Middleton took that picture," explained Miss Hicks. "It's my favourite one of him. It catches his artistic nature so well, I think. Of course, he was a very good photographer himself – as you might expect. Most of the pictures they brought back from their trips were his."

Julianne peered at the picture. "Did they go to Venice a lot together?" she asked.

"It was one of their favourite places," said the old lady. "That and Naples. I think it was Mr Smedley who introduced Miss Middleton to them in the first place. He was a well-travelled man."

"It's a bit odd," put in Jamie, "that a man of Mr Smedley's parts should have spent his days working as a milliner's assistant here in Scarborough, isn't it? Don't get me wrong," he added hastily to Miss Hicks.

"Exactly my thought too," said Julianne. "He should have studied at the Slade or the Royal Academy and moved up and on, shouldn't he?"

"Oh, he did study in one of those places," replied Miss Hicks. "But he never finished it. It was a question of money – and his mother was a widow. He had to get out and earn a living. Remember life could be very hard for people like him then."

"I'm sure that's true," said Julianne.

"And then he was so fond of Miss Middleton," went on Miss Hicks. "He worshipped her and they both had this passion for Italy."

"We certainly knew of it in her case," said Julianne's father. "But virtually nothing about Mr Smedley, I must confess. I think this is the first picture I've ever seen of him."

Miss Hicks gave what, for her, passed as a wicked smile. "I don't think her people entirely approved," she whispered. "I mean of them taking holidays together. You see, Mr Smedley was – how shall I put it – out of a lower drawer. People were very particular about those things then."

Dear Miss Hicks, thought Julianne. "Tell me, Miss Hicks," she resumed, "did Mr Smedley have a name? I mean one like Kevin or Bill?"

"I never heard anyone use one, though I suppose he must have done." There was a faint note of disapproval in Miss Hicks' voice as if it was too personal a matter to be touched upon.

And Julianne found herself wondering if Miss Hicks had ever been called anything else either. It would have been appropriate somehow if she hadn't because 'Miss Hicks' fitted her like a glove. More than that seemed superfluous.

"I tell you what," suggested Jamie. "If you're game, Miss Hicks, I'll drive you down to Huntriss Row tomorrow and you can see these heads for yourself. Just tell me a time that suits you."

"Goodness gracious, I don't think I've ventured there since Mr Smedley left, all those years ago," she shrilled with a clap of her hands.

"Then it's high time you paid a visit, Miss Hicks," insisted Julianne's father. "It's long overdue."

"Tomorrow afternoon?" said Jamie.

"Done," answered Miss Hicks.

"One thing," put in Julianne. "What happened to Mr Smedley? I don't suppose he's still alive, is he?"

Miss Hicks frowned, rather defensively she thought.

"She's studying to be a lawyer," explained Mr Middleton, "so she's always asking awkward questions."

"It's not an awkward question," replied Miss Hicks, "but I don't know the answer to it. My word, you must be a clever young lady if you're studying to be a lawyer! Not many girls do that, do they?"

"More than you think, Miss Hicks," said Julianne. "You'd be surprised."

"Yes, I suppose I would," answered the old lady.

"But tomorrow you'll come out of your retirement and visit Middleton's that once was," said Jamie. "Half past two? Don't be late, Miss Hicks, because I won't be. I'll be here on the dot."

And he was true to his word. Miss Hicks had even put on a Middleton hat for the occasion – a wide-brimmed affair in straw with a lilac ribbon.

"It was one of Mr Smedley's creations," she explained when Jamie congratulated her on it.

In Huntriss Row, they were met by Julianne and her father.

"I love the hat, Miss Hicks," said Julianne.

"Thank you," said Miss Hicks. "It was one of Mr Smedley's."

"I'm sorry about all the mess," Jamie apologised. "We're in the throes of a conversion."

"What's it going to be?" enquired Miss Hicks politely.

"An Italian bar," put in Julianne. "Something very cool and trendy."

"Oh," said a slightly mystified Miss Hicks. "Miss Middleton might have liked that."

"Are you all right with the stairs?" Jamie asked her as he led the way to the back of the premises.

"Of course I am. I've climbed them enough times before," retorted Miss Hicks. Her eye wandered over her surroundings as she tried to recapture them as they used to be in the piping days of Miss Middleton and Mr Smedley.

Once they were in the attic, Julianne's father provided Miss Hicks with a chair and Jamie placed himself before the cupboard door.

"Ready?" he said.

"Ready," replied Miss Hicks.

"Close your eyes, then," commanded Jamie.

"Oh dear, do I have to?" said the old lady.

"Of course you do."

She did as she was told while Jamie yanked the door back and it grated against the bare boards. Then he thrust his arm into the cupboard and drew forth a bust. He placed it on the floor before fishing out another one and placing it next to it.

"When am I allowed to open my eyes?" enquired Miss Hicks.

"When I tell you to," said Jamie. "Just bear with me a minute, Miss Hicks."

When all the busts had been set out to his satisfaction, he told her to open her eyes. Miss Hicks' mouth fell open.

"Good gracious," she exclaimed.

The others watched her, saying nothing.

"That's Miss Middleton," said Miss Hicks pointing to the bust in the middle. "It's her to a T."

"And this is the first time you've set eyes on it?" asked Julianne.

"It's the first time I've seen that one," declared the old lady. "My word, isn't it lifelike? But I do remember the others. They were used to display the hats in the window."

"So who made them?" put in Julianne's father.

"Mr Smedley, of course. Who else?" said Miss Hicks firmly. "That's why they look so real. He was so clever with his hands."

"What happened to Mr Smedley?" enquired Julianne, returning to her question of the day before which had not been properly answered.

"He went to America." The old lady emitted another of her wistful sighs.

"To America?" said Julianne and Jamie simultaneously.

"Why? Is that so surprising?" replied Miss Hicks with some asperity. "Remember, he was a much travelled man. And his talents were never properly appreciated here, in his own country. You know what they say about a prophet in his own country."

"Did you ever find out what happened to him over there?" asked Julianne's father.

"He sent me a couple of letters from New York and I got a Christmas card." Miss Hicks' jaw wobbled. "But then I'm sure that he was much too busy with his new life to think about me."

"Did he have friends in America?" enquired Julianne.

"I'm sure he must have done. But I don't really know. The two letters he sent me just told me about the wonderful things that he was seeing there. He seemed so excited. Like a little boy really."

"And then you heard no more?" said Mr Middleton.

"Apart from the Christmas card. That came from Chicago. I've still got it at home and the envelope it came in, if you'd like to see."

"And you've no idea what he did there? How he earned his living?" Julianne asked.

Miss Hicks shrugged her shoulders and shook her head. "Before he went he told me that he knew some artists there – friends he had made in Italy. I think he wanted to escape from hats and fancy dress and to be a real artist himself."

"Perfectly understandable," said Julianne.

"I confess I have never heard of him – if he ever made it," said Jamie, who thought he knew a bit about the post-war art scene in New York.

"And he certainly wouldn't have had time for boring old me." There was a faint hint of bitterness in Miss Hicks' voice – for the first time.

"He simply disappeared into God's Great Crucible – the melting pot of the nations," Julianne's father mused. "How many went to America and did just that?"

They fell silent and looked at the row of busts.

"Do you know any of the others?" Julianne asked Miss Hicks.

The old lady shook her head. "I believe they were Italian girls," she said. "That's what Mr Smedley told me. He and Miss Middleton had some sort of a studio out there, or knew somebody who did. He did a lot of his work there – where he felt inspired."

"And what about Aunt Constance?" put in Mr Middleton. "The family certainly haven't got anything like this to show for her days in Italy."

"I really wouldn't know," replied Miss Hicks. "I only ever saw the busts."

"Were there any more of them?" asked Jamie.

"Oh yes, I'm sure there were. He was making them and bringing them home over a period of what? Ten years."

"Crikey," said Jamie. "I wonder where they could have got to?"

Miss Hicks shrugged her shoulders. "He was such a wonderful artist," she sighed. "I would dearly like to believe that he finally became successful."

For a moment, no one spoke.

"Time for a cup of tea," said Mr Middleton. "I'm sure you're ready for one after all these questions, Miss Hicks. You've certainly earned it."

The old lady smiled. "What a good idea. You were always the perfect gentleman. I remember it so well."

Julianne smiled too. "In his burgundy blazer and grey flannel shorts, Miss Hicks?"

"And none the worse for that," retorted Miss Hicks.

They had tea in a cafe further up Huntriss Row before Jamie took the old lady home.

"Tell me about Aunt Constance's accident," Julianne asked her father as they strolled back to Belvedere Road." It was a warm evening in early summer with the softest southerly breeze. "She was knocked down by a mad Italian motorist, wasn't she?"

"In Rome," said her father. She had just come up from Naples and it happened outside the railway station."

"Was she by herself?"

"You know, I don't remember anything being said about that. But the name 'Naples' stuck in my young mind, and the railway station of course. That was all. And it all seemed so far away. Italy was still a bit like that in the fifties."

"When you were such a good-looking boy and the perfect gentleman in your burgundy blazer and grey flannel shorts?"

Mr Middleton smiled. "Dear Miss Hicks," he said. "She really is a gem, isn't she? But she seems to have forgotten the school cap – that was burgundy as well, but with yellow rings round it. I was terribly proud of that."

"It sounds very dashing, Dad. And Aunt Constance was buried in Italy?"

"Apparently, that's the way she wanted it. She'd made it clear in her will – if she died there, she was not to be shipped home. By that time, she was no chicken."

"And where was Mr Smedley when all this happened? Or should I say Albert?"

"Why Albert?"

"Because he looks like an Albert – despite his attempt to look raffish," said Julianne.

"I've simply no idea where he was at the time," replied her father. "I expect he arranged the funeral – if he was out there with her."

"Has anyone ever visited her grave?" asked Julianne.

"Your mother and I did once – when we were in Rome. It has quite a decent little headstone in the British cemetery there. It seems to have been properly done and bore a perfectly acceptable inscription, but nothing very memorable. Discreet, merely. Her dates and name, that's all. Perfectly tasteful."

They continued their walk in silence.

"So what are you going to do with the busts, Dad? After all, they're yours," said Julianne at length.

"Jamie can have them for his whatsit – Italian bar."

"They would add an appropriate touch of continuity, certainly."

They had crossed the Spa Bridge and were ascending to the Esplanade when Julianne spoke again.

"I'd dearly like to know more about Mr Smedley, Dad. I'm a bit surprised that no one in the family ever mentioned him – when they talked about Aunt Constance, I mean."

"Perhaps it was as Miss Hicks said. They were prodigious snobs in those days and Mr Smedley was – well – below the salt."

"But surely, Dad, a milliner in a place like Scarborough was nothing very special either."

"True, but people are seldom very rational about these things, are they?"

"He fascinates me. So artistic, apparently, and yet I keep wanting to call him Albert."

"There you go, my girl, you're every bit as bad as your Middleton and Cox forebears." Julianne stuck her tongue out at her father, who, like cousin Jamie, enjoyed the way she did it.

And there the matter seemed to rest – for the time being at least. Jamie completed the Italian bar and placed the busts at suitable points round it, closely advised by Julianne. He had given the place a thirties ambience, which they fitted in with very well. There was some discussion about what should be done with the bust of Aunt Constance – whether she ought to be included with the others or to take up residence in Belvedere Road – but it was decided that, as she was the genius loci of the place in Huntriss Row, she should remain there for the time being at least. As for her companions, no one had the remotest idea who they were – probably just Italian girls as Miss Hicks had suggested.

The old lady was brought down to inspect the completed scene and, though the delights of an Italian bar eluded her, she pronounced the display of busts very tasteful.

"Mr Smedley would be pleased," she declared. "And it would have been recognition of a sort, at least."

Jamie had even named the place the Constanza and, with the lady herself looking proudly out from behind the bar into the Italianate setting, it seemed an ideal memorial to Aunt Constance and, moreover, to provide an historical continuum into which the period of Wyndham's seemed a rude intrusion. If she haunted the place, it was as a benign tutelary deity. A smile playing about her lips, she radiated a serene contentment as she presided over the cafe clientele enjoying themselves in the Italian manner.

No one enthused about Aunt Constance's new tenure more than Julianne did.

"She was a cunning old bird," she told her cousin, "hiding all that time in the attic cupboard until her time came round again. And yet …" a note of doubt crept into her voice.

"And yet what?" said Jamie.

"I can't help thinking about those other ones – the so-called Italian girls – and who they were. Were they the Neapolitan poor, children of the slums posing to make a little money? Modelling was often a wretched business, you know. They may well have been prostitutes."

Jamie shrugged. "Who knows and so what? They look happy enough now. Not a bit like the guillotined heads you once compared them with"

"No." Julianne frowned. "And there's Albert."

"Albert? You mean Mr Smedley?" Jamie laughed.

"It's just that buttoned-up look he has in Miss Hicks' photograph. We really know nothing about him, do we?"

"Maybe it's better that way."

"I'd dearly like to know how they all fit together."

"You know something, Julie-A? You're doing just the right thing."

"Oh?"

"I mean by becoming a lawyer. You must make crime your speciality."

"Do you really think so?"

"Yes I do. You assume that there's an unpleasant secret lurking behind every smile."

And, in a way, that seemed to match the discovery of Aunt Constance and her companions in the attic cupboard, the affair took an unexpected lurch forward.

The Italian bar took off and, in a flippantly superstitious way, Jamie put its success down to the benign influence of its resident goddess. Her smile, which radiated from the shelf above the counter, was so commanding, yet reassuring. But it was Julianne who decided to mark the first anniversary of the opening with a brief ceremony celebrating Aunt Constance. By now, the cafe was attracting a regular clientele, so a number of these were invited to its birthday party with the first drinks on the house and a mountain of Italian delicacies to go with them.

The climax of the evening was to be the crowning of Aunt Constance with a garland of summer flowers put together by Julianne herself. She had thought of asking Miss Hicks to do it, but in the end had decided against it because, inevitably, there was an element of lightheartedness about the occasion, of which she was not sure that the old lady would entirely approve even if she was still up to it.

The turnout was good and the Tuscan wine was flowing when Julianne called the company to order for the coronation ceremony. Indeed, she had to raise her voice to make herself heard above the hubbub, while Jamie perched himself on a stool, ready to place the garland round the neck of the goddess. He was rather flushed and not a little giggly, delighted with how the evening had gone so far and the entire year that the Constanza had been in business as well.

He had thought of making a speech but, at Julianne's suggestion, had ruled it out. Instead, he ordered the recharging of glasses and a toast, or 'libation' as he preferred to call it, in honour of Aunt Constance. Glasses were raised and everyone called out "Aunt Constance!" one guest even adding facetiously "and all who sail in her!"

And then it happened. The thing that probably was fated to happen. As he was placing the wreath round the neck of the bust, Jamie slipped on his stool. He was tipsy and the wreath was a tighter fit than had been anticipated, requiring a little pressure to get it over the bridge of Aunt Constance's nose. There was a gasp and in some quarters a low shriek as Jamie fell bringing the bust down with him.

He was unhurt, his fall broken by the bar, but Aunt Constance wasn't. For the face of the bust had sheered clean away and, instead of the serene smile of a presiding goddess, there was the all-too-mortal leer of a skull.

It was a shocking revelation, but one Julianne was not entirely surprised by and, quite naturally, she wanted to know what lay behind the plaster features of the other busts as well. Needless to say, her suspicions were confirmed. Classical Roman castes from the British Museum took the place of the original ones in the cafe, which, despite the scandalous discovery, remained The Constanza.

Miss Hicks, who by now had retreated from the little house in Osgodby to a nursing home, was never told. When Julianne went with her father to see her, no one even mentioned Mr Smedley. Instead, the old lady looked fondly at Mr Middleton and gave one of her little sighs. "Such a nice young gentleman you were."

"In his burgundy blazer and grey flannel shorts, Miss Hicks?" said Julianne.

"Indeed," the old lady replied. "Just so."

"But you've forgotten the school cap, haven't you, Miss Hicks? That was burgundy too, with lovely yellow rings round it," protested Julianne's father. "I was frightfully proud of that cap. As a milliner you surely can't have forgotten it, can you?"

14   The Fall of the Roman Empire

"I'm not sure it's such a good idea," said Mirabel. "You know the kind of things that have been said about him."

"But he's expecting us, Bel, and it won't be for very long," Peregrine replied. "And anyway, I want to see the place."

"You may well do," retorted his wife, "but it's the kids I'm thinking about."

"You're getting a bit stuffy in your old age, aren't you, Bel? They'll probably be more amused than anything. I mean at the sight of Uncle Orlando dressed up as a Roman. And it'll be good for their education as well since we've kept them out of school for this trip. Then we'll be off. He's probably quite harmless, a bit dotty, perhaps, but hardly a dangerous paedophile – if that's what's bothering you. It's the witch-craze of our time – assuming that anyone who's a bit offbeat is a menace to children."

"You're the head of the family and they're your kids," said Mirabel sarcastically.

"You know that's not what I meant, Bel. We don't have to stay longer than five minutes if it doesn't smell right. And anyway …"

"You want to see the place."

"Yes, I do rather."

"Be it upon your head then."

Peregrine kissed his wife.

Peregrine and Mirabel Crocker had spent three days in Lucca with a couple of bored kids, Will and Naomi, gazing up at Romanesque facades among other cultural delights. But after a rebellious outburst in a restaurant on the third evening, which had annoyed the other customers, they had decided to move on and look up Peregine's brother in his villa a day or two earlier than planned.

For several years there had been only minimal communication between the Crocker siblings, whose lives had taken sharply divergent paths. Orlando was older than his brother by ten years – Peregrine was very much an afterthought, with their sister Emerald coming between the two boys. Word filtered through to Peregrine from time to time via the occasional mutual friend who visited his brother in his Tuscan retreat but, for the most part, their communication was reduced to Christmas cards with brief, scrappy messages. Orlando's last one consisted of a picture of himself kitted out like a Roman emperor, in profile with a "sunburst" crown on his head.

Orlando, while in many ways something of a traditionalist and a fogey, had always been considered the family screwball, which his sister Emerald put down to his being given a name like Orlando. He had surprised them all, however, having hardly had a girlfriend in his life, by marrying in his early thirties an American property tycoon's daughter quite a bit older than himself. It had left the normally voluble Crockers lost for words. And then, after seven years of marriage, he had managed to lose his partner in a road accident and, being childless and the heir to her share of her family's millions, had settled into a mode of existence that enabled him to indulge his curious fancies exactly as he pleased.

Back in the nineteen-eighties, it was good to have a fortune to play with and not to have to work for it. From an aesthetic viewpoint, Orlando found his own times distasteful and to have the opportunity of shutting them out of his existence as far as possible was irresistible. So he went ahead with a fine disregard for anyone else's opinions on the matter. His late wife's family had been bemused by Beatrice finally settling down with a guy like Orlando – while, at the same time, mildly flattered by what they considered to be his upper class polish – but interestingly, they had never thought of him as a gold-digger. He was a dreamy kind of fellow who had struck a chord with Beatrice's own whimsical nature just at a time when most of her generation were finally coming to their senses and she was expected to do the same. She had been a flower person back in the sixties, but since then her tastes and style of life had mutated into something more modernist while Orlando's remained stubbornly rooted in the world of classical antiquity. Outwardly, he looked conservative – if anything, like a mildly poetic young schoolmaster of the fifties, if such a concept is not too paradoxical – with an untidy mop of blond hair, a trim figure and leather patches on the elbows of a decently cut tweed jacket.

Needless to say, he had been inspired by a classics master at his public school, while feeling perfectly at home under its Spartan regime at the same time. Both things had blended with a romantic imagination to give him his own very particular neo-classical outlook on life. Such was the brother who now contrived to live the life of an upper class Roman ...

It was a shimmering day of high summer when the Tuscan countryside was drained of the more subtle tones, which are one of the glories of Quatracento painting. As the people carrier climbed the winding road to the villa, Peregrine and Mirabel tried to explain to their children that despite Uncle Orlando being a bit odd, they were under no circumstances to tell him so directly.

"In what way is he odd?" enquired Will.

"Well, for a start," said Peregrine, "he'll probably be dressed up like a Roman. But I've explained that to you already"

"Is he a nutter?"

"No, I don't think so. He just likes pretending to be a Roman."

"Does he wear a toga? The same as Julius Caesar?"

"What's a toga?" Naomi, who had just broached seven, demanded to know.

"A costume that Roman men used to wear – a kind of robe, a bit like being wrapped in a sheet," supplied her father. "But no, he probably doesn't wear a toga. A tunic more likely. Not such a bad idea in this heat, as a matter of fact."

There was a small stand of cypress trees near the gates of the villa and, as they drew up, the noise of cicadas rushed to meet them. Peregrine sounded his horn. There was no reply so Mirabel jumped out and opened the gates. The hinges were rusty and protested painfully, which gave her the feeling that it was something that hadn't happened for some time.

Then they drove up the short sweep of drive into the courtyard of what had once been a farm. It was shady and cool in front of the house, which had been refashioned as a Roman villa.

"Because he wanted to live like a Roman, he rebuilt his house to look like one of theirs," Peregrine explained.

"How did he know what Roman houses looked like?" asked Will. "There aren't any of them left, are there?"

In the south there are," said his father. "Remember what I told you about Pompeii and Herculaneum – how the houses there were buried under the ash when Vesuvius erupted. We'll see those places sometime."

They sat in the car for a minute having sounded the horn once more, and waited for someone to emerge from the house. Silence reigned, apart from the rattle of the cicadas – not even the sound of a solitary bird.

"I'm dying to see Uncle Orlando dressed up as a Roman," declared Naomi. "Look, there's a cat."

Sure enough, a lean-looking tabby cat slunk from under the colonnaded porch and loped off into the bushes near the entrance to the yard.

"I didn't tell you about Uncle Orlando's cats," said Peregrine. "He's supposed to be almost as mad about them as he is about the Romans. Well, there's no point hanging about here, is there? We'd better see if anyone's at home."

He climbed out of the car and went to the double door behind the colonnade where he turned the big ring handle. He gave the door a push but it didn't budge. He banged on the panels, producing a hollow reverberation on the inside. There was no reply, so he repeated the performance three more times.

There doesn't seem to be anyone about," Mirabel called from the car.

"Someone must be here, surely. He was supposed to have a large household – quite the Roman gent. With all his money he could afford it," said her husband.

He stood back in the courtyard. "Hullo? Anyone at home?" he shouted at the house in Italian.

Only silence. He glanced round the courtyard. "Come to think of it, the place doesn't look as if it's been swept for months." He called again. "It's almost two months since I told him we might be paying him a visit. He may have forgotten. Perhaps we should have reminded him nearer the time."

Mirabel got out of the car and joined him. "Stay where you are," she ordered the children. "It's funny," she went on, "but I had the feeling that the place might be empty when we arrived."

"Maybe they're all out somewhere," said Peregrine, scuffing his feet in the dust. "But you may be right, darling, it does look as if they haven't been around for some time."

"Abandoned ship?" said Mirabel. She turned to the children in the back of the car.

"Alas, you're out of luck, kids. You may not be seeing your Uncle Orlando dressed up like a Roman after all."

"But I saw that cat," insisted Naomi. "So there must be someone here."

"Good thinking, my child," said Peregrine. "I'll see if there's a way in at the back."

This meant going out of the courtyard and onto the terraced walk at the side of the villa. The beds were parched and the grass running to seed. The others trailed after Peregrine. "Hullo!" he called out again. "Is anyone there?"

The back could have been the work of Alma Tadema, the nineteenth century painter of Roman genre scenes. It was terraced in marble with benches set in alcoves at suitable vantage points, overlooking stands of cypress trees and wisteria and vine-festooned walkways. But, like a barbarian army, the weeds were on the march and the beds dried out. Inexorably, it was sliding into a wild state.

"This hasn't been touched for a while," said Mirabel. "It's a shame. It's a beautiful garden."

"The Fall of the Roman Empire," mused her husband. "Let's see if there's a way in."

A door leading onto the upper terrace was firmly shut and, indeed, seemed to have been wedged on the inside. A couple of windows were shuttered.

"Why not climb over the wall, Dad?" suggested Will.

His father looked at the tiled roof of the rooms at the back of the villa.

"Don't do anything daft," Mirabel warned him. "We don't want you breaking a leg – or your neck, for that matter."

Peregrine stood back. "Clearly, there's no one here and we're not meant to get in," he said.

"There was that cat," Naomi reminded him. "Look, there's another one."

Sure enough, what looked like a Persian, its long coat a knotted mess, appeared on the tiles. It glared at them with wild eyes, baring its fangs.

"Wherever Orlando has got himself to, his cats are at home," said Mirabel. "But hardly in the best of condition, by the look of them. This one looks distinctly feral."

Peregrine decided to have another go at the door and hurled himself at it. Suddenly it gave way and he landed in a heap on the other side.

"Have you hurt yourself?" Mirabel called after him anxiously.

"Nothing that won't mend," he replied, picking himself up. "Anyway, we're in. You'd better wait here."

"Do be careful," urged his wife. "It looks a bit spooky to me."

"Spooky?" said Naomi anxiously.

"A Roman ghost in a bloody toga?" suggested her brother. "I mean a bloodstained one, of course."

"Not literally spooky," said Mirabel. "It's just that when a house has been empty for some time it feels a bit that way, that's all."

Peregrine advanced into a little garden surrounded by a peristyle. The vegetation was already invading the colonnade, climbers twisting themselves round its Ionic columns. In a patch of sunlight, two lean cats were stretched out licking their paws.

Peregrine crossed to the far side of the peristyle where there was a big double door leading into the main body of the villa. An architect himself, he had an idea of the layout of the building, being familiar with the plans of various villas at Pompeii – which had inspired architects working in the neo-classical style in the eighteenth and nineteenth centuries as well as his brother. The big bronze door opened readily enough, though not without complaining.

It was the smell that he first noticed: the trace of something that not long before had been very much stronger. It reminded him of a Camembert cheese that had started to dry out. The dim interior was illuminated by a shaft of sunlight falling through the light well of an atrium at the centre of the building's axis. Everywhere he looked there was a mess of smashed furniture, its coverings in shreds, scattered marble and mosaic tesserae, broken vases and fragments of dismembered sculpture.

"The Fall of the Roman Empire." Peregrine repeated the idea out loud to himself again. But that tart, lingering, smell ... He advanced further into the house ... then rapidly retreated. He dragged a wing of the big double door back behind him, but as he did so, a cat that had been shut up inside the house darted out between his legs into the sunshine where it yawned and stretched itself out on the warm pavement. It began to lick its rich golden coat, which was stained with something dark and congealed ... But unlike the others, it looked sleek and well fed.

*****

Orlando Crocker had first become fascinated by the works of Laurence Alma Tadema, the nineteenth century painter of ancient genre scenes, when, as a boy, he came across them serving as illustrations in an encyclopedia. Later on, he had discovered the real thing and bought himself a lavish coffee table book that did some justice to their meticulous beauty. The archaeological exactness and sensuous rendering of surface textures, above all of marble, appealed to him just as they had done to the artist's original public. The authentic, scrupulously-researched detail, the sense of a different world in its entirety beyond the bounds of the picture – aided, in part, by the use of a "cut-off' effect that gave the paintings something of the quality of photographs – conjured up an alternative existence in the mind of an impressionable young man – one that he would have preferred to his own. Above all, perhaps, rather than the interiors, it was the outdoor scenes set in the mid-afternoon of a Campanian summer that attracted him most.

    At Oxford he had read Greats and hung colour prints on his walls. At the same time he had been a keen oarsman and had trained his body hard, though he was never really a man's man in the strict sense. His love of the arts – especially those of classical antiquity – had distanced him from the usual male bonding rituals, as did his comparative indifference to women. Not that he was manifestly gay. There was nothing camp about Orlando. In many ways he would have been an ideal schoolmaster, though possibly one a couple of decades before his own time. Yet it was a route he chose not to take: it was something he set aside as a possibility for later in life after he had spread and tested his wings in a wider world first.

Orlando made no claims to scholarship – he was never going to write a doctoral thesis – but his love of things aesthetic was serious. His degree was a lower second – something that was sniffed at as being worse than a third, which at least had a cache of loucheness about it – but he had friends who could open doors for him in the world of the fine arts. One was an Oxford friend, Edmund Hopkirk, with whom he took himself off one long vacation on a grand tour in the eighteenth century manner, a journey through Gaul, Spain, the Roman provinces of North Africa and, of course, Italy. There was something engagingly old-fashioned about this pair of handsome English undergraduates exploring the works of classical antiquity together.

And it was through Edmund that Orlando met Oswald Freeman-Attwood, a London dealer in mostly nineteenth century paintings and prints, who decided that he was sufficiently knowledgeable and keen, as well as looking and sounding presentable enough, to be "given a whirl'.

But Orlando did not feel entirely happy in the cut and thrust world of marketing works of art. He felt it diminished them, and the element of Spartan austerity that was a part of his character disdained anything so mercenary. At the same time, he dreaded the prospect of an Alma Tadema coming his way and being forced to sell it on to who-knows-what kind of a buyer. In a way, selling beautiful things was like being engaged in the slave trade. Not that he didn't want them for himself, of course – but to be placed in the setting of his ideal classical world, one that combined a Stoic sense of discipline with the taste of Maecenas.

Then, one day, he bumped into Beatrice Flynn – quite literally, as they both happened to be in the Uffizi looking at Botticelli's *Adoration of the Magi* at the same moment when she stepped back for a fuller view of the picture and stood on Orlando's toe. The resemblance of the young Englishman to the artist's self-portrait in the painting was striking. Indeed, it was one that had occurred to Orlando himself and possibly the thing that kept drawing him back to the picture.

"God," exclaimed Beatrice after apologising, "you might have stepped out of the picture!"

Orlando felt flattered that someone else had noticed it and was willing to tell him so. Despite his fair-haired good looks, he was not a lady's man, but he found himself immediately warming to Beatrice and her lively and apparently spontaneous attitude to works of art, which seemed miles away from the sneery, pretentious kind he had come, perhaps unfairly, to associate with the trade. They had lunch together and, before they separated, Beatrice had invited him to her home near Pisa – a converted Tuscan farmhouse that had belonged to her family for a couple of generations.

The house had a fine view towards the Tuscan hills from a terrace that had been added at the back. The rooms, which were high and airy, Beatrice was busy transforming into a more modernist style. Italian Futurists and an early Picasso were among its highlights – a taste not shared by Orlando, but not too far removed from his own ideas of classical purity. Her enthusiasm was infectious and her apparently sympathetic understanding of his aesthetic proclivities aroused in him uncharacteristically warm feelings towards her.

And, if the truth be told, Orlando basked in the friendship of someone who owned such beautiful things. Money had never been in great supply in the Crocker family. Beatrice had the house all to herself, she assured him, since her brother, who had a share in it, never came there.

"He's such a bloody philistine," she told Orlando, "and doesn't give a damn about this place. He spends half his life in business meetings in the States and the other half living what he likes to think of as a Scott Fitzgerald kind of existence on the French Riviera. It's not bit like that now, of course – but it's fine if it means leaving the joys of Tuscany to me."

Both Beatrice's parents were dead despite her only being in her mid thirties, but there were various cousins and an aunt or uncle or two who made occasional visits to Italy. All this was explained to Orlando. At the same time, she was terribly rich, owning, as she did, a very sizeable chunk of Flynn real estate in the Californian Sunbelt where she disdained to live. She seemed to enjoy having her cake and eating it at the same time. To Orlando, she appeared interestingly pre-war, even though she felt inclined to cherry-pick from her sixties past when it suited her.

But Orlando, she sensed, was not a sixties person – he seemed to pre-date the permissive society and she liked him for it. He fitted in rather snugly with her own emerging preferences for what had gone before the great liberation. And then there was his name.

"I adore the name Orlando," she trilled. "Whoever thought of giving you one like that?"

"I guess it was my parents. There aren't any others in the family that I know of."

"It slips off the tongue so beautifully: Orlando Crocker. Perfect."

Orlando nodded. She was quite right – he couldn't think of a better name for himself either.

And so the relationship built up – with remarkable speed. Orlando gave up his job – a reckless move, according to his family – and settled into a life with Beatrice – all within three months of that first encounter in the Uffizi. It was a curious relationship – based more on mutual aesthetic appreciation than anything very sexual. But Orlando, who normally felt rather threatened by women, was perfectly at ease with this one, especially as she took his ideas seriously. And as for Beatrice, if she occasionally let her eyes wander in other directions it didn't matter to Orlando. Sexual jealousy seemed to be foreign to his nature. Together they made a hospitable and interesting couple in the sort of circles they both enjoyed moving in.

And there was the money – bags of it. Orlando greatly enjoyed the access he had to the Flynn millions, which Beatrice managed to make available to him without letting him feel that he was a kept man. Discretion was a quality she possessed in bucketfuls, not least in the case of the man she elected to live with. Not that she needed much of it with Orlando – he enjoyed the opportunities she provided without a great deal of soul-searching. Orlando was not sybaritic – he was no seeker after luxury – the austerity of the English public school had been engrained in his psyche – but the chance to pursue an aesthetic vision with unlimited means at his disposal, that was another thing altogether. While he interfered little with the inside of the house, they came to an agreement that the garden was to be Orlando's to do with as he liked. He had visited a number of famous Italian gardens, but it was the Campanian vision of Alma Tadema that he was determined to bring to life. Above all, he wanted to indulge his love of marble, the creamy-white substance of the paintings, which amounted almost to a lust – if such a word could be applied to Orlando. He took his time: visiting museums, acquiring photographs, even making his own drawings, as well as consulting masons. He visited the famous Carrara quarries that had supplied

Michelangelo and arranged for a shipment of roughly dressed stone. That was why it was good to have loads of money.

Beatrice was generally supportive. A Roman terraced garden did not offend her own ideas in the least and the clean lines of well-dressed marble rather appealed to her. They sat well with Italian Futurism – a view shared by the dictator Mussolini – and she continued to buy her own pictures and pieces of sculpture while her partner set about reordering the garden with a team of young men – a not disagreeable feature of the enterprise.

It seemed an ideal arrangement with no openings for conflict. Each kept to his or her own and seemed to take pleasure in what the other provided. It was the way civilised people ought to arrange their lives – assuming that they had the means of doing it. And yet ... inside Orlando something gnawed: his longing for the world of Alma Tadema was not going to end in a perfectly re-created Roman garden. It was bigger than that, and the seed had been growing since those far-off childhood days when he had sat with the already old-fashioned encyclopedia on his knees and peered into another universe, one where he felt he truly belonged.

And then Beatrice was killed. It came out of the blue, of course, but considering the way she drove, it was not entirely surprising. As a devotee of the thirties, she loved speed – the sort associated with fast cars and streamlined railway trains. She drove an old Lamborghini much too fast, despite Orlando's warnings, but she wasn't driving that when she died. Instead, she was on her way into Pisa in her runabout Fiat when she shot off the road on a sharp bend. Her demise was said to have been instant, though Orlando was duly devastated and needed all the stoicism he could muster to hold back the tears at her graveside.

Several members of her family came out to Italy for the funeral, though none of Orlando's, of course. He met Beatrice's brother, Jefferson, for the first time, who was amiable enough, taking a sober, "I-always-thought-it-might-happen-one-of-these-days" attitude to his sister's demise. It was clear that they had never been close but without any particular animosity between them. They had agreed to differ and had gone their separate ways. Jefferson was married with two teenage sons – a pair of preppy American boys whom Orlando, when he met them, dressed like athletic young Romans in short tunics with naked limbs in his mind's eye.

And then when Beatrice's will was opened came the big surprise. She had left her entire share of the Flynn family fortune to Orlando. He was flabbergasted. Beatrice had never discussed sordid matters like wills and, in a way, he was surprised that she had even got round to making one, let alone include him in it. But include was scarcely the word. She had left the whole lot to him.

His amazement – and, indeed, embarrassment – registered favourably with the Flynns who had so much money anyway that it would have been difficult to begrudge him Beatrice's share. The fact that he showed a positive, rather schoolmasterly, interest in Jefferson's two boys probably helped too.

Beatrice, of course, had not been the sole owner of the house in Tuscany, but again, there were no problems. Jefferson allowed himself to be bought out, though he was not over-generous, which suited Orlando who, despite everyone being so reasonable, still felt a bit of an interloper.

But now the house was his to do with as he pleased. In his wildest dreams he had never envisaged such a situation arising in his life. And he wasted no time. The ex-public schoolboy who looked back with feelings of nostalgia to the time of wholesome austerity, as he perceived it, of his own schooldays, which had been blended with a love of classical antiquity, given visual expression in the works of the nineteenth century painter Alma Tadema, realised that he was one of those uniquely privileged human beings who possessed the means of bringing his personal dream to life. He had no false modesty about it. If anyone was to be favoured by fortune, it was fitting that it should be him. Wealth should be in the hands of those rare spirits whose refined sensibilities would see it put to the best possible use.

He wasted no time. The garden, which had been virtually completed when his wife died, was rounded off and then he addressed the house itself. Orlando had long been pouring over plans and photographs of Roman villas at Pompeii and Herculaneum where the best-preserved examples could be found, and he had even considered a reconstruction of Pliny the Younger's famous villa at Laurentum, but decided that it would be too speculative. He wanted to be on surer archaeological ground, while the interiors of Alma Tadema were his most obvious source of inspiration. So, with the help of an architect friend of his brother Peregrine, he set about recreating the House of the Silver Wedding from Pompeii. He approached his task with the same thoroughness that the nineteenth century painter had himself put into his work – except that this was to be a complete Roman house, not simply a picture of one.

The original house had to be taken down in stages as the new one took its place. Orlando, with his architect, a classicist in the traditional mould, went about it paying attention to the smallest details. For example, traditional Roman bricks were specially commissioned and only cement prepared according to the ancient recipe could be used. The stucco that was applied to the walls was mixed according to an ancient formula as well, while wall paintings and mosaics were based on ancient patterns. It seemed as if most of the museum restorers of Tuscany were involved in the enterprise at one time or another. Indeed, the opportunity of making a completely faithful replica of a Roman villa was irresistible to many of them – not to mention the handsome fee that went with it. Despite this, the word kitsch was bandied about in some quarters, but Orlando didn't care.

Some of Orlando's friends, met through his late wife, were inevitably dubious about the enterprise, especially those who shared her modernist leanings, seeing it as a betrayal, but they were intrigued by the experiment nevertheless. They sneered that the thing was tacky and too redolent of the big screen, yet were still eager to see how it turned out.

Most of the time the villa was being built, Orlando lived on the site and it was then that he started to affect Roman dress – tunics made from linen or light wool and sandals designed specially for him by one of his museum experts. He had his hair cut in Roman fashion too, though, as yet, he eschewed the laborious business of shaving in the ancient manner. Later, perhaps, he would arrange for a slave to do that.

After more than three years work, the villa was virtually completed and Orlando tentatively set about living in it as he thought a Roman aristocrat might have done. It was entered through a wide porch leading into an atrium with an open skylight over a pool, which collected rainwater. A series of rooms ran along each side with a dining room, or tablinium, at the far end. A pair of bedrooms were arranged on each flank while beyond, a big double door led onto a peristyled courtyard with a kitchen and slaves" quarters on three sides of the cloister. Ionic columns supported the roof of pantiles surrounding the planted space with its terracotta urns in the middle. A door at the far end led out onto the terrace, which overlooked Orlando's garden.

Not that Orlando could go the whole way, of course. A Roman bathhouse was under construction behind the villa, but when it was completed it would need slaves to service it, and anyway, Orlando liked his cold shower first thing in the morning with a hot bath at the end of the day – and a modern lavatory, needless to say. So one of the rooms off the courtyard was given over to these while the kitchen provided him with wholesome Italian fare, though, in due course, he thought he would experiment with some Roman recipes. For the time being, he cheated with electric light too – one room leading from the dining area, designated his bedroom, was fitted with a modern reading lamp – otherwise the place was to be lit and heated in the Roman manner – even with an under-floor hypocaust, should he feel the need for central heating. But, as far as the latter went, Orlando had decided to make his life as a Roman a strictly seasonal affair – something for the spring and summer months – and to take off elsewhere for the winter.

Slaves were vital to the running of a substantial Roman villa and this is where the schoolmaster in Orlando at last came into his own: in the summer months, when he was in residence, he decided he would offer the authentic Roman experience to keen young classicists and others of that inclination who were prepared to accept the authority of the master of the household. It was to be a strictly boys only thing, however, with its roots in the Spartan Utopia of his own schooldays. In a nutshell, it was to be an English public school dressed up in Alma Tadema's clothes.

Orlando did his homework carefully, reading everything he could lay his hands on about Roman domestic life – disregarding its womenfolk, it went without saying, yet attempting to draw up a blueprint for life as it might have been lived in a Roman villa at the same time. It was to be no mere costume frolic under the Italian sun, however – there was real work to be done: in the garden, laying out an orchard and creating a vegetable garden, as well as the day-to-day running of the house.

A steward – he did not quite like to say slave master – who could also supply him with willing young men would have to be found – on the face of it, a daunting task, but Orlando had money and was ready to pay whatever it cost.

In fact, he found what he was looking for in Lucca with astonishing speed. It was a place he had grown very fond of in Beatrice's time. What he wanted was a man, probably in his late twenties or early thirties, who could command the obedience of men younger than himself and, if possible, supply them. Orlando was cautious about advertising his scheme too brazenly, fearing that people might get the wrong idea about him. To turn art into life was what he wanted – or at least, that is what he told himself.

What caught his eye was not an Italian but a German whom he saw in one of the outdoor cafes in the Arena. He was with another young man, but with much less pleasing looks than his. Germans and slaves – they went well together in the Roman context. Blond German slaves … he fancied that idea, just as many Roman aristocrats – including the emperor Tiberius – had done.

He looked at the two young men. They might have been mature students, not all that long out of university. Orlando settled at the table next to them and eyed them more closely. One was certainly nothing to look at, but the other, the fair one …

"God, what would Beatrice make of me now?" he suddenly asked himself. But what the hell. She had probably worked it out anyway. Though it was strange, he reflected, that he had never discussed such things with her despite her apparent openness to anything. He admired her for that – taking him the way he was and respecting his likely hang-ups. She was an altogether remarkable woman.

Orlando knew just a little German and could only catch snatches of the conversation. He realised that he would have to break into it when, no doubt, he would find that like most young men of their kind they would speak English. He decided to take the bull by the horns.

He spoke to them in English and they replied in the same language. When they learned that he lived in the country and wasn't another tourist like themselves, they invited him to join them.

"I'm Orlando," he said.

"Lothar," replied the blond boy. "My friend is Ernst."

"Pleased to meet you. You speak good English," said Orlando.

Lothar shrugged. "Of course."

"I'm afraid my German is pretty poor, but I get along well enough in Italian." Something Orlando proceeded to demonstrate by ordering a fresh round of coffees.

Lothar's blond thatch came low across his forehead. He was a trifle on the plump side, but not disagreeably so, sturdily built, if anything. His eyes were an intense cornflower blue. A good Nordic specimen, Orlando decided, knowing that he really oughtn't to be thinking things like that. Ernst was a different kettle of fish: dark, lean, narrow-featured, a sharp academic face –hardly a tribal warrior of the Teutoberg Wald.

Both young men were intrigued when Orlando told them about the villa and took little persuading to go back with him to see it. They both knew their Roman history and had time on their hands – a leisurely two months of travel together stretched ahead of them.

And, on the drive back, Orlando made another discovery: Ernst was to return to Munich to complete his degree in the new semester, but Lothar had already finished his and was hoping to extend his travelling time before settling down to the inevitable German doctoral thesis.

Orlando's mind raced at fever pitch. Lothar was sitting beside him in the passenger seat with Ernst in the back. He and the young German next to him exchanged an occasional glance, which seemed to say more than words might have done, but as yet, Orlando didn't quite know what. Meanwhile, he told him about Beatrice and then his fascination for the works of Alma Tadema.

"Have you ever heard of him?" he asked Lothar, expecting a reply in the negative.

"Of course." It seemed that knowledge of the Anglo-Dutch painter was something that any civilised young European with more than a passing interest in art ought to possess.

"What do you think of him?" Orlando went on.

Lothar shrugged without offering an opinion. "It depends what kind of thing you like," he came up with at length.

"I'll be interested to see what you make of the garden," said Orlando.

"I'm looking forward to seeing it," the other replied. He sounded as if he meant it too.

Ernst, Orlando noticed, had nothing to contribute, which was fine.

They drove into the courtyard and drew up in front of the porch.

"My God. Have you done all this yourself?" Lothar said.

"Put it this way, it's my idea."

"Alma Tadema brought to life?" said the German.

"I'll show you the house, which isn't quite finished, and then we'll look at the garden – that bit's done."

The rooms were complete except for the work on the frescoes and mosaics, which was still in progress.

"I've settled for the later Pompeian style for the paintings, though several of the mosaics are based on some good third century examples," Orlando explained.

He showed his visitors into his bedroom that led off the tablinium "Do you like my gladiators?"

Lothar inspected the wall closely. "Are these copies?"

"Not quite. I like to give my artists a bit of room for self-expression."

"Your artists?"

"Sure. He who pays the piper calls the tune."

"An English proverb?"

"An English proverb."

It was a gory gladiatorial action fought between Samnites and Thracians. There was also a fisher who was spearing a man entangled in his net.

Ernst wrinkled his nose. "How do you English say it? Not quite my cup of tea – that is right?"

Lothar, meanwhile, was identifying the different types of gladiator. "It reminds me of something," he said.

"A boy's bedroom wallpaper?"

Lothar eyed Orlando for a second but turned away from the mosaic without saying anything.

"In many ways the world has changed very little since then," Orlando went on. "But come and see the garden. That's where Alma T really comes into his own."

The day was kind: the sky was a deep azure as in Alma Tadema's world, and the pathways were shaded by rapidly maturing wisterias and vines. The garden was spread out below the terrace where they were sitting.

"It needs a couple more years to grow in properly," Orlando explained. "That'll be the time to see it." He looked closely at Lothar who nodded.

"I'd like very much to see it then," the German said at length. "But this marble is beautiful!" They were sitting on the carved bench set into the projecting terrace bay.

Even Ernst added his pennyworth, while Lothar sighed with a sensual satisfaction that sounded real enough as he ran his fingers along the smooth surface.

"That's what Alma paints best of all. Marble," said Orlando. "I want the real thing to look as good as it does in his pictures. And to feel like it, too."

"It feels warm … like human skin," mused Lothar. He closed his eyes as his fingers continued to caress the masonry.

"What do you plan to do after you've left Tuscany?" Orlando asked him rather abruptly.

Lothar opened his eyes and closed them again, his fingers still playing on the surface of the ballustrade. "Who says I'm leaving?" he chuckled.

"It's seducing you the way it did me," said Orlando. "What about you, Ernst?"

"I have to finish my degree," he replied methodically. He stood up and set off down the steps from the terrace into the garden.

"He can't stay still," explained his compatriot, opening his eyes and seeing him halfway down the steps. "He's always on the move."

"Would you like to stay here?" said Orlando. "I mean it seriously. You can, you know … if you want to."

"What? To live inside your pastiche of an Alma Tadema painting?" Lothar laughed. "But I don't look Italian."

"Nor did most of the people in his pictures. You don't need to."

"It would be like living inside a dream. Somebody else's dream. Your dream."

"There are worse places to live than that. It could be your dream too. We could share it."

"A shared dream?"

"Exactly so."

"You're a strange man," said the German. But the way he said it made it sound like a compliment.

"Think about it," said Orlando. "It could be an amusing experiment – for a month or two at least – living in the ancient world."

Lothar laughed. "And what happens when you get a ruptured appendix? Are you allowed to call an ambulance?" He shook his head. "It's not really possible, I'm afraid."

"Never completely possible," Orlando conceded, " but a beautiful kind of game all the same ... like one of Alma's pictures. Like the games the Romans themselves sometimes played. Mind you," he went on, "it would be a game with rules ... quite strict ones ... a disciplined sort of life. I'm no hedonist – if anything, I'm a Spartan ... or a Stoic."

The German opened his eyes at that. "It might be interesting ... for a month or two," he mused. "But how do you say it in English? Where's the catch?"

"There isn't one, though we'd need to define our roles."

"Our roles?"

"Our roles and those of the others as well. Because it would need to be properly thought out – like the house. It's the kind of game a lot of people would probably like to play – the right sort of people. Where's Ernst got himself to?" Orlando could hardly believe that it was only two hours since he had first met Lothar.

They went down the steps and found Ernst in an arbour at the end of one of the paths. He was leaning over the balustrade gazing at the hazy blue hills.

"Strictly speaking, we should be looking out onto the sea at Antium," Orlando explained, "but the Tuscan hills do pretty well."

"And where are Alma T's beautiful Roman girls?" remarked Lothar with an ironic wink. "But I mustn't forget – they weren't Roman beauties at all, were they? They were English ones."

Orlando shrugged his shoulders and frowned. "You can't have it all ways."

Lothar looked at the hills. "I think we can manage without the girls, don't you?"

"We?"

Lothar pursed his lips and glanced at Ernst then back again at Orlando who took the hint.

"Time for a drink, don't you think?" suggested Orlando. "I'm afraid that's where I cheat as well. I do like my white wine chilled."

They drank a light Tuscan wine on the terrace.

"I suppose I am a bit of a fraud," admitted Orlando. "I want to live like a Roman without too many of their discomforts."

"Perhaps it's good to take the bits you like and leave out the ones you don't," said Lothar. "The privilege of living in the times we do. If you can afford to do it," he added.

"It's an interesting existential question," said Ernst pedantically.

"One for our time," observed Lothar.

"But not only our own time," said Orlando. "People have tried it before."

A dreamy look came into Lothar's eyes. "This is a terrible thing for me to say – especially as I'm a German. It's the one thing I approve of about Hitler."

Neither of the others spoke.

"Have I said something terrible?" Lothar asked.

"Go on," said Orlando.

"It was his attempt to bring back the heroic virtues of the past. A futile dream, of course, and one with terrible consequences – but all the same ... I would have loved to have been a member of the Hitler Youth. It was Sparta ... you called yourself a Spartan, Orlando ... or a Stoic ... I suppose you can be both ... and the Spartans were Aryans ... the Romans too ... nature's leaders ... warriors ..."

Ernst looked away, pained.

The talk of Aryans was nonsense, of course, but Lothar's reference to the Hitler Youth struck a spark with Orlando – the stern appeal to self-sacrifice, the bonding male virtues ... those godlike young men, brimming over with fitness ... their physical perfection ...Sparta ... a beguiling myth if ever there was one ... something he could understand and go along with ...

Ernst, who was embarrassed by the turn the conversation was taking, glanced at his watch.

"We must talk more about this another time," Orlando said to Lothar in a low voice as he patted the back of the German's hand.

It was time to take them back to Lucca.

The two Germans were going on to Rome and then to the south – Lothar wanted to see Calabria and Magna Graecia – so they were leaving Lucca after just one more day. Not a lot was said on the drive – Ernst's presence probably restrained his companion – but Orlando exulted silently. Lothar obviously liked him and he could see that their minds, and probably their instincts too, ran on similar lines. If he could put a practical plan to him he felt confident that the German would work with him. He dropped them at the Santa Anna gate where he exchanged telephone numbers and e-mail addresses with them – something Lothar seemed very happy to do. He promised to call by and look him up again before the end of the summer.

"We have much to talk about," he said, getting out of the car and patting Orlando's knee lightly at the same time. He flashed him a big smile and Orlando's loins throbbed while he remained firmly glued to his seat.

Orlando drove back to his villa. The timing seemed perfect. The next three weeks were spent happily with a couple of mosaicists and fresco painters – Orlando was impressed how well supplied Italy still seemed to be with such craftsmen. They seemed to have lost none of their old Tuscan flair. A week later, a postcard arrived from Taranto in the south – signed by Lothar and not by Ernst, which was exactly the way he wanted it to be. Lothar would be back in Lucca before the end of August – by himself this time.

And that is what happened. He rang Orlando from the Universo Hotel in the middle of town, saying that he wanted to "discuss future arrangements'.

In the meantime, Orlando had been giving a lot of thought as to how his Roman household would be organised. Without women, it could hardly be very typical. In fact, he based his thinking as much on the house system of his old public school as on anything he read up about Rome – which, in a way, made a kind of sense, as the classical tradition of the English public school with its system of prefects and fags and strenuous physical exercise was inspired by Rome and, possibly even more, by Sparta… Sparta… the idea of which so gripped the imagination of Lothar …

When they met again in Lucca, he found that Lothar, who was alone this time, had been giving the thing as much thought as he had. The thing would have to run as a commercial venture – not a term that Orlando liked very much, but he saw the force of the German's argument. Lothar, for all his Ayran ideas and dream of Sparta, was surprisingly practical about such matters. Students or any other young men who wanted the 'authentic experience' – as he phrased it – could live as members of a Roman household for one month on the understanding that they knew what they were letting themselves in for and accepted it without demur. It was to be a regime of communal living with work and healthy open-air activity and the kind of discipline that might be expected in a well-ordered Roman household. A sort of youth camp in a Roman setting was how Lothar saw it – which chimed with Orlando's own ideas of the house system in an English public school.

A disciplined communal life is what they both envisaged. They agreed, for instance, that there was to be a uniform consisting of a simple woollen tunic, leaving the limbs free, and that they should all go barefoot. Orlando pushed that last point: he remembered once seeing a film about the old Dr Barnardo's home for orphan boys where they went barefoot all through the summer months to toughen the soles of their feet for a possible life at sea.

Lothar liked that idea too, and the idea of the Roman bathhouse that Orlando was working on. A communal latrine of the kind that could still be seen in some Roman settlements was also agreed upon. This was not to be for the squeamish. For boys mucking in together there was no room for such inhibitions.

"There are plenty of German boys who would enjoy this kind of thing," Lothar assured Orlando.

"And probably English ones too," he replied.

It was agreed that while Orlando was the master of the house, Lothar was to be his steward with the powers of a slave master. However, while strict obedience was to be part of the deal, discipline would be properly regulated and its nature fully understood in advance by the participants. There could be no room for any misunderstandings.

"You can leave this to me," said Lothar, his eyes alight with the prospect of bringing ancient Sparta back to life again

"It won't always be very nice for them," Orlando pointed out.

"Of course. That is what they will expect and be paying for. It will be a total experience as far as is practical. Not completely so – it cannot be. And you never know … it might be … how do you say it?"

"Say what?"

"Be a pointer? Who knows how it might inspire young people and lead them in a new direction ... a better ... a healthier one ..."

It was cloudy, German stuff – a little dangerous, perhaps, but Orlando liked it all the same.

"And all inside your beautiful Alma Tadema world. That itself will be an education!" enthused Lothar.

Orlando, of course, was well enough versed in the work of the painter to realise that below his exquisite surfaces there sometimes lurked hidden messages – innuendoes – of things morally dubious, but tacitly understood by his clients.

"But that," he told himself, "has been the way the public school system has always worked. A degree of hypocrisy masked by a decent reticence. That is part of its essence."

It was the way his own life had worked so far, too.

Lothar was off to Germany in a couple of days to spread the word. Orlando, meanwhile, looked after the Italian end of things. He needed regular staff to set the place up and to provide some continuity between the visitations. Stefano, who had worked on the garden with him, was a young man in his twenties and had been an enthusiastic supporter of the scheme to bring the ancient world back to life. He was also prepared to play the game the way Orlando wanted it played – to take his part as a member of the household. So he was recruited at a generous rate –which, no doubt, was also an inducement.

Part of his job would be to look after Orlando's cats. Orlando was not a great animal lover, but had a soft spot for cats – partly because they were self-sufficient creatures and yet did not spurn the occasional attentions of humans. He did not see them as particularly Roman but, padding softly in and out of the house and in the garden, they added something to the serenity of the place. And in the winter months he could go away and leave them in the care of someone else. He acquired no less than five of them, his favourite being a tom with a beautiful silky golden coat that he loved to stroke. He had called it Cupid.

It was Stefano who produced Marco.

My God, thought Orlando, looking at the Tuscan eighteen-year-old for the first time, where on earth did he come across such a perfect creature? You can forget about your Aryan blonds – this is a cupbearer fit for a god!

Marco had recently left school in Pisa and had hopes of studying to be a painter, so was intrigued by Orlando's enterprise. He had a mild manner with gentle trusting eyes and, as he gazed about him, emitted little sighs of appreciation and wonder, which somehow added an extra lustre to his beauty if, indeed, it could leave any room for improvement.

He was slightly built with not an ounce of spare flesh on him – poised perfectly between man and boy, but with a guileless quality more suggestive of the latter. To Orlando, he was a boy and no question about it. He was olive-skinned and dark-eyed while his thick, rather untidy mop of hair had a hint of fairness – the Aryan strain, perhaps, that Lothar liked to talk about?

Orlando could not wait to dress him in his slave's tunic and make him his cupbearer and personal attendant. Stefano and another Italian boy, Silvio, made up the tablinium servants who attended the master of the house and his steward as they relaxed on their couches and drank their wine before retiring for the night.

And it all went swimmingly well. As Orlando had hoped, Lothar rounded up his German boys with no apparent difficulty – mostly students with a few older schoolboys – and delivered them in batches of twenty at a time. This was an ideal number – enough to run the household and for a full programme of activities, most of which were arranged on a team basis. Lothar, whose own academic speciality was athletics in the ancient world, modelled it largely on fifth century BC and Hellenistic Greek practises – which included naked wrestling, with bodies oiled and scraped down afterwards with a strigulus in the proper manner, running, and discus and javelin throwing. Lothar was especially fascinated by Sparta and its programme for bringing up its boys to form a warrior caste, so he arranged war games with battle lines modelled on Greek hoplite rather than Roman legionary practise. This quickly became popular with the young men who were barely out of their adolescence and happily regressed back into it. Lothar's Germanic sense of discipline was considerably tested in keeping control of his mock battles, so he devised a system of point scoring to give them a sense of order, but it was bliss for him. And for Orlando too, as he watched the young men from the terrace overlooking the field. They usually fought with their tunics on, but like true Hellenes they sometimes stripped them off to fight naked.

Other activities included gardening chores, scything the grass in the orchard and other day-to-day things that needed doing. And Orlando, who regulated the day's programme with the aid of a sundial on the terrace, insisted on a reading hour, which he liked to supervise himself. Usually he read aloud from a classical text and discussed it with the young men, many of whom were studying the classics. Orlando felt that it stretched him and he found that he enjoyed the cut and thrust of sharing ideas with bright young people. He was discovering a vocation, but in a setting that was altogether more satisfactory than any he might find through orthodox educational channels.

And then there was the bathhouse and relaxation and a meal taken together in the triclinium. This consisted of plain Italian fare. Orlando had studied the famous book of Roman recipes by Apicius, which included the liquamen garum, a highly pungent fermented fish sauce to which the Romans of all classes were strangely addicted, but perhaps wisely, decided against attempting such things. Instead, he settled for a diet of bread and olives, different pastas with simple fish or meat sauces, cheese, and fruits in season, which included apples, pears, figs and grapes. They drank Tuscan red wine – usually watered – or fresh spring water and, occasionally, milk. Since the appearance of the thing mattered most to Orlando, the meal was eaten in the authentic Roman fashion, reclining on couches, each one made to accommodate three people.

Not long after, it was early to bed in the quarters round the peristyle court, the gathering darkness relieved only by the light of oil lamps, for a start to the new day at first light or dawn. It was then that Orlando would settle down to drink wine with Lothar, attended only by their cupbearers and one other so-called slave, usually Silvio. And that hour or two of fading light with oil lamps lit was the time he enjoyed most of all. Marco came up to his expectations – assiduous in his attentions, yet with a suggestion of merely acting a part betrayed by the satirical gleam in his eye and the smile, which hovered on his lips and threatened to break out in open laughter. Nonetheless, his master took his show of respectful affection to be genuine enough. He even appeared to be fond of Orlando's cats, so the responsibility for feeding them was transferred to him.

But the test was going to come after the season ended in September – which was a full eighteen months after Orlando had first met Lothar. The final year's batch of twenty was due to depart then and the next was not due until the following July. Would Marco come back to him? As well as with his master, he seemed to be popular with some of the Germans too – a point not lost on the sharp-eyed Lothar, even if it may have been on Orlando who saw him as utterly without guile, despite his dangerous beauty.

And the following summer, Marco did come back as soon as the term at his art college was finished – drawn in part, no doubt, by the bait of a generous wage.

There were four separate intakes planned for that summer and everything seemed to be running on a settled basis. It confirmed something that Orlando had long suspected: that youth, despite its claims to the contrary, actually preferred a disciplined existence, which channelled its energies in a healthy manner. Or was it that German boys were particularly susceptible to this kind of ordered existence? They certainly threw themselves into it, working and playing with a will while engaging in a rough masculine humour at the same time – the latrine sticks providing an obvious opportunity for this. Instead of using lavatory paper they did things the Roman way with sponges or pieces of rag fixed to the end of a short stick, which gave rise to much pawky horseplay in the communal latrine.

"You must admit, Hitler did have a point," remarked Lothar, as he and Orlando watched the young men stripping off their tunics to wrestle in the sunshine.

Orlando wasn't prepared to admit as much openly, but tacitly agreed.

And Marco fitted into this like a regimental mascot. During the day, when he had time to spare from his domestic chores, he sometimes joined the others in their games and in the bathhouse, which Stefano was responsible for. He had a gracefulness that most of the German boys fell short of but respected, so that they handled him with a special gentleness missing from their own rough and tumble.

And then there were the photographs. At times, a camera and video recorder were allowed to intrude upon the purity of the Roman world, though their use was strictly limited to set occasions when Orlando would try to recreate the world of Alma Tadema on film. He strove for total verisimilitude and the young cupbearer was his favourite subject: usually stretched languidly on a marble bench – in the manner of one his cats – or leaning on a parapet gazing out at the Tuscan hills. Occasionally, he would be caught, almost Pan-like, in the dappled light of one of the bowers, a roguish smile playing on his lips. Orlando took photographs of the other boys too – most of the young Germans demanded a record of their stay – and there was always a house photograph at the end of each term, like the ones that Orlando remembered from his own school days. He would sit in the housemaster's place in the midst of his flock with his head prefect, Lothar, on his right while Marco sat cross-legged at his feet.

But best of all for Orlando was the time after supper when the boy served as his cupbearer. Once the rest had been fed and turned out into the garden, Lothar and Orlando would sip their wine together, reclining on couches with their three attendants at hand and discuss their charges and the day that had passed. Orlando, of course, reserved Marco to fill his cup from a ewer that he carried. Much of the time, he stood behind his master ready to answer his bidding, while Orlando and Lothar picked at a few pieces of fruit left over from the meal. Occasionally, they washed their hands in bowls of water and Marco would supply his master with a cloth to wipe his fingers and Stefano would provide a similar service for Lothar.

Lothar might even break into an incongruous German drinking song – but Orlando preferred it when Stefano, who had a good tenor voice, sang something from an Italian opera. It was then that his master would tap the side of his couch lightly and nod to his cupbearer to sit beside him where he ran his fingers through the boy's hair and planted gentle kisses on his forehead. The performance was strangely chaste and not unlike Orlando's attentions to his favourite cat, Cupid, whose silky fur he liked to stroke as it lay purring in his lap and to drop the occasional light kiss on its nose.

And that was as far as Orlando allowed it to go. The self-restraint added piquancy to the pleasure. It was a brief, contained license, which was acceptable to the boy. Part of the pleasure it gave to Orlando to toy with his cupbearer in this gentle fashion was that it went unchallenged. Whatever Marco may have got up to when he was away from him did not concern Orlando in the least, but here, under his own roof, he was in sole possession of him and he prided himself on doing the right thing by keeping his passion within bounds.

The penultimate intake, in the last week of August, was a party of twenty, which included an English boy called Harry who was in Germany as part of his degree course in modern languages. He had the rather louche manner of a certain type of public schoolboy, which immediately drew Orlando's attention to him as well as the fact that he was English. With his fair-red hair and light-brown eyes he seemed to fit in well enough with the general run of Nordic young men who enjoyed being Romans for a few weeks of their summer vacation, but it soon became clear that he was not quite the same as the others. At first, Orlando put it down to his being the only one who wasn't a German.

One morning, when he found him sunning himself on the warm marble bench on the terrace, he admonished him.

"Oughtn't you to be out with the others?" he said "That's what you're here for, isn't it?"

The young man smiled, almost conspiratorially. "You don't really go along with all that Germanic rubbish, do you?"

"This isn't Germany," Orlando retorted. "It's Rome. Possibly Sparta even, if you prefer to see it that way, but not Germany."

The boy grinned but said nothing.

"Tell me," went on Orlando "which school did you go to?"

"Canforth."

"Good God, did you really? It just had to be, hadn't it? That's where I went."

The boy only smiled. "Well, that explains Sparta, I suppose. It works like an English public school – as they may have been once, perhaps, back in my grandfather's day."

Orlando felt uneasy that a boy from his old school, of all places, should sound this cynical note.

Harry went on. "I mean this business of opting out of the real world and pretending that you belong to a quite different one. It's a bit of theatre. A game."

"Of course it's a game – but one with rules. There's a challenge – and escapism as well, that's true – I won't deny it," explained Orlando. "Anyway, what are you here for? What makes you so different from the others?"

Harry shrugged. "Idle curiosity."

"Not such a bad reason if you leave the "idle" bit out of it, but you do have to try to enter into the spirit of the thing, you know. It's only fair on the rest. You have to work at something."

And it was agreed that Harry should serve at table instead of Stefano. Orlando did not take to the young man despite the bond of the old school – he felt he was mocking his enterprise – but Lothar, who rather fancied the idea of a British slave, was keen enough to make the change, and it meant that Harry gave something to the community, at least, which, after all, was what was supposed to lie behind all the play-acting. To appoint Harry a cupbearer, of course, brought him into close contact with Marco and also to observe the flirtatious intimacy that went on between the Italian boy and his master. Not that he registered any reaction to it – after all, he had been to an English public school – and he adopted the kind of deadpan manner that once would have been expected in a good valet.

Marco spoke some English and Harry, who was more or less fluent in German, was soon picking up the Italian language as well. Sometimes, Orlando would come across them in animated conversation in the shade of the peristyle at the back or in the atrium. They rattled away, clearly at home in each other's company, but occasionally they would break off and spring to their feet looking mildly shamefaced when they saw the master watching them.

Orlando told himself that it was right that the young men of his household should be friends – to a large extent, that was what it was all about – but after seeing these two clearly so happy in each other's company a couple of times with the hint of something brewing up between them that they were not ready to share with him, he felt a jealous pang of a kind which, until now, had been foreign to his nature.

Their youth was the problem: while his own physical charms were starting to fade, theirs were just reaching full fruition and Orlando sensed that he had a rival. Then, one day, he came across the pair of them lying together – on his own bed, of all places – with their clothes off. It was the middle of the morning and everyone else was out, sweating under the hot sun in an athletics competition, which Lothar had laid on in the field beyond the garden. Orlando had noticed that neither boy was present and went up into the garden where he strolled round the shady paths, looking out for them in an uneasy kind of way. A sense that something was going on that he wasn't meant to know about oppressed him, and he went up into the house where it was agreeably cool after the strong sunshine outside.

Orlando went into his own bedroom and there were the two of them – stretched out on his own bed, side by side, naked and apparently asleep – two flawless creatures poised on the brink of manhood. Orlando – though he was not yet far advanced into middle age – suddenly felt horribly old. He did not disturb them, but stole quietly away.

He said nothing about it immediately and toyed with the idea of letting the matter pass. After all, he could hardly deny the homoerotic element that underpinned the whole enterprise and he did not want to introduce a sour note, especially when the Spartan cult of young manhood was something he felt so strongly about. But that evening he felt a coldness creep into Marco's attentions to himself. For the first time, the boy seemed to be pre-occupied and he watched him and Harry closely to see what signals might be passing between them.

As luck would have it, Lothar was at his most boisterously German – in a Bacchanalian mood, as he rather ponderously termed it – and Harry, who was rather good at that sort of thing, had even woven a garland of roses for his hair – his tongue firmly in his cheek, no doubt – which was a shade too camp for Orlando's taste. And when the time came for Marco to sit beside him on the couch, his master sensed the lad's muscles stiffen while he turned his face away, reluctant to be kissed in the usual manner. Abruptly, Orlando pushed Marco from him and ordered him to re-fill his cup, and, despite Lothar's convivial mood, the evening ended earlier than usual.

Worse was to follow: on the following night he saw what was clearly a conspiratorial glance pass between Marco and Harry who was sitting on the edge of Lothar's couch. Moreover, the glance had come from Marco and had been picked up by Harry. It was the merest lift and drop of an eyelid on the part of each young man and probably would have passed unnoticed by anyone else, but Orlando, in his charged state, felt a chill grip his chest.

"Wake up, boy, and fill my cup," he ordered Marco sternly.

Orlando looked across at Lothar with his garlanded hair. The German was peeling a fig in his normal fastidious manner. He had appeared not to have noticed anything amiss about the boys" behaviour, but he glanced back at his friend when he heard the harsh tone with which Orlando addressed his Ganymede. It wasn't the arch master/slave one that he usually affected. This was serious displeasure and made the German think.

Orlando knew he was excluded from the mutual enjoyment that bonded the two young men. The pleasure that they so obviously took in each other's company – and, indeed, in their bodies – was something that he, as an older man, was shut out of, and it was unreasonable of him to expect it to be otherwise. But, all the same, the green-eyed monster had gone about its work only too well, raising his longing for Marco to a fever pitch. Before he had paddled along unchallenged, indulging his feelings for the boy in an indolent fashion: the massage in the bath-house – the performance of which seemed to come naturally to Marco – the management of his simple wardrobe – something he left entirely to the boy – and the gentle petting on the couch at the close of supper were as far as he allowed it to go. These, together with the odd small present and the games of dice or draughts he played with him, had been for Orlando the boundary he had set himself in the expression of his love. In a way, it had been paralleled in his life with Beatrice, though in that case there was hardly any question of having to rein himself in.

But now the fires were well and truly raging as Orlando ordered Marco into his bedroom while Lothar slipped away. Harry and another slave cleared the tables, looking at each other anxiously and saying nothing. Then they tiptoed out, leaving Orlando alone.

When Orlando retired to his bedroom, he found Marco waiting for him and straight away he crossed to the chest and took out a rod he had cut from the garden earlier in the day. The cupbearer, without saying a word, started to draw back the cover of the bed as he usually did.

"Leave that," Orlando commanded him sternly. He sat down on the chair at the foot of the bed. "Marco, I'm displeased with you."

The boy hung his head submissively. "Why master?" he said, still affecting the manner of a slave.

"Yesterday, when I came in here, I found you lying with the English boy – on this bed, my bed."

Marco did not speak and looked away.

"Look at me, Marco."

Sullenly, the boy looked at him. He bit his lip and shifted his gaze again.

"I'm not pleased with you Marco." Orlando felt himself impelled to act out the part of a heavy housemaster, but the lines sounded hollow as if they had been written for him by someone else. "Have you anything to say? What you did was wrong, very wrong." The pomposity of the words struck Orlando, and probably the boy too, but he found himself uttering them just the same.

The boy tossed his fine head of hair and still said nothing.

"Bend over the bed, Marco," went on Orlando, or rather the demon that was speaking through him. The boy gave him a startled glance then did as he was told.

Orlando hesitated for a second before folding back the boy's tunic and exposing his naked buttocks. It seemed an act of vandalism to damage something so exquisite but, at the same time, an overpowering sense of mastery, of total dominance possessed him. This perfect creature before him was entirely his own – to do exactly what he pleased with.

Then he began to beat the boy – not particularly hard, but with short crisp strokes, which brought up ugly red weals on his buttocks, nevertheless. Small gasps escaped from Marco as each stroke struck home, but he managed not to cry out. Orlando, as he applied the cane, felt tainted – he knew what he was doing was sordid – but, at the same time, he told himself that the punishment was controlled, more fatherly than brutal. After all, it was not in his nature to lose control of himself.

After dealing out six strokes he placed the cane over the chair at the foot of the bed. Marco lay still, making no effort to move. Orlando stretched out a hand and ever so gently started to massage the bruised flesh. At this, the boy flinched, twitching his buttocks and causing him to desist.

"I'm sorry, Marco," Orlando said thickly. "Truly I am, but it had to be done. You can stand up now."

The boy stood up without a word but stopped in the doorway as he left and turned to him. "Thank you, master," he said.

"Good God, whoever taught him to say that?" Orlando said to himself. "It's just the thing an English schoolboy was expected to say after he had been beaten."

Orlando threw himself down on the bed and buried his face in the pillow. A great surge of disgust for what he had just done swept over him – a feeling of shame and self-loathing, that he had polluted something pure and destroyed it once and for all.

Then the thought occurred to him. Why only Marco? Shouldn't he have beaten the English boy as well? He knew the answer to that, of course, and shied away from the thought.

The night that followed was sleepless. And in the morning when his personal slave normally appeared with water for his morning ablutions, no one came. With a sense of foreboding, Orlando rose to find Lothar already up and sitting in the atrium where he was dipping a piece of bread in a bowl of warm milk.

"I had to punish Marco last night and this morning he hasn't come to me," Orlando explained stiffly.

Lothar said nothing but went on dunking his bread.

"As the steward responsible for the discipline of my household you must take the necessary steps."

Lothar stared at him. "The necessary steps?"

"Yes. The necessary steps."

Lothar bit his lower lip and climbing to his feet ambled off towards the slave quarter at the back of the house. He seemed in no hurry. Orlando waited in the atrium where he picked up Cupid, and began to stroke the animal's fur. It purred sensually in his lap. Lothar returned shortly afterwards to report that Marco was nowhere to be found. The English boy, Harry, had vanished as well.

"Oh my God," groaned Orlando, tipping the cat from his lap.

"Two runaway slaves," said the German.

"Oh my God," said Orlando again. "What have I done?"

"What have you done?"

"I beat Marco – for his insolence."

Lothar sighed. "And broke the spell?"

"Slaves were regularly beaten by their masters in ancient times," said Orlando.

"The same as English schoolboys?"

"And German ones too, no doubt – especially in the days of your beloved Uncle Adolph. But what are we going to do? The conditions were understood, surely?"

"Call the rest together – for a history lesson – the harsh reality of the ancient world – and what they're here to learn."

Orlando buried his face in his hands. "I love that boy – that's the trouble – that's why I did it."

Lothar placed his hand on his shoulder. "Would you like me to talk to them?"

"Would you mind?" mumbled Orlando in a pathetic voice.

And that is what Lothar proceeded to do. He assembled the entire household and informed them that Marco had been punished in the proper Roman manner for what he and the other boy had done. That the latter had escaped punishment, he did not mention. But Marco had willingly accepted to play his role of slave in a Roman household and for his master to beat him was entirely appropriate.

There was no dissension and Orlando felt that he had been a bit cowardly in not addressing the troops himself, as his own housemaster would have done, instead of leaving it to his head prefect. But with the loss of Marco, a deep lassitude took a hold of him. He did not care a fig about the departure of Harry – good riddance, if anything – except for the possible scandal he might cause. But he mourned the passing of his slave boy in a way he had never done with his wife. A hole had been torn in the fabric of his existence, leaving a wound that, for now at least, refused to heal.

And the summer wore on. Another consignment of German boys was due at the end of August – Lothar's supply seemed inexhaustible – all eager to take part in a recreated ancient Rome combined with the traditional rigours of an English public school. Meanwhile, Orlando found such solace as he could in his garden, brooding on a marble bench beneath a spreading vine, silently mourning his lost Marco and blaming himself bitterly for what had been done to him.

In the middle of September, the household broke up and, with the onset of autumn, Lothar took off for Germany, leaving Orlando alone in the house. Free at last to give full vent to his feelings, Orlando paced the length of the villa from front porch to the end of the peristyled courtyard, dressed in a rough woollen tunic that Marco had once worn, and lamenting loudly.

After three days of this unrestrained self-indulgence, he shut up shop and departed, arranging only for someone from the village nearby to sweep the leaves in the garden and make sure that the house itself was secure. The locals, who were quite used to the foreigners settled in their midst with strange ideas about the world, regarded Orlando with easy-going tolerance, apparently without putting an unfavourable gloss on the goings-on in his house. Looking on during his absences was merely a notional business anyway.

Orlando travelled through Europe and returned to Tuscany in the following spring. Lothar was to provide another consignment in the middle of July and by now, Orlando was finding his feet again. He was determined not to repeat last year's mistake, though he did allow himself a little agreeable speculation about the fresh intake. The prospect of a good-looking German boy did not go amiss – a taste shared by the Emperor Tiberius, after all.

Then the letter arrived from his brother Peregrine, announcing that he was coming with his wife and two kids early in June. He was using a half-term break and extending the holiday ten days beyond it – something the schools rather frowned upon, but Peregrine, who disliked travelling in Europe at the height of the holiday season, made a great song and dance about Italy and its educational spin-offs. He talked of projects on the Roman world and, if what he had heard about his seldom-seen brother Orlando was correct, he too would offer a splendid insight into that very thing. Orlando, who had lost all meaningful contact with his own kin, was nevertheless pleased as well as surprised to hear from his brother. He was curious to see how his nephew and his niece were growing up and he felt that Peregrine, who was an architect after all, might be sympathetic towards his experiment. In fact, he wondered why the trip hadn't been made sooner. Early June was a good time too – safely before Lothar's return and the start of the new "term'.

The wound left by the incident with Marco was almost healed. Nothing more was heard of the boy – nor of his English companion, for that matter, who was probably the more dangerous of the pair – and no exposure seemed imminent while Lothar reported nothing untoward as he made his round-up.

Orlando spent his time working in the garden – with the aid of a couple of men from the village – and feeding the cats. There were several of these by now – all good mousers – though the golden-haired Cupid remained the privileged occupant of the master's lap.

He thought about his brother's visit. He had told Peregrine that he intended to look "Roman" and suggested a costume re-enactment that the children might enjoy. Peregrine leaped at it as excellent project material, which might even interest their schools. Orlando smiled to himself at the thought. But what about Mirabel? He would have to kit her out too and he had no women's costumes. She would probably want to know why, knowing the little he did of her.

It was late in May and, pleasantly tired after a day spent in the garden on his own and a plunge into the frigidarium of the bathhouse, Orlando settled down in the atrium with a large goblet of red Tuscan wine and Cupid on his lap. He felt at peace with the world and in no hurry to prepare himself a simple meal. Having lit an oil lamp, he watched the daylight begin to fade through the open doors beyond the dining area.

From where he was sitting, he could see a pair of cats stalking some tiny unseen creature in the courtyard. The light was fading rapidly and at last he stood up, having had his fill of wool-gathering, and wandered across to the open doorway. It was quite still outside, the silence only broken for a second by the sound of a twig snapping somewhere in the garden beyond.

He turned back into the house. He would have a cold snack and another glass of wine, then doze on the couch once he had eaten Roman-fashion. Meanwhile, stretching his limbs along the length of the couch, he lay back and thought rather wistfully of Marco. "It would be nice to have him here right now," he reflected mournfully.

As if in answer to his wish, Cupid leaped up beside him and he lay there stroking the animal's fur. The cat settled itself on his stomach and started to purr, a sound that increased his feeling of drowsiness and he drifted off into a light slumber.

So he did not notice the figure that slipped through the open doorway from the courtyard. It came with the soundless footfall of one of his cats while Orlando went on snoring, and tiptoed into the atrium. Orlando stirred when the cat sitting on his stomach jumped down to the floor and he felt a torch shining directly in his face.

"Signore Crocker?"

"Marco!"

He saw the face in the torch's beam leaning over his own. But it wasn't Marco's. It belonged to someone like him, only a little older. His brother, perhaps? He started to sit up, but a hand pushed him down again and pressed hard against his mouth. It was all that was necessary – the knife plunged in and did its work, instantly, expertly.

Then the intruder tiptoed back the way he had come and beckoned to a companion outside, who joined him. The second one carried a holdall and together the two of them emptied it, spreading its contents on the floor. Then, having selected their implements, they set about attacking the house – slashing at the wall paintings, gouging mosaics and toppling and shattering urns and statues. They took their time and were not particularly bothered by the noise they made, knowing perfectly well that they were out of earshot of the nearest human habitation.

After three quarters of an hour, they packed up and left the way they had come, taking care to shut the doors that opened onto the courtyard behind him.

Meanwhile, once silence was restored, Cupid emerged from the shadows and, jumping up, settled comfortably once more on Orlando's stomach.

And it was a few years later that the English boy, Harry, became one of the inventors of something new in broadcasting called reality television.